Books in the AGENCY Series
Eve of War
The Favor

Books in the PANTHEON Series
Hecate
Tridyma

Books in the COLONY Series
QUANT
ARCADIA
GALACTIC SURVEY
SILK ROAD
LOST COLONY
EARTH

Books in the EMPIRE Series
by Richard F. Weyand:
EMPIRE: Reformer
EMPIRE: Usurper
EMPIRE: Tyrant
EMPIRE: Commander
EMPIRE: Warlord
EMPIRE: Conqueror

by Stephanie Osborn:
EMPIRE: Imperial Police
EMPIRE: Imperial Detective
EMPIRE: Imperial Inspector
EMPIRE: Section Six

The Favor

An Agency Thriller

by

RICHARD F. WEYAND

RICHARD F. WEYAND

ISBN 978-1-954903-12-8
Printed in the United States of America

Cover Credits
Cover Art: Luca Oleastri and Paola Giari,
www.rotwangstudio.com
Back Cover Photo: Oleg Volk

Published by Weyand Associates, Inc.
Bloomington, Indiana, USA
December 2022

THE FAVOR

CONTENTS

THE FAVOR

An Informal Assignment

Elina Stavros woke in a strange bed, in a strange position. She was draped, nude, across the body of a man, also nude.

Memory came back, and she sighed and snuggled closer.

Bert Mangum woke mid-morning, as was his usual when not on assignment. Officially a trade representative for the Association of Planets' Agency for Interstellar Trade, that was in fact a cover. The Agency for Interstellar Trade was actually the Association Intelligence Agency, and Bert Mangum was a direct-action operative of that organization.

Of course, the Association of Planets denied the Agency – the AIA – existed at all, but people in the know knew better.

People such as Elina Stavros, a police detective for the Crossroads space station, the massive hub of the hub-and-spoke freight and passenger system that served the six star nations of the local cluster. Centrally located, but not a part of any of the six star nations itself, it was a perfect central hub.

Mangum had just successfully completed an assignment to head off an interstellar war. He and Gloria Dent, of Gaston's Bureau of Investigation and Espionage – the BIE – had followed the trail from Crossroads to Abelon, then Mystik, a planet in the Star Nation of Abelon.

On that assignment, Bert Mangum had killed seven people more or less extra-legally, and participated in the legal executions of hundreds more as the Coordinator of the Star Nation of Abelon had used Dent and Mangum to clean out his traitorous intelligence agency.

Now Mangum was back on Crossroads awaiting his next

assignment. Gloria Dent had gone off on a new assignment of her own, and he found himself at loose ends.

That is, until Detective Elina Stavros had shown up the evening before. She had not come in any official capacity, however, and at the moment she was seriously out of uniform.

Mangum thought back over the night before and smiled. The beautiful redhead was not sexually inexperienced so much as she was out of practice. Her frustration had grown on the space station, which had only a hundred thousand inhabitants. Two-thirds or so of them were men, most of whom, it seemed, were intimidated by the female police detective.

Stavros had sought Mangum out for the pure sexual release of a willing partner with no strings attached.

It seemed to have worked out for her. There had been several times last night when Mangum was glad the first-class accommodations on Crossroads were so well soundproofed.

"Good morning, handsome," Stavros said when Mangum opened his eyes and stirred.

"Morning, beautiful."

Stavros smiled and kissed his chest. She had a beautiful smile. Mangum stroked her side where she lay across him.

"How about some breakfast before we try to improve on last night?" Mangum asked.

"Improve? Oh, my."

Mangum smiled, and Stavros rolled off of him.

"Order me whatever for breakfast, then you can have the shower after me," Stavros said as she headed for the master bath.

"Deal," Mangum said.

Mangum was dressed by the time room service showed up.

Stavros, by contrast, was wearing a big terry-cloth robe that was supplied in the first-class suite.

With the room-service waiter gone, Sam came in from the kids' bedroom of the suite, in the persona of a large golden doodle, one of the few breeds allowed on spacecraft. Sam walked up to Stavros for some scratching between the ears, but his gaze was very much on the table and the meal thereon.

"I didn't forget you, Sam," Mangum said.

He put a plate of eggs and sausage on the floor, and followed it up with a fruit bowl. Sam dug in, wolfing it all down in seconds.

Stavros laughed.

"So he's your dog?" she asked. "I couldn't tell from the surveillance recordings of you and Ms. Dent boarding the shuttle and returning. Ms. Dent left without him, but I didn't see him during the Van Dyke investigation."

Morton Van Dyke, contract killer for Evelyn Barnes, whom Sam had captured in Mangum's room and Mangum had subsequently killed.

"No, I kept Sam in the bathroom while the police were in my apartment."

"I see. Well, he's a beautiful dog, Bert."

"Thanks, Elina."

Of course, what Stavros didn't know was that Sam wasn't a dog. He was a shape-shifting alien who took the shape of a dog – and other things – when around anyone but Mangum. For only Bert Mangum knew Sam's race existed.

Mangum had found the first sentient alien race humanity had run into out in space, but, by arrangement with the aliens who saved him from the crash of his courier ship ten years ago, he had kept their existence secret.

Sam had been curious to go along with Mangum when he

left, however. Spying out humanity for the aliens, no doubt.

"So what is your status, Bert Mangum?" Stavros asked as they set into breakfast. "And how long am I welcome?"

"My status is 'between assignments.' I'm literally a phone call away from leaving for who knows where. But that phone call could be weeks away, or it could come this afternoon. I just don't know."

Stavros nodded.

"And me?" she asked.

"You're welcome to stay with me as long as I'm here, with the caveat I may have to leave at any time on short notice."

"I understand. In which case, I need to go to my apartment and pick up a few things. All I have along is the clothes I was wearing last night. Nothing casual. No supplies."

Mangum glanced over at the seating area of the combined living room/dining room where Stavros had shed her clothes last night. Her 'work clothes' of a business suit reminded him of her occupation. He turned back to Stavros.

"So what does a police detective do on a space station, Elina? I had the impression most police activity on Crossroads was in the nature of breaking up bar fights between transient spacers and the like."

"Most of it. That's what all the patrolmen are for. To make sure everybody understands that we mean it when we tell them to stay out of trouble. Still, we get our little mysteries now and again. Like when Jaeger, and Carmen, and Van Dyke got killed."

Mangum nodded. Van Dyke had killed Jaeger and Carmen, the prostitute, to hide what Evelyn Barnes was up to. Mangum had been next on Van Dyke's list, but that didn't work out for Van Dyke.

"That was a few months back. What now?" he asked.

"Indeed. Well, there's something I've been working on, and I can't make heads or tails of it."

Stavros looked at him and tipped her head.

"I don't know. Maybe you could even help me with this one."

Mangum shrugged. He was between assignments, so his time was his own. What's more, if he helped out the Crossroads station, they would owe Febo one. Chairman Isabela Febo, chief executive of the Association of Planets, liked to have people owe her favors.

"Depends. What's going on?"

"That's just it, Bert. We don't know."

"Hard to help, then."

"I understand, Bert. Here's the gist of it. Remember that Morton Van Dyke used RDT on Jaeger and Carmen, right?"

"Yeah, and he was a user himself, I think."

"Right. We have things like that happen once in a while. Someone overdoses, or someone gets pulled in for something else, and they have RDT on them."

"OK, Elina. I'm with you."

"But where's the shit coming from, Bert? We don't know. We never find it in incoming shipments – and it's not like we don't look for it – and we even chemically scan inbound passengers for RDT in their systems."

"You do?"

"Oh, yes. Remember where you stand in front of the inbound customs agent and he asks you your name and all that shit? We could do that over the network, but we don't. We need you to stand there for a minute. He'll pretend not to find you on the manifest until the chemical analysis clears. It's built-in to the counter, in that design on the front."

"Wow. I never knew. It's that simple?"

"Oh, yes, Bert. It comes out in people's sweat. The byproducts do. It's pretty easy to pick up. On their skin. On their clothes."

"And once you identify them, Elina?"

"We search them. Them and their luggage. Thoroughly. The thing about RDT is, it's so addictive, there is no way anyone addicted to it would travel without a supply of it. And we don't want it on the station. On Crossroads."

"I can see that."

"Yeah. So we isolate them, Bert. Them and their drugs. Until their ship leaves, then we pack them aboard. Under extreme surveillance."

"You don't confiscate the drugs, Elina?"

"No. We tried that. If we do, they often die without them."

"Wow."

"Yeah. RDT gets across the blood-brain barrier. It remakes the brain. If they don't get the drugs forevermore, they have significant cognitive losses until they get it. Even once they get it, the losses aren't completely made up. And those losses are cumulative. It's nasty shit."

"I see that. But it looks like you have it under control. What's the problem, Elina?"

"How the hell is it getting here, Bert? On Crossroads? Not the stuff in isolation, but RDT uncontrolled among station personnel, like with Van Dyke. We see it all the time, and I can't figure it out."

"How do you think I could help?"

"One thing is that we can't do surveillance in the transient crew spaces. We promise, as part of being a welcoming shore-leave host. Same with our accommodations of prostitution and most drugs. So I'm blind in the transient crew spaces. But you could. Do surveillance, I mean."

THE FAVOR

Mangum nodded. He had wondered how that would work. You sort of expected to be under surveillance pretty much constantly in a space environment. It was too important to keep an eye on all the equipment and sealed spaces. A small micrometeorite puncturing a pressurized space was something one didn't want to miss. An equipment failure was a huge potential for disaster. Everything had to be kept under close watch to ensure safety.

So spacers got used to it. Planetary shore leave, though, got you out from under that. Crossroads, to compete with planetary shore leave, offered the same sort of thing. To make it work, transient crew quarters were interior to the station, and had a minimum of operations equipment.

It did create a problem for police trying to suss out what was going on, though. No surveillance was no surveillance. If they broke that, and word got out, they would lose massive amounts of business to border planets. The whole hub-and-spoke system could break down.

Running something like Crossroads was an expensive proposition. They needed a certain amount of traffic to make it work financially.

But Mangum was not bound by the rules binding station personnel. Was it a cheat? Yes, of course. But it wasn't – quite – breaking the rules. That was a space Mangum was comfortable operating in. Always operated in, in fact.

"All right, Elina. Let me work on that and see where I get."

"I appreciate it, Bert. And I need to go pick up some other clothes."

Breakfast was over, and Stavros stood up from her chair. As she did so, she let the bathrobe drop from her shoulders and remain in the chair. She stood before him in all her naked splendor.

"But I don't need clothes just yet, Bert. I think it's time to work on those improvements you mentioned."

A couple hours later, with Stavros run off to her apartment to pack a vacation bag for her stay with him, Mangum sat in the kids' bedroom talking with Sam.

Sam was in his utility persona, which was sort of like an unfinished statue. There was no detail. No pores or fingerprints. No eyebrows or eyelashes. No buttons or zippers on what looked like a jumpsuit, but was just a different color.

The utility persona was easiest for Sam. It was like hanging out in one's pajamas, without getting all dressed for the day.

"So it looks like we have a roommate for a couple of weeks, Sam."

"That's OK, Bert. I like Ms. Stavros. Like me, she seems to have a couple of different personas."

Mangum chuckled.

"She does at that. Who expected the prim and demure police detective to be a wildcat in sheep's clothing?"

"Isn't the idiom a wolf in sheep's clothing, Bert?"

"Yes, Sam, but describing her as a wolf wouldn't do her justice."

"Ah. I see. Changing the metaphor in the idiom to emphasize the difference. Clever. Yet another trick of English."

Sam nodded, then continued.

"So you will help Ms. Stavros with her problem?"

"Yes, Sam. If I solve a problem for Crossroads, then Crossroads police will owe Chairman Febo a favor. Not a small thing. And it's sort of an interesting problem."

"I see that, Bert. How are the drugs getting onto the station if they have such tight entry controls?"

"Right. Clearly, the people transporting the drugs can't be

users as well, or they would be caught out in the entry procedure."

"That's certainly one option, Bert. I have another, perhaps. What if the drugs are being sourced here? How hard is this drug to make?"

Mangum stopped with his mouth open, then closed it. Could RDT be manufactured on the station itself? What were the raw materials that would be needed? How big would the manufacturing setup need to be? And how would one hide it?

"I don't think so, Sam. These things normally take a lot of equipment, so it would be hard to hide. It's an interesting possibility, but I don't think that's what's going on."

"Just asking, Bert. Covering the bases, as you say."

"It's a good thought, and I'll keep it in mind. Right now, I think it's a low probability option."

Sam nodded and sat quietly for a while. Mangum sipped his drink and just enjoyed the quiet time.

"Bert?"

"Yes?"

"I had another question for you. Since we're apparently on the station for a while. I've been considering reproducing."

"Having a child?"

"That's one way of saying it, I suppose, though it's a little different for me."

"How do you even do that, Sam? Do we need to go back to your planet? So you can find a girl?"

"What? Oh. No, that's not how it works. I can do it by myself."

"How is that possible, Sam? Would it be a clone, then? Without a second set of genetic material, you wouldn't have evolution. How did your species even evolve?"

"I need to go into a little more detail, Bert. First, I am not one organism."

"You're not?"

"No, Bert. Our basic lifeform is more like an amoeba or something. Reactive, but not intelligent. If two of us join together, we get up to the intelligence of, say, a frog or something. If three join, we get up to the intelligence of a small mammal, like a dog. But if four of us join together, we become sentient at the level of a human being."

"So you're a committee in there?"

"Not in the sense that we vote or something like that. We do not have differentiated organs, or we could not assume shapes like a flat wall or a carpet on the floor. Instead, our intelligence – our brain, if you will – is distributed among all our cells. They aren't anywhere near as powerful as your brain cells, but we have a lot of them."

"OK, Sam. I'm with you so far."

"If two of us join, the brain gets bigger. When enough of us join together, we hit the sentient level."

"What about five, then? Has that been tried?"

Sam shuddered.

"Yes. It– Well, it didn't work. The resulting creature was insane. It did successfully split into a two and a three, and then merged into two sentient creatures of four each. We have the memories of what it was like to be that creature. It was not pleasant."

"You have the memories, Sam?"

"Oh, yes. We are born with all the memories of our forebears."

"So your child would remember everything you and I have done together? Know English and everything?"

"Sure. We don't have anything like basic education. It took me a long time to figure out why humans had schools."

"So it would basically be an adult right off."

"No, Bert. It would be smaller, so it would have fewer brain cells overall. It would have all the memories, but its decision-making would be, um, less than ideal, shall we say. Immature."

"So it would act like a child?"

"Yes, in some ways."

"Could it assume the shape of a golden doodle, like you?"

"Yes, but more of a puppy than an adult dog. And it would act much like a puppy. For a while, anyway. Until it grew up."

"And how long is that process?"

"Shorter than for humans, by a lot. Shorter than a dog, too, for that matter. It would be full-grown within a few months."

"Wow. That's different. So how do you get genetic mix?"

"Well, there are four basic creatures that merged to form me. So that's four pair-wise combinations. Each pair would create one basic creature, then those four basic creatures would merge to form a sentient individual."

"What's your family life like, Sam? Does your child stay with you a long time, or do they go off on their own when they grow up? How does that work?"

"That I can't tell you, Bert. Back home, we were all together all the time. There was no concept of leaving. Of going somewhere else. Everybody stayed within the local area. I'm the exception there."

"Huh. So we don't know what your child would decide to do. He could go off and tell everyone about your home planet if he had a mind."

"Actually, that I am not worried about. Because he would also have all the memories of why that is a really bad idea. He might let something slip accidentally, and I would have to watch for that, because he would not have personal experience. But he would not consciously do that. I'm sure of that."

"I see."

Mangum thought about Sam's question, and Sam was content to wait.

What would it do to their partnership? Would Mangum end up with two Sams accompanying him around? To do otherwise meant letting someone else in on the secret, though. Someone who could cover for the second alien. Who could Sam even trust with that knowledge?

Then again, Sam was not stupid. His thought about RDT being perhaps manufactured on the station was brilliant, and a possibility that Mangum – and probably Stavros – had missed. So if he thought it could work, it probably could.

The negative consequences of a leak, moreover, would not accrue against Mangum, but against Sam and his fellows. So it was really his decision.

"I think you know what the possible problems would be more than me, Sam. And it's your decision, anyway. So if that's what you want to do, I would say to go ahead."

"Thanks, Bert. I could have just gone ahead, but I didn't want to inconvenience you in some way I couldn't see. I've enjoyed traveling with you, and it's been a lot of fun. That's not something I want to jeopardize."

"No, go ahead. We're good. It'll be weird to have a puppy around, but we'll make it work."

Placement And Collection

When Stavros got back from her apartment, Mangum ordered lunch from room service. While they waited, they reviewed their status.

"Mission successful?" Mangum asked.

"Oh, yes. You see?"

Stavros pirouetted for him in the casual clothes she had worn back from her apartment, slacks and a pretty blouse. With her hair down and minus the severe glasses she wore at work, she was unrecognizable from her official persona as a police detective.

"Very nice. I approve."

Stavros beamed her beautiful smile at him, then grew serous.

"How about you?" she asked.

"I had some other things to take care of, but after lunch I'll go place some cameras. Get things started, at least. Once we see what we're getting, I'll place some more."

"Sounds good. Oops. There's lunch."

The door buzzer had sounded, and Mangum went over and admitted the room service waiter with their lunch.

"If this plate is mine, and that one yours, who are the two hamburgers for?" Stavros asked once the table was set and the waiter left.

Sam got up from the sofa and trotted over, sitting next to the table.

"Oh, of course. I almost forgot."

"Yup," Mangum said. "Two hamburgers with everything, but hold the onions."

Mangum set the double hamburger plate on the floor and Sam wolfed them down greedily.

Stavros laughed.

"Manners aren't his strong suit, clearly."

"No, enjoyment is his strong suit, and he really likes hamburgers."

As Mangum and Stavros started their own lunches, the conversation turned back to surveillance.

"As for where to place surveillance cameras, I have some ideas. Let me call up an engineering plan of that section."

Stavros called up the plans on a roll-up display she flattened out on the table, and pointed out specific areas.

"These are based on our own arrests for possession when we were about other activities. We would arrest some brawlers, and, when we searched them, we found RDT. So we think it would be most prevalent in these areas."

Mangum followed along as they ate.

"Looks good, Elina. I guess I'll start placing cameras this afternoon, at least in the most obvious places."

"Then we can sit back and relax while we wait for surveillance imagery to build up."

Mangum nodded.

"And once police arrest someone and find drugs on them, we can follow that person back through the surveillance and see where they've been. See who they hang out with."

"Then what do we do, Bert? There are limits to what I can do within my regulations."

"Oh, I can question them."

Stavros raised an eyebrow, and Mangum nodded.

"Your regulations don't apply to me, Elina."

Mangum walked the transient crew quarters for his first

pass placing cameras on Crossroads. The question was, Where would his limited supply of surveillance gear be put to best use?

Knowing this would leave him short for his next assignment, Mangum had already put in an emergency request for more clandestine surveillance cameras. It would take two weeks to get them to him, but, if he had to leave Crossroads in the meantime, the shipment would follow him to his next assignment.

With carte blanche to use what he had remaining from the Abelon assignment, where should he put them?

Mangum dressed down for this first pass. It wouldn't be appropriate to wander the transient crew sections dressed as a first-class passenger. It wouldn't be particularly safe, for one thing. Though Mangum looked, at the best of times, like someone one simply did not want to mess with, there was no sense glossing that over.

Second, he would stand out like a sore thumb. The people in the corridors in the transient crew sections were almost entirely transient crew, with a few station staffers thrown in. A first-class passenger simply didn't go for a casual walk in those sections of Crossroads.

Mangum also had the advantage of having been a bartender in the transient crew bar, so he had experience in those sections of the station.

"Hey, you!" someone called behind him.

Mangum ignored him.

"Hey! I'm talkin' to you."

Mangum stopped and slowly turned around. The fellow was clearly transient crew, out to cause trouble. Mangum gave him a ten-mile stare as he considered distances and the space about him.

"Yes?" Mangum asked in a deadpan voice.

"Uh. Nothin'. I thought you was somebody else."

"I see."

Mangum continued to watch him, and the man turned and walked away.

"How was your afternoon?" Stavros asked over dinner.

"Good. I got the easier cameras placed. In planters. On some doorknobs. I'll do some of the harder ones tomorrow."

"Harder ones?"

"Yes, I have some signs I can use," Mangum said. "Replace existing signs with new ones."

"With cameras in them."

"Right. But that's a little more involved. In the meantime, we are getting feeds from the ones I placed today."

"Excellent," Stavros said.

She looked at him with a sly smile.

"We'll just have to think of something we can do while we wait."

Mangum was having a late night drink in the kids' bedroom. Sam was there in his utility persona.

"I thought you two were busy," Sam said.

"I needed a break."

"It sounded like you were having fun."

"Oh, yes," Mangum said with a sigh. "Elina's been on Crossroads for four years. She has some serious catching up to do."

"And you?"

"I just hope I survive."

Sam laughed.

THE FAVOR

"I have to say, our method for reproduction is much less work than yours. Less practice as well, come to think of it."

Mangum nodded.

"How's that going, by the way? Have you started?"

"Oh, yes. We have four basic organisms under way. It's very early on, and they're very small. A couple of cells each."

Mangum nodded.

"That makes sense, Sam. It's a geometric process."

"Yes. Exactly. So it will be a couple of weeks."

"That's all?"

"Yes, well, it's easier with us, because we don't have functionally differentiated organs to deal with. We just need size."

"I see. That would make things go a lot faster. I'm surprised you never overpopulated your planet."

"We did at one point, Bert. It was not pleasant. The memory of that has stayed with us, and we're very careful now. Famine is not pretty. Or enjoyable, for that matter."

Mangum shuddered. There had been famine on some of the colony planets early in the colonization of space. That was more of an issue of crop failures than overpopulation. But Sam was right. It hadn't been pretty.

Sam's pregnancy – if you could call it that – brought up another issue, however.

"Thinking about it, Sam, you might want to start putting a bit of a belly on your golden doodle persona. So when the puppy appears, Elina isn't wondering where this new dog came from."

"Ah. Good point, Bert."

"And you need to not have male genitalia."

"Well, I originally copied a male dog that had been fixed, so the external genitalia was minimized, at least on a dog as hairy as a golden doodle. But I get your drift. You'll have to show me some samples so I can copy the appropriate shape."

Mangum nodded and went to get his display. When he got back, he and Sam went through various images of pregnant dogs at various stages.

"These changes are all easy," Sam said. "Let me try it."

Sam shifted into his golden doodle persona, but now looked seriously pregnant. End-of-term pregnant.

Mangum compared to the images.

"Yes, that looks right, Sam. You need to get to that point by the end, but start out subtle. It accelerates toward the end."

Sam changed back into his utility persona.

"Not a problem. What about my name, though?"

"Sam? Short for Samantha, obviously."

"Ah. English again. Your language is delightfully slippery, Bert."

"What about the baby's name, Sam? Have you thought about that?"

"No, Bert. I haven't decided. I know what his identity would be in our own language. It's derivative of mine. But in English? No. I just haven't thought about it."

"You might want to think up something similarly slippery, Sam. In case this comes up again."

"Ah. Good point. You might need to help me with that."

The next morning, Stavros came out from the master bedroom in the big bathrobe to where Mangum was drinking a cup of coffee and reading the newsfeeds.

"I woke up and you weren't there," she said.

"I needed some liquid energy," Mangum said, lifting his coffee cup to her.

"Ah. Good idea. Is there any more?"

"Yeah. I made a pot."

Stavros went over and poured herself a cup of coffee, then joined Mangum at the table.

"So what's for today?"

"I'll place those harder cameras. Some of them, anyway. I want to hold some back so we have options for additional placements later."

Stavros nodded.

"I will be very interested to see if we can figure out what is going on. It's got me stumped."

"Well, clearly there are only two options. They're using couriers who are not themselves users, or they're making RDT on the station."

Stavros shook her head.

"That's not possible. At least, I don't think it is. I think you probably need a pretty big setup to manufacture something as complex as RDT."

"What if you had precursors that were closer to the finished product?"

"Perhaps. I'll look into that while you're out placing cameras."

Mangum considered that he might have figured out how to derail Stavros' amorous proclivities for a time.

Bring up an interesting work problem.

Having placed a few of the easier cameras on his first pass, Mangum dressed in coveralls and went back to the transient crew section that morning to place more surveillance cameras. The more difficult ones.

Coveralls and a tool bag were a great disguise for most any situation. You effectively disappeared. Just a maintenance guy, doing some kind of maintenance job. Didn't matter what.

Factories, office buildings, and space habitats like Crossroads had maintenance going on all the time. In a coverall, you could stop anywhere, mess around with anything.

Mangum wore a T-shirt under the coveralls, and had the zipper down a bit in front. Crossroads was kept at a comfortable temperature round-the-clock, but it also gave Mangum easier access to the 8mm pistol in his shoulder rig.

The 8mm was a bit big because it had integral suppression, but he was used to it.

And you never knew when you might need it.

Mangum was replacing a bathroom sign when he heard a gruff voice behind him. He had just taken down one sign and was putting the new one up.

"What's with replacin' the sign? It's the same as the old one. Different color is all."

"Hell if I know," Mangum said over his shoulder as he continued working. "The guys gettin' the big money make the decisions. I just do what I'm told. You know?"

Gruff Voice laughed.

"Yeah, I get that. Anyways, just wonderin'."

"You and me both."

Another laugh.

"All right, take it easy."

"Thanks. You, too."

Mangum finished installing the new sign, put the old one in his tool bag, and moved to the next location on his list.

Mangum was hours changing signs. Part of it was just getting around the big transient crew area of the station. One could forget just how big a space station with a hundred thousand permanent residents and thousands of transients could be.

He got back to the first-class suite after normal lunch time, and found Stavros at the table deep into something on her roll-up display. She waved a hand in his direction as he came in, but didn't say anything, so he let her be.

Instead, Mangum sat in an armchair and took out his own roll-up display. He checked his video feeds from his newly mounted cameras. They were all uploading to his memory in the station's systems. He checked the stored recordings, and they all looked fine, so check that box.

He switched to checking the newsfeeds. In particular, he was following the continuing events in Abelon as Jack Sturm set to rebuilding the Abelon Intelligence Service after they had cleaned out Nina Lato's treasonous conspiracy.

It was another hour before Stavros surfaced from her display. She came over and sat next to Mangum in the other armchair. Sam came out of the kids' bedroom and curled up on the sofa opposite.

"So, what do you know?" Stavros asked.

"I have all the cameras placed and they're uploading."

"Ah, good."

"What about you?" Mangum asked.

"Well, it turns out it's not that easy to find out how to make RDT. I guess they don't want to put the recipe out there for anybody to find."

"That makes some sense."

"Yes, Bert, but it makes it harder for me to answer your question. Could RDT be made here on Crossroads?"

"Any feel for it?"

"I think it would likely take a laboratory structure about the size of a small suburban house. That's including the chemistry, storage of the precursors and components, and storage of the end product and waste byproducts."

"That's a pretty big widget to hide, Elina."

"Yes, but with a resident population of a hundred thousand, plus transients, Crossroads is the equivalent of fifty thousand such homes, plus all the infrastructure required to support them. I'm not sure you couldn't hide something that big."

"OK. I can see that."

"Two things I am sure of, though, Bert. First is that you couldn't hide such a structure without active collaboration of some of the management and staff of Crossroads."

"Ouch. And the second?"

"Such a plant could produce all the RDT in the whole cluster."

"Really?" Mangum asked.

"Oh, yes. RDT is not something you make in small batches. Once you have a production facility capable of making it at all, you could make all the RDT we think is circulating in that single facility. Which raises a big concern."

"Oh, yes. If we shut it down, every RDT user in the cluster is going to be debilitated or dead."

"Exactly," Stavros said.

"Well, for what it's worth, I still think the non-user courier scenario is the most likely. That is something to keep in mind, though."

Waiting for things to develop, Bert Mangum, Elina Stavros, and Sam settled into a comfortable rhythm. Mangum and Stavros watched various surveillance recordings off and on during the day, getting in tune with the rhythm of the transient crew spaces as ships came and went from Crossroads.

Stavros, her immediate desperate need slaked at last, was

content with cuddling in bed or on the sofa during an after-lunch siesta, punctuated by merely occasional episodes of more physical affection.

Comfortable days passed as the surveillance library built up.

And Mangum and Stavros read the police blotter every day, watching for the break they needed.

Analysis And Visualization

"You lost your razor," Stavros said one day.

"I stopped shaving the day we started looking into this."

"Why?"

"Easiest disguise in the world. Just stop shaving. And a lot of the transient crews have facial hair, or stop shaving while on shore leave. I fit in better in the transient crew spaces."

"Well, at least you're past the scratchy part. Furry I can deal with. Scratchy is something else entirely."

Mangum chuckled, and Stavros looked over at Sam.

"Is it my imagination, or is Sam getting pudgy?" Stavros asked.

She and Mangum were cuddled on the sofa after lunch, her head on his chest. Sam was curled up in one of the armchairs opposite.

"No, I think she is, actually."

"She?"

"Yes, Elina. Sam is short for Samantha."

"Oh, and here I've been saying 'Good boy' all the time, and you never corrected me."

Mangum shrugged.

"Doesn't matter usually. I call her 'he' and 'him' a lot myself. But I think Sam's pregnant."

"How?"

"How else? On Abelon, when we thought the assignment was over. I think it's going to be a small litter, though. One, maybe. Two at most. She's just not getting that big for this late in her term. She's coming right up."

"Oh, Sam! You're going to have a *puppy*?"

THE FAVOR

Sam got up and came over to the sofa, sitting on the floor next to Stavros so she could pet the dog.

Mangum chuckled. Stavros was clearly very excited about having a puppy to play with.

He hoped the inexperienced baby alien didn't try to eat her.

The next morning's police blotter in the newsfeed reported an incident in the transient crew quarters. An argument among some crew members in the transient crew bar had escalated, and they had taken it outside into the corridor. Two people were knifed and ended up in the hospital. Several were arrested. All were tested for RDT, and three were positive.

Stavros saw it first, just as they were finishing breakfast.

"OK, Bert. This might be it. Check the police blotter."

Mangum tracked down to the article.

"Looks good. We have three leads to follow. Can we run those against the surveillance recordings?"

"Sure. Let me get their customs imagery together from their names, and then I can run those images against the recordings. That will work better than mug shots, what with them all beat up."

"Good. That's not my specialty. I'm more of the 'drug the guy and question him' type. Gloria Dent always did the computer work. I mean, I can do it – most of it, anyway – but I'm not very fast at it."

"This won't take long to set up. It will take a while to run, though, with almost a week of recordings from multiple locations."

Stavros bent to her task, and Mangum grabbed a last nosh from breakfast and wandered over to an armchair where he sipped his coffee and continued to scan the newsfeeds.

It was most of an hour later when Stavros came over to join him in the other armchair.

"That's all set up and running now," she said.

"Excellent. What do we do while we wait?"

"We could go for a walk in the gardens."

"The gardens?" Mangum asked.

"You've never been to the gardens?"

"No. I didn't know there were gardens on Crossroads."

"Oh, sure," Stavros said. "They generate oxygen, and give you more of an open-air feeling than being in cabins and offices all day."

"Can we take Sam, too?"

"As first-class passengers? Sure."

Sam looked up from the couch.

"What do you think, Sam? Walk in the park?"

Sam got up off the couch and trotted off to the kids' bedroom.

"Where is she off to?" Stavros asked.

"You'll see."

Sam trotted back into the living room of the suite carrying his leash and collar in his mouth, and sat on the floor in front of them. Stavros laughed.

"Well, I think you have her answer, Bert."

The gardens were at the far end of Crossroads, so they took a transit pod the several kilometers to the closest entrance. Mangum's first-class key let them through, and they walked out into a tropical wonderland of plants.

The chamber itself was thirty feet tall, and perhaps a hundred and fifty feet across, running all the way around the inner corner of the huge drum of Crossroads. The red dwarf sun shone dimly in through the far windows.

THE FAVOR

"Wow. This is something, Elina."

"It runs all the way around the station. There's a path, and some people jog the circuit every day."

"But it's very dark here. How do the plants grow?"

"See all the lights in the ceiling, Bert? Those simulate a normal day. They cycle the lighted portion of the lights around the gardens, so they use the same amount of power all the time. If they turned all the lights in here on and off at the same time, it would be a huge draw part of the time."

"Ah. Got it. Looks like it's dusk here, then."

"Or pre-dawn. Actually, it could be the middle of the night. It never gets truly dark because of the light from the sun, wan though it is."

"This is incredible," Mangum said as they walked. "I didn't even know these were here."

"They don't generate all the oxygen the station needs, but they do limit the 'stale processed air' smell you normally get on a ship."

There was also a bit of an occasional breeze, as fans on the ceiling rotated back and forth, mixing the air to be sure the plants got enough carbon dioxide. All the fans pointed in the same general direction, down the length of the gardens.

They got to the main path and started walking around the inner circumference of the station. Others walked or jogged the wide path. Sam smelled around at everything, and was very happy to be finally out of the cabin.

Mangum had been getting a bit of cabin fever himself. He had been on Crossroads almost a month by this time, and two weeks before that on the *Abelon Sky* for the transit from Abelon to Crossroads with Dent.

It was nice to be out in something approaching open air for a change.

They spent two hours in the gardens, walking toward the approaching light as the lights sequenced around the station. They left at a different entrance, and took a transit pod back to the suite.

"That was wonderful," Mangum said when they got back. "I don't even mind being back in the suite. How about you, Sam? Did you have a good time?"

Sam wagged his tail, then took the leash and collar from Mangum's hand and set them on the coffee table in the living room. Stavros laughed.

"It's amazing how much she can say without saying anything, Bert. She's leaving the leash and collar out where they're handy."

"Well, I wouldn't object to a walk like that every day. At least until the action starts."

"As to that...," Stavros said.

She walked over to her roll-up display and checked the progress indicator and hits count.

"We have several hits on those guys already, but it's nowhere near done. It will probably run all night."

"Well, let's start thinking about lunch. All that fresh air – as fresh as it gets on station, anyway – left me with an appetite."

They lingered over lunch, a series of tapas plates they shared. Even Sam got in on the action, liking the Jamón Serrano, some sort of ham and cheese on toast points, and the Salmón Querado con Queso, smoked salmon on toast points with sour cream.

After the morning walk and a lazy lunch, Mangum and Stavros were both yawning.

"Wow. Time for siesta," Mangum said on his third yawn.

"Agreed. But in bed. I want to cuddle more."

THE FAVOR

"That works for me."

They took their siesta in the bed, nude, cuddled up under the blankets. They inevitably got frisky when they woke, but it was different. Slow and relaxed, gentle and tender.

Stavros had finally calmed down, and their more relaxed lovemaking was even more enjoyable for both of them.

When they got up in the late afternoon, Stavros checked the status of her scanning.

"It's about twenty-five percent through the recordings now," she said. "It's gonna take most of the night to complete."

"I had an idea. You showed me those engineering diagrams of the station. Given that we have the locations of all the cameras, can you program something up to put traces on the diagrams? With a different color for each guy, maybe?"

"Yes, I think so. Gonna take a little work, but that would make some things pretty obvious, wouldn't it?"

"Yes. If nothing else, where I can best intercept them."

Stavros nodded and bent over her display. They already had point-mapping software in the system. And she already had the point locations of the cameras and their orientation. Now, if she could calculate a point location for the individual from the camera images, and lay those points down in sequence. Play connect the dots....

With Stavros off into her programming problem, Mangum went and checked his weapons and drug caches. He would likely be needing them soon.

Mangum paid particular attention to the dart airgun.

Hitting someone with Com-Ply from a short distance might be required.

Stavros took a break for dinner. Mangum ordered, and they

sat waiting for room service.

"So how's the programming going?" Mangum asked.

"Well, the bones of it were easy. Now it's time to debug the darned thing. I've got some wires crossed somewhere."

"How so?"

"Well, unless someone can go from over here to over there in seconds, or walk through walls, there's something wrong." Stavros shrugged. "I think I have the AM/PM handling messed up, so the matched images are not in proper time order. People are bouncing around like ping-pong balls. It's a mess."

"Why not convert all the timestamps to 24-hour time, and rip out the AM/PM handling in the code altogether?"

Stavros looked up at him sharply.

"There's an idea. Pre-process the time stamps, so I don't have to handle them in code. That will work."

She thought about it.

"That's probably not the only bug, though. We'll have to see."

"One at a time," Mangum said. "Only way to do it."

Stavros nodded.

The door buzzer sounded.

"And there's dinner," Mangum said, getting up to go to the door.

The room service waiter laid out dinner. There were three hamburgers at the third position tonight, along with two bowls of fruit salad. Sam came out from the kids room and looked hopefully at the table.

"Three hamburgers? And fruit salad?" Stavros asked after the server had left.

"Eating for three, remember."

"Oh, yes."

"Here you go, Sam."

THE FAVOR

Mangum put multiple plates down on the floor. Sam alternated, demolishing one hamburger first, then a fruit salad, then another hamburger and a fruit salad, then the final hamburger.

"Funny how she stages the food like that," Stavros said.

"As an aid to digestion, I think. Getting crowded in there."

Stavros nodded, and Sam walked over to the couch and jumped up. He laid out on the couch with a sigh.

"Not a lot of trotting around anymore, either."

"Not on a full stomach, no," Mangum said.

Stavros got up and went over to the sofa, then knelt down and petted Sam.

"You're a good girl, Sam. Taking good care of your babies. Good girl."

Sam wagged his tail, and Stavros gave him a last pet, then got up and came over to the table.

"OK. Now dinner," she said.

After dinner, Stavros went back to her software on her roll-up display. She was in the zone for two hours before she looked up and stretched.

"Finally," she said.

"You got it?"

"Yeah, I think so. I'm getting answers that make sense at least."

Mangum got up and came over and sat at the dining table where Stavros had been working. She manipulated the display and pointed out the tracks the computer had made.

"So we have red, blue, and green tracks for our three RDT addicts. What do you see?"

Overlaid over the station's engineering map, the tracks ran back and forth across the display. Stavros rotated the three-dimensional map slightly, so Mangum could pick up on the subjects' activities across multiple levels.

"OK, so this location where they all go once in a while is the bar where I used to work, right? That looks like the right location."

"Yes, that's right."

"Then these must be their quarters. Here, here, and here."

"I think that's right, Bert. That's in a resident section."

"Boy, you can really see where we have coverage gaps from this. The tracks are all segmented. But it looks like our most worrisome gaps are here, here, and here. Oh, and probably here as well."

"I think that's right, too."

"All right, Elina. I'll look into that and see if I can place some cameras there tomorrow."

"Well, we aren't going to catch this crew with those. As RDT users, they're in isolation now until they leave the station."

"Yeah, but that won't be the last brawl in the transient crew section. We'll have coverage in those areas for the next bunch. And if it's really an area of interest, they'll go there as well."

Stavros nodded.

"Sounds good, Bert. Whatever are we going to do while we wait?"

"Oh, we'll think of something."

Mangum was sitting with Sam, in his utility persona, later that evening. Stavros was sleeping, and Mangum was having his customary nightcap.

"So your surveillance scheme is working, Bert?"

"For the most part. Elina has the software running, and we can track people in the areas where there are cameras. We found some more places I need to have cameras. Apparently

RDT addicts go to or through those places, and we can't track them there."

"So you'll be placing more cameras?"

"Yeah. We need coverage there."

"I see."

Sam sat quietly for a few moments before changing the subject.

"It's very interesting, Bert. Ms. Stavros is more solicitous of me now that she knows I'm reproducing."

"Yes. Take care of the pregnant females. That's very deeply ingrained in humans. Most other higher mammals as well. Especially in other females."

Sam nodded.

"I can see where that would be survival enhancing among humans, but with dogs?"

"Sure, Sam. Dogs were humans' companions for a very long time. Their hunting companions. Their watchdogs. Survival of the dogs was important to human survival as well."

"All right. I can see that. I find all this fascinating."

"Just wait until you have a puppy. Humans are programmed to think baby animals, including humans, are cute, even when they're ugly as sin."

"Really?"

"Oh, yes. Babies need a lot of care, and humans are programmed to care for them."

"Even inter-species?"

"Absolutely. Bunnies, ducklings, baby chicks. Everybody thinks they're adorable and fusses over them."

"Even though in a year or two, they'll kill and eat them."

"Yup."

"Fascinating."

Refinement And Breakthrough

Bert Mangum, for all his complaining to Sam, was enjoying his layover on the Crossroads station. He had a beautiful and enthusiastic sex partner. He had an interesting problem to solve. He was living high in first class, as opposed to slumming around in some cover identity, and the suite, the food, and the liquor were all top-notch. He wasn't getting orders from the Agency. It was turning into a great holiday.

He hadn't had to kill anyone yet, but you couldn't have everything.

The morning after Stavros had cleaned up her tracking software, Mangum went back into the transient crew section of the station to place cameras in the blind spots of interest. The spots where the RDT addicts had gone and were not yet covered by Mangum's surveillance cameras.

Mangum again wore coveralls and carried a tool bag. Together with his growing beard, he was just another maintenance guy on the huge station.

Mangum placed half a dozen more cameras and was back in the suite in the first-class section in time for lunch.

When Mangum got back to the suite, Stavros was hard at work on her display. She looked up as he came in.

"All set?"

"Yes. Six more cameras placed. You should see their feeds in your setup right now."

Stavros checked, and she had access.

"Got 'em."

"What have you been up to, Elina? You looked pretty engrossed when I came in."

Stavros looked embarrassed.

"Something of a wild hair. What if the RDT was being manufactured on the station? I can't get the idea out of my head. So I decided to find it. If it's there. You know."

"How do you even do that with the computer?"

"Well, Crossroads is pretty well documented, right? I mean, it has to be if people are going to maintain it. Keep it safe for everybody aboard. All that documentation is splattered around all over the place, but it all exists. Every system, every space."

"So you gather up all the documentation and look for where the hole is?"

"Exactly, Bert. With my detective status, I can access all that stuff, where any individual on the station can't. The plumbers have their bit, the electricians have their bit, and so on, but I can get into them all."

"Nice. What about private spaces? Rooms and suites and such?"

"They're all going to have an occupant listed, right? And Crossroads, even the so-called permanent staff, is pretty transient. I mean, if you get a new job, you're going to leave the station, because Crossroads is the only employer here. The station itself."

"And so, if that's where it is, the residency records will show some room or suite or something that never changes hands. Do you have access to those records as well, Elina? Historically, I mean. Going back several years?"

"Yes. Of course. As a detective, I do. Anybody else, probably not."

"So how's that going?"

"Slowly. It will not be a quick effort. Don't forget how big the station is, Bert. I'm looking for a twenty thousand cubic foot space in a volume measured in cubic *miles*."

Mangum nodded. The largest human artifact in space, it had been called, and it likely was. In the cluster, at least.

"How about lunch?"

Stavros pushed back from her display.

"Sounds good. This is going really slowly. It's very frustrating, and I could use a break."

With more cameras placed, Mangum, Stavros, and Sam settled back into routine. It would be a while before the new cameras had any store of surveillance data to search, and then they needed more suspects with RDT addiction.

They walked the gardens every morning. They used different entrances to see different portions of the large circular space. There was a playground for children in one portion. A dog run in another. A big hill, twenty feet high or so – to within ten feet of the ceiling – with a climbing wall on one side. The plants on top of the hill, close to the lights and with less irrigation, were dry-country plants. There was a dirt path among them.

Stavros worked on her search for the potential RDT lab on the station. Mangum watched his surveillance recordings from the transient crew section of the station, trying to see any anomalies in behavior or traffic.

Sam let Mangum know he was growing short of certain nutrients, and they looked over the room service menu to see what would fit the bill. Liver – no onions – started turning up for Sam every couple of days, as well as guacamole. Mangum had had no idea how many nutrients there were in an avocado.

Sam got bigger every day as he adjusted his golden doodle persona to appear pregnant. He often now curled up on the

THE FAVOR

floor in niches and protected spaces like corners, rather than in the open on the couch.

It was a quiet time, waiting for the next shoe to drop, and the trio made the most of it.

"How are you doing, Sam?"

"I'm good, Bert. I really enjoy the walks in the gardens."

"And how is your little project going?"

"It's going well. A few more days, I think, before we separate. Then a couple of days before the basic organisms merge into an intelligent individual. They'll be a handful until then."

"I still can't get over how you're not one person, in some sense."

"One person, but not one organism. I had the hardest time getting pronouns right when I learned English. We couldn't fathom that you were a single organism. How could you possibly be intelligent?"

Mangum recalled how hard it was to explain to the aliens that he was a single organism, born that way, and never merged with another.

"I remember. I thought all of you were using the royal 'we' when you used the plural to refer to yourselves."

Sam nodded, and Mangum sipped his nightcap.

"Sam, when you separate, just take over this room. I'll keep Elina out, but you should probably lock the room anyway. Bolt the door. You know. Just to forestall any curiosity on her part."

"Oh, yes. That won't be a problem, Bert. I'll want to make sure the youngsters don't go off wandering anyway. They're remarkably stupid until they merge."

The days dragged out. One evening, Stavros commented

about it.

"I can't believe your employer lets you hang out for weeks on Crossroads in first-class luxury. That's really expensive, and you could have easily been home by now."

"Oh, sure, but that means I have to take two weeks to get back here before I can go anywhere else. Unless they want to send me point-to-point on a courier ship. And if you think Crossroads is expensive, you wouldn't believe what it costs to run a fast courier ship out to move one guy around and then deadhead home."

"So you're pre-positioned for the next move, and that's cheaper."

"Exactly, Elina. Cheaper and faster. On that scale, Crossroads just isn't that expensive."

"OK. I guess I see that. And I'm not complaining, mind. I'm having fun."

"Me, too. The company's nice, and we have an interesting problem to deal with, so I'm not just sitting idle."

"Well, we're sitting idle now, Bert, waiting for surveillance."

"Yes, but surveillance always takes a long time."

Stavros nodded. Long periods of tedium punctuated by moments of frenetic activity. It was a detective's life. A spy's, too, she supposed.

It was the next morning that the station's newsfeed had something interesting. Stavros was sitting at the table with a cup of coffee when Mangum finally wandered into the living room.

"There you are, sleepyhead."

"Hey, if you want me to get up early, you shouldn't keep me up so late. Besides, Sam was kind of clingy last night. I think she's close."

THE FAVOR

Stavros looked across the living room to where Sam was curled up on the floor between the two armchairs.

"Sam is such a good girl."

Sam wagged his tail, thumping it on the floor, but did not come over to her or even lift his head.

"Yeah, she's close," Mangum said. "She'll probably set up shop in the kids' bedroom soon, and not come out until her puppy or puppies are mobile on their own."

"Protective mommy."

"Oh, yes."

"Well, it's probably just as well, Bert. I think we have our break."

"Really."

"Yeah. A brawl last night, then the knives came out. We don't mind a bit of roughhousing, but when the knives come out, we get involved."

"We get any RDTers in this bunch, Elina?"

"Oh, yeah. Four. It was a big melee, in one of the bigger open spaces in the section."

"We have good face images on them?"

"Oh, sure. Computer matching is already running against the newer surveillance recordings."

"Excellent." Mangum rubbed his hands together. "Then I guess it's time for breakfast."

Stavros laughed.

"More like brunch."

Mangum shrugged.

"That works, too."

After breakfast – and another double order of guacamole and a fruit bowl for Sam – Mangum and Stavros got ready for their morning walk.

"Walk in the gardens, Sam?" Stavros asked.

Sam looked up at them for a few seconds, then put his head back down and heaved a deep sigh.

"She's really close now," Mangum said. "She doesn't want to be away from home when her time comes."

Stavros nodded. She went over and sat in the chair next to where Sam lay on the floor. She reached down to scratch the back of his neck and between his ears.

"OK, Sam. Good girl. Taking care of your babies. We'll be back soon."

They were walking the ring path in the gardens. The wan light from the distant red dwarf star was all they had in the night portion of the ring. That and some pathway lights along the walk.

"It's not the same without Sam," Stavros said.

Mangum nodded. He was clearly distracted, and Stavros let the conversation drop. It was several minutes before he spoke up.

"Elina, I was wondering. What kind of chemical analysis do they do on the RDT you find? What level of precision?"

"It's a go/no-go test. Like a piece of litmus paper, but treated with other chemicals. They put a drop on it and look for the telltale."

"So you have no idea how pure it is."

"No. Why, Bert?"

"Because it seems to me it would be more pure the closer you were to the source. That is, if it got diluted somewhere along the way in distribution, maybe more than once, that would be one thing. But they won't be diluting it at the source."

"I see what you're saying."

Stavros thought about it.

"But if you're going to ship it interstellar, I wouldn't think you'd dilute it, Bert. You certainly don't want to increase its bulk or weight in that case. You would ship it as pure and concentrated as you could."

"Yeah, you're probably right. So everything you would see here would be full strength anyway."

"I would think so."

"OK. It was just a thought."

"Keep 'em coming, Bert. We won't solve it if we aren't open to possibilities. It's nothing obvious, or we would have figured it out already."

When they got back to the room, Sam was nowhere to be seen, but the door to the kids' bedroom was closed. Stavros was concerned.

"I'll go check on him," Mangum said.

"Her. You'll go check on *her*."

Mangum shrugged.

"Pronouns don't matter."

"You're impossible."

Mangum went into the kids' bedroom, closing and locking the door behind him. Stavros did not have a key to the suite, she only had permission on the front door.

Then again, as a police detective, she probably had an override on every door on the station.

Sam was in the bathroom, in his natural state, in the bathtub. There were four nodules – lumpy masses – around his periphery, but still connected to his main mass.

"How are you doing, Sam?"

A mouth on a tube extruded from the alien's central mass.

"Good, Bert. Working up toward separation."

"When?"

"Oh, it will be hours yet. Or tomorrow."

"What do you want for lunch?"

"Fruit plate. Double order of guacamole. Maybe three hamburgers. Oh, and throw in a pizza."

"All for you?"

"No, as they prepare to separate, they're going to be very hungry. Better make that four hamburgers."

"You got it, Sam."

"Thanks, Bert. I gotta get back to work here."

Mangum just nodded and backed out. He closed the bathroom door, then closed and locked the door of the kid's bedroom as he left.

"How's she doing?"

"Good. She's curled up in the bathtub on a blanket. But she's just getting started. It's going to be hours yet. Maybe not till tomorrow."

"Is she going to be all right?"

"Oh, sure. This isn't her first. She knows what she's doing."

"Are you going to help her?"

"Oh, no. Sam's a very good dog, but you don't mess around with an animal that big when she's having her babies."

"Oh, I hope she'll be OK."

"Sam will be fine. I need to get her food, though. You ready for lunch?"

"Sure. That walk always makes me hungry."

When the server came, Stavros watched him set out the food in growing disbelief. Fruit bowl, double order of guacamole, four hamburgers, and a pizza. Just for Sam?

When the server left, she put it to Mangum.

"All that's for Sam?"

THE FAVOR

"A variety of things. She can eat whatever she wants and leave the rest. Hard to say what she will want to eat. Or when."

"I see."

Mangum arranged the other plates on the pizza box and headed to the kids' bedroom.

"Can I help?"

"No, Elina. Just stay here."

Mangum went through into the kids' bedroom and locked the door behind himself. He went into the bathroom and set the food down on the bathroom vanity.

"How you doing, Sam?"

"Good, Bert."

"I have all the food."

"Great. Just put it all in here with me."

Mangum put the fruit bowl and guacamole on the platform of the tub, then put the four hamburgers and the pizza down on Sam, but clear of the nodules at the edges.

Sam extruded a hand and mouth, picked up a hamburger and took a bit of it, then deposited that bite next to one of the nodules. As Mangum watched, the nodule extended toward the food, and started to pull it in.

Sam put a bite next to each of the other nodules as well, then started distributing the fruit, one piece at a time.

Mangum just nodded and backed out.

It was one thing to disturb an animal that big when they were having babies.

Disturbing an *alien* that dangerous when they were having babies was a whole 'nother thing.

Tracking And Confrontation

Stavros was nervous the rest of that day.

"I can't believe you're not more worried about Sam, Bert."

"I am worried, Elina, but what can I do? I certainly don't want to get in the way, or distract her from her business. We're best off just letting her carry on with it."

"I suppose. It just seems like we could do something."

"We can. We can wait."

"O-o-o-oh."

"In the meantime, have you been checking your matching run?"

"Yes, Bert. It's more than half finished. We should be able to map the contacts tomorrow morning."

"Excellent."

"What are you going to do then?"

"Look for the common element."

"Is there some place they all go? Someone they all see? That sort of thing?"

"Exactly. They're all getting RDT from somewhere, Elina. That's the common thread, after all. They're all hooked into the distribution network. What's the common element? If I can find that, I can tap into the distribution network and start tracing up the tree."

"This is going to get messy, isn't it?"

"Oh, yes. There's a lot of money involved, and the people making all that money are not going to want us finding out who they are."

"I suppose at some point I need to get my colleagues involved."

"Not yet, Elina. After all, you said if the chemical plant is on the station, station management and staff have to be involved. The police have to be involved, too. Probably even if it's coming in from outside."

Stavros' eyes widened, and Mangum nodded.

"The real reason you haven't been able to find the source, is that your superiors aren't interested in finding it. Are, in fact, actively working against you."

"That's a disturbing thought. But you must be right. It explains a lot."

Stavros pounded the arm of her chair.

"Actually, it pisses me off," she said.

Mangum nodded.

"So no colleagues. Not yet."

"Agreed. We'll bring them in on it when we start locking them up."

Mangum raised an eyebrow, and Stavros gave him a 'just tell me I can't' look.

"I came here to enforce the law, not aid and abet criminals."

Stavros pounded the arm of her chair again.

"Fuck."

That night, when Mangum climbed into bed and curled up to Stavros, she turned around and clung to him. She began to cry.

"I've been living a lie," she said through her tears.

"No. You've been living honestly within someone else's lie. There's a big difference."

Mangum held her until she cried herself to sleep.

Sleep evaded him for another couple hours while he considered what he knew so far, and what he could reasonably surmise.

Things were about to heat up. He was sure of it.

Which direction it would go was another matter.

The next morning Stavros was all business. She'd gotten past the frustration and betrayal, and had bent her anger against those who had manipulated her.

While waiting for breakfast to arrive, Stavros bent over her display. She engaged her mapping routine on the face matches returned by the pattern-matching program, which had completed processing all the surveillance recordings overnight.

When breakfast arrived, Mangum took Sam's breakfast – a double order of eggs and sausage with toast, two fruit bowls, and a double order of guacamole – into the kids' bedroom.

Looking into the bathroom, Mangum was surprised to see Sam sitting on the cover of the stool in his utility persona, watching four amoeba-like creatures splashing about in a quarter-inch of water in the tub.

"Morning, Sam."

"Hi, Bert."

"Separation last night? You sound pretty beat."

"Yes. It was a most grueling process, Bert. And now I have to watch them constantly."

"Very similar to human infants, or so I've been told. They wake up every two hours to be fed."

Sam nodded, then sighed.

"At least it's done. Thanks for breakfast."

"No problem, Sam."

Sam started tearing apart pieces of toast and tossing the pieces into the tub. It was much like someone feeding ducklings in a pond, which forced a chuckle from Mangum.

"So now what?" Mangum asked.

"I feed them almost constantly over the next several days

while keeping an eye on them. Keeping them from getting out and about."

"And then?"

"Once their body mass about doubles, we see if they will attempt a merger. They should, if they're together all the time."

"All right. Well, you let me know anything you need, Sam. And congratulations."

"Thanks, Bert."

Mangum went back out into the living room, locking the door behind him.

"How's Sam doing?" Stavros asked.

"Fine. Exhausted but happy. One puppy."

"Ooo. I wanna see."

"No. Not yet, Elina. Wait for Sam to come out. She just wants to recover for right now."

"Oh, all right. Spoilsport."

She smiled, making it clear she was just ribbing him.

"Did your matching software complete?"

"Oh, yes. Bert, I want these guys. I want them bad."

"OK, but let's not make any mistakes in our haste."

"No, no. I want to be successful. I want to see the looks on their faces when we bring them down."

"So the mapping routine is running now?"

"Yes."

"Well, let's eat then, before it gets cold."

Mangum's breakfast this morning was a lot of protein and fat and not a lot of carbs. He thought things would break soon, and he would be moving about. He didn't want to be loaded down.

So no donuts or cinnamon rolls this morning. No cereal or

pancakes. No hash browns or English muffins. Four eggs over easy, half a dozen bacon strips, half a dozen sausage links, a chunk of cheese, and a cup of espresso, black.

"Action breakfast this morning?" Stavros asked when Mangum uncovered his plate.

"Yeah."

Stavros raised an eyebrow in query.

"I just have this feeling," he said.

After breakfast, they cleared the dishes on the table to the bar for housekeeping to pick up, and Stavros rolled out her display.

"So let's see what we have," she said.

Stavros scrolled through her status display.

"OK, so the mapping routine completed."

Stavros pulled up the engineering diagrams of the station.

"Overlay all four suspects' traces, in different colors, Elina," Mangum said.

"Yeah. I can do that."

"And go to a three-dimensional representation."

"All right."

A floor plan appeared in the display, then multiple floors appeared, all rendered on top of each other. Traces overlapped and ran back and forth through the representation, without being able to tell which floor they were on.

"Now rotate the display slowly."

Mangum stared into the display as Stavros rotated the view, first on one axis, then on another.

"Well, look at that. What level is that?"

"A-12."

"Isolate A-12."

Only one floor plan was rendered now. Multiple traces in

different colors went to the same hallway, then re-emerged.

"That's suggestive," Stavros said.

"Can you reference that back to the surveillance recordings?"

"Sure, Bert."

Stavros marked one of the facial match traces, then shoved the floor plan off to the side. A video surveillance recording appeared, frozen at that point. She scrolled the recording forward in slow motion.

"So that's one of our guys?" Mangum asked.

"Yeah. Red trace."

The camera location had a view down the hallway. Red Trace went down the hallway maybe halfway, and buzzed at a door. He talked to whoever opened the door for several seconds, then went in.

Stavros speeded up the recording to him emerging from the room.

"Looks like he was in the room for maybe five minutes? Something like that."

"Can we tell which door that is?" Mangum asked.

"Not really. Not from this angle."

"OK. Let's look at Green Trace and Blue Trace."

"Sure, Bert."

Stavros walked the video recordings through the same sequence for the other two traces, which repeated exactly.

"OK, so maybe that's our RDT retailer, Elina. One of them, anyway."

"What about Orange Trace, Bert?"

"Maybe he didn't need any refills during the surveillance period. Or went to a different supplier."

"OK. That would make sense. But how do we know which room it is? We can't really tell."

"Run through the occupancy records for the spinward side of that section of the hallway. Which hallway is it?"

"A-12-27."

"Can you reference those records, Elina?"

"Sure. Let me see."

Stavros swept the video recording off to the side, then pulled up the occupancy query.

"A-12-27," Stavros said as she typed. "Got it."

She scrolled down the list.

"All of these are shown as recent occupancies by transient crew, Bert. Oh. Except one. A-12-27-122."

"What have you got on that?"

"Long-term reserved. For Maintenance, it says. They sometimes do that, to have a room to store equipment and such. They're all over the station."

"Uh-huh. Elina, can you check Maintenance and see what *they* think their reserved rooms are?"

"Yeah. I think so."

Stavros swept the occupancy records to the side and pulled up the Maintenance Department. She went to equipment stores, and keyed for location.

"That's strange, Bert. A-12-27-122 isn't listed. A-12-27-217 is, though. That's further down that hallway on the other side. In the next section."

"So it's reserved to Maintenance, and Maintenance doesn't know anything about it. Are Maintenance stores rooms normally that close together?"

"No. I don't think so, anyway."

"All right. That's our room then. A-12-27-122. Easy to remember anyway. Probably why they chose it."

"What are you going to do, Bert?"

"I'm going to go down there and ask them what's going on."

THE FAVOR

"Oh my God. Bert, they'll kill you."

"As it turns out, Elina, it's been tried before."

Mangum shrugged.

"I'm very hard to kill."

Bert Mangum walked though the A section of Crossroads on the twelfth level. He was dressed down, way down, like transient crew on leave. That and his full beard made him just another crewman out for some fun between runs.

He also carried the 8mm semiautomatic pistol and the small six-shot dart gun.

Mangum remembered corridor A-12-27. He had placed a surveillance camera in the lobby at the nearby intersection of several hallways, which is why they had surveillance recordings of the area.

Mangum found A-12-27, and walked down the corridor to room 122. He leaned up against the doorframe on his forearm, the dart gun in his hand. He pushed the door buzzer.

After several seconds, the door slid aside. Standing in the doorway was a very large man. He filled the doorway. Mangum shot him in the neck with the dart gun as the door opened.

The giant let out a roar and grabbed at Mangum, who spent a nervous ten seconds evading his grasp. Mangum was glad he had skipped carbs this morning. It was a close thing as it was.

When the Com-Ply started to kick in, the big man seemed confused for a moment.

"Tiny, is everything OK?"

"Tell him yes, you were confused for a moment," Mangum said softly.

"Yeah, it's OK. I was confused for a moment," Tiny called back over his shoulder.

"How many people are in the room behind you?" Mangum whispered.

"Two."

"Are they armed?"

"Yeah."

"You know what I think would be fun, Tiny? Go back in the room and take their guns away. Sneak up on them, though. Don't let them know what you're up to. You can hit them first if you want."

"Oh. All right."

Tiny turned around and strode into the room. He took the one man who was standing, picked him up and threw him at the other, then wrested both of their guns out of their hands when they tried to pull them.

Mangum walked into the room behind Tiny and shot the other two men with darts, then closed the room door behind him. The Com-Ply kicked in as they were trying to figure out what was going on.

Mangum pulled up a chair and sat.

"Why don't we all just have a seat? Get comfortable."

"OK," one of the men answered.

"You can just put those guns on the table there, Tiny."

"All right."

The big man put the two guns on the table and then took a seat himself.

"So what are your names?"

"I'm Sam Skinner, that's Matt Carson, and the big guy is Tiny McCord," the senior of the three said.

"What do you guys do here?"

"We sell RDT to staff and transient crew."

"Where does the RDT come from?"

"We don't know."

"Yeah, it's just always here," Carson said. "It gets replenished when we're not here. We're only open specific hours."

"And everybody knows they can get RDT here?"

"Yeah. It sort of goes through the addict community that this is where to come for it," Skinner said.

"It's an all-cash business, I assume."

"A lot of it is. But we can bill their accounts, too. It goes down as prostitution services, I think."

There was a buzz at the door, and Tiny looked toward the door.

"Ignore the door buzzer, Tiny. They'll come back later."

"OK."

"Who pays you guys? I mean, what do you do for a living?"

"Crossroads pays us. This is our job, right here. We make pretty good money, too."

Skinner had been doing most of the talking, but Carson spoke up again.

"Yeah. I got a big pay raise for this job. And it's easy. Mostly we just sit here."

"Why three of you?"

"I do the money work," Skinner said. "Carson there gets the drugs from the cabinet, and Tiny takes care of any trouble."

"The drugs are in the cabinet?"

"Yeah."

"Show me."

Skinner got up and went over to the cabinet in the room. It was a typical office supply cabinet. He opened the doors, and Mangum could see the interior was thin half-wide drawers maybe two-thirds of the way down, with an open area underneath that held a cash box and an account reader.

Mangum walked over to the cabinet and opened one of the

drawers at random. Dozens of ampoules. He picked another one. Dozens more. There were dozens of drawers.

"Hey, can I buy one of these?"

"Sure. That's what we do here."

Skinner opened a specific drawer and pulled out an ampoule.

"This is the current working drawer. We rotate stock, you know?"

"Sure. I get it. What do I owe you?"

"Going rate is twenty credits for that size ampoule."

"Sounds good."

Mangum pulled out a twenty-credit bill and passed it to Skinner.

"Thanks."

Skinner put it in the cash box.

"All right. You can close the cabinet."

Skinner closed the cabinet, and Mangum and Skinner both went back to their chairs and sat down.

"Well, that's all I wanted to ask you guys about. Thanks for being so helpful."

"No problem," Skinner said.

"I have an idea, though" Mangum said. "Your bosses would probably be upset if they knew I was here asking questions. You know, they get all bent out of shape about stuff like that. Be mad at you, too, I bet."

"Yeah. Probably."

"So I have an idea. Let's just not tell them. I mean, I bought RDT, but nothing else happened. I won't say anything about it if you don't. We'll just keep it between ourselves. How does that sound?"

"Would you do that?"

"Sure. No sense getting them all upset about nothing."

THE FAVOR

Skinner looked to the other two, and they were both nodding.

"Sounds good to me," McCord said.

"Yeah. Thanks," Carson said.

"Looks like we're agreed," Skinner said. "We appreciate it."

"No problem," Mangum said. "I just bought some stuff, and didn't ask any questions. You wouldn't recognize me again if you saw me."

"OK."

"I'll just leave now and let you guys carry on with business."

"All right. And thanks a lot."

"No problem."

Mangum got up and left the room.

"Nice guy," Carson said.

"Yeah," Skinner said. "And remember. Nothing happened. Just a normal sale, to a normal customer."

"You got it," McCord said.

He looked over at the table.

"Hey. You guys want your guns back?"

Surveillance And Testing

With Mangum out of the suite, Elina Stavros couldn't help herself. She walked over to the door of the kids' bedroom and opened the door quietly.

"Sam?" she said softly.

Stavros didn't see the dog in the room beyond, but the bathroom door was ajar.

The golden doodle stuck its head out and looked at her around the corner of the partially open bathroom door, then shut the door and locked it with the lock paddle.

"Huh. Well, I guess that's that."

She backed out of the kids' bedroom and closed the door behind her.

Mangum got back to the suite just before lunch.

"You survived," Stavros said.

"Clearly. Should we order lunch?"

"Sure, but then I want to hear everything that happened."

They got a lunch order together, and Mangum called it in.

"OK, now out with it. What happened?"

"It's an RDT retail outlet, no doubt about it. They have hundreds of ampoules in stock, and their stock is periodically refreshed by persons unknown when they are otherwise closed."

"An RDT store?"

"Yup."

"So what did you do?"

"I bought some RDT."

Mangum took the ampoule out of his pocket and set it on the

table.

"What are you going to do with that?"

"Do you have access to secure mail off-station, Elina?"

"Sure. 'Special Handling - Diplomatic Pouch' works. I can do that. Where would you send it?"

"Back to my boss. Get it properly tested."

"You're going to send it to the Agency, Bert?"

"There's no such thing as the Agency, Elina."

Stavros waved that away.

"So you send it to headquarters?"

"Yes. They can do a proper chemical test there, not just a go/no-go test."

"Well, I could do that, too."

"Without giving away what we're up to?"

"Well, no, that I couldn't do."

Mangum nodded.

"All right, Bert. So I send it off to wherever, and then what do we do for two weeks?"

"Someone is replenishing their stock. We figure out who that is, then I question him."

"How do we figure that out?"

"I put a surveillance camera in the RDT store."

"You did?"

"Yup. You know those office cabinets? The ones with two doors?"

"Yeah."

"The locking ones only have a keyhole on one door handle. The one in the RDT store now has a keyhole on both door handles."

"Nice."

Mangum shrugged.

"It'll probably get discovered pretty quickly, but we only

need one facial match."

"Yeah. If I get one good shot of his face, I've got him."

Mangum nodded.

The door buzzer rang, and Mangum opened the door for the server. The server set the table, then withdrew, and Mangum collected Sam's things to take into the kids' bedroom. Fried liver – no onions – a double order of guacamole, and two fruit bowls.

"Bert, I have a confession to make."

Mangum raised an eyebrow.

"I thought I would peek in on Sam. See how she's doing."

"And?"

"She was in the bathroom. She stuck her head out, and, when she saw it was me, she closed and locked the bathroom door."

"As I told you, Elina. She doesn't want to be bothered."

"Yeah, I thought you were just being selfish. Keeping all the cute to yourself."

Mangum chuckled.

"When the puppy is big enough, in her view, Sam will introduce you. In the meantime, you and I are just going to have to wait."

"You? But you're taking her food in."

"Yes, and she guards the puppy behind her till I set out the food and leave."

"You haven't seen her puppy yet?"

"No, Elina."

"That makes me feel better."

What he said was strictly true, Mangum thought. The four alien organisms had not yet merged, had not yet tried to generate a puppy persona. Misleading as hell, but true nonetheless.

THE FAVOR

"I'll be right back."

Mangum went over to the kids' bedroom, went in, and closed the door behind him. He knocked twice on the bathroom door.

"It's me, Sam."

Sam unlocked the door and let Mangum in. Sam was in his utility persona.

"Sorry, Bert. Elina tried to peek in before."

"I know. She told me. I reminded her that I said you weren't ready."

Mangum put the tray down on the vanity.

"So for lunch we've got liver, guacamole, and fruit."

"Perfect. Thanks, Bert."

Mangum just nodded and headed back out to the living room. He heard the bathroom door close and lock behind him.

After lunch, Stavros went into the bedroom and came back dressed in office wear. In fact, it was the outfit she had worn to Mangum's suite a month ago, after Gloria Dent left Crossroads.

"I'm going to go mail this, Bert."

"Let me put a note in with it."

Mangum scrawled on a piece of paper and put it in the envelope with the ampoule. Stavros would ship it all in a small box.

"And this is the address?"

"Yes. That's it. It's a drop box."

"All right. See you in a bit."

Crossroads had post offices, just like any other city its size. This one was also a shipping center, with boxes and packing and such. Stavros selected a small box – though not small enough to get lost – and placed the envelope with the note and ampoule in the box, surrounded by packing wrap.

She taped it up, taped on the address, and took it to the counter.

"Special handling. Diplomatic pouch."

The clerk raised an eyebrow and Stavros produced her badge. He nodded.

"Very well, Detective. Cash or account?"

"Cash. I'll expense it later."

He nodded and rang it up. Stavros paid, and he gave her a receipt.

She turned and walked away.

"Next."

"Any problems?" Mangum asked when Stavros got back.

"No. I paid cash for it as you said. So it won't get reported back to my superiors."

"Good. Now let's see what we're getting on our new feed."

Stavros unrolled her display and pulled up the stream.

"Feed looks good."

She watched for a bit.

"Oh, my. Is that guy as big as he looks?"

"Yeah. They call him Tiny."

Stavros chuckled.

"He looks like he could pull you apart like a chicken."

"He could. It was pretty dicey staying out of his clutches long enough for the drugs to kick in."

"Drugs?"

"I shot him with the dart gun no sooner than he opened the door, but it took ten seconds or so to kick in."

"Ah. And the other two?"

"I had Tiny take their guns away, then shot them as well."

"Then you had a chit-chat."

"And I bought some RDT. Yup."

"Are you in trouble then?"

"No. I left them with a post-hypnotic suggestion to keep it all between us so they wouldn't get in trouble with their bosses."

"Will that hold?"

Mangum shrugged.

"I'm not worried about it."

"We're actually getting footage of all the purchasers as well. Do we round all these people up and arrest them?"

"No, Elina. That's how police always do it. Arrest users and small-time dealers. Lock up a bunch of people and ruin their lives, but the big fish never get in trouble. Nothing changes. You bust an operation, and then the real troublemakers get off scot-free and go set up another operation. I'm not interested in the little fish. I want the boss."

"I see. I agree, I think. So what now, Bert?"

"Now we wait for restocking. Can you set up a scanner to watch for after-hours activity in that room?"

"What are their normal hours?"

"Don't know, but we should learn that today."

Stavros nodded.

"Once we have that time, I can set up the scanning."

"Good."

"In the meantime, we're back to waiting?"

"Yeah. Surveillance sucks, but there's no other way to do it. At least the computers can keep track of it for us, and we don't have to sit and stare at a screen twenty-four hours a day."

"So what then, Bert?"

"Walk in the gardens?"

"Works for me."

That evening, Mangum held Stavros in the afterglow until she was asleep, then got up for a nightcap. He went in to the kids' bedroom to check on Sam.

Mangum found Sam sitting on the cover of the stool in the bathroom, watching the alien infants in the tub. They were larger now, maybe fifty cubic inches each. Ten percent of their adult volume.

Sam occasionally dropped some food into the tub from the plates from dinner. Just from the way he moved, he looked pretty tired.

"Hi, Sam. How's it going?"

"Good, Bert. Damn, I'm beat, though. At home people take turns watching bigger groups so you can take a break. And we lose some. They're just so damn stupid at this stage."

Mangum looked back into the tub and nodded. They just kept crawling around, looking for food.

Sam looked up at him.

"But I can't afford to lose one, Bert, or they won't be able to merge into a sentient creature. I don't have any margins in this operation. There are no others around."

"When will they merge?"

"They should attempt a merger soon. In this limited space, they keep running into each other, so they're aware of each other."

Sam shrugged.

"Maybe tonight. Maybe tomorrow. Then I can at least reason with them. They can keep themselves out of trouble at that point. In the meantime, it's twenty-four-hour monitoring."

"Wow. All right. Well, I thought I would check in."

"No problem, Bert. It's all going well."

Sam sighed.

"I will be glad when this stage is over, though."

THE FAVOR

It was clear they did not replenish what Mangum and Stavros called the RDT store every night. Several days passed without any after-hours action in room A-12-27-122. They spent their time walking in the gardens, taking siestas, and enjoying each other's company.

Mangum checked in on Sam when he took meals in and when he had his nightcap every evening once Stavros was asleep. Sam's offspring merged the day after Mangum's visit to the RDT store, but Mangum couldn't see any difference other than that there was only one creature now, as big as the other four combined.

Sam had disagreed.

"Oh, it's a huge difference, Bert. This combined being is now sentient. It understands who it is, and who I am. It understands that I want what's best for it, and is willing to obey my restrictions."

"That's unlike a human child, Sam. They always want to test to see if those restrictions make sense."

"Yes, Bert. But they already have all the memories of why those restrictions are necessary. That's a big difference."

Mangum nodded.

"Have you thought about a name, Bert?"

"There are a bunch of choices. Things that are ambivalent with regard to sex. The one I keep coming back to, though, is Jules. It's a French male name, but the French pronunciation is the same as the English female name Jewel."

"Which is a precious stone. I like it, Bert. Jules it will be."

Over the next day or two, Jules practiced shifting into various personae. A utility persona, like Sam's, and the persona of a golden doodle puppy.

Mangum was asked to judge the puppy persona one evening. Sam fed the puppy persona some bits remaining from supper, and Jules properly ate it, chewing it with his mouth rather than by simply enveloping it. Looking good. Mostly.

"We've been watching videos of puppies on your display, Bert," Sam said.

"Well, I think he almost has it, Sam."

Mangum offered some advice, which Jules incorporated. Mostly about how clumsy puppies were, and how energetic and enthusiastic about everything, at least until they wore themselves out.

"OK, that's about perfect right there, Jules."

The tail formed a mouth on the end.

"Great. Thanks, Bert."

"Now don't do *that* in front of anybody else."

"I understand, Bert. I'll be good."

The next morning, once the server had set for breakfast and left, the door to the kids' bedroom opened. Stavros looked over, and Jules came out of the bedroom walking like he owned the universe, Sam walking along watchfully behind.

Then Jules got his feet tangled up and fell on his face. Typical puppy stuff.

Stavros laughed.

"Sam, what a beautiful puppy. What's his name?"

"Jules," Mangum said, pronouncing it 'Jewel.' "Like Jules Verne."

As Jules approached, Stavros leaned down to pick him up, but he decided it would be more fun to play keep-away from her hands, running behind her legs or under her chair.

Stavros laughed.

"So cute!"

Sam sat down by the table and looked at the food. Looked at Mangum, then back to the food.

THE FAVOR

Mangum put two plates and two bowls down on the floor. One double order of eggs and sausage, one single order of eggs and sausage, and two fruit bowls, one a double. Both dogs set to them, gobbling hungrily.

"Oh, this is so fun," Stavros said. "But what are we going to do about walking in the gardens, Bert? We only have one leash."

"I actually have two, Elina. In case I can't find one, or one breaks. I think one of them will close down enough for Jules."

"Excellent. It will be fun to see what he thinks of the gardens."

Stavros wasn't disappointed. Jules was all over the place while Stavros, Mangum, and Sam walked the path through the gardens. This way to the end of the leash, that way to the end of the leash, the puppy was all over the place.

At some point it was clear Jules had worn himself out. He lay down on the path, put his head down, and sighed.

Stavros laughed.

"Now what do we do?"

But Sam lay down on the path next to Jules, and Jules climbed up on Sam's back, his legs sticking out to the sides. Sam got up carefully, and Jules lay his head down on Sam's neck and napped.

"That'll work," Mangum said.

Stavros nodded. She scratched Sam between the ears.

"Good girl, Sam. You're such a good girl."

RICHARD F. WEYAND

An Official Assignment

After lunch, Mangum and Stavros were at loose ends. Sam lay on the couch and watched Stavros, who was down on the floor playing with Jules. He would attack her hand, then she would advance on him and he would run away, then turn to attack her hand again.

Mangum sat in one of the armchairs, deep in thought. He had kept headquarters informed on his activities, at least once things had gotten more serious. Waiting was never his game, though he understood the need, and he kept wondering what else they could be doing with the time.

At some point, Jules got tired. He lay down on the floor and sighed. Sam saw that and got down from the couch, picked the puppy up in his mouth and trotted off to the kids' bedroom.

Stavros got up off the floor and sat in the other armchair.

"Wore him out, I guess," she said to Mangum.

"It's good for him."

Stavros nodded.

"Elina, I have a question. We found this RDT store, right?"

"Right. Waiting now for the surveillance to show us the supply clerk who keeps the stock full."

"Right. So how many RDT stores are there on Crossroads?"

"What do you mean, Bert?"

"Do you think there is only one store like that for the whole station? How many are there?"

"You think there's more than one?"

"Yes. I would actually be surprised if it was only one."

"How would we go about finding them?"

"A-12-27-122 is a reserved room, right? Reserved to

66

Maintenance. But it's not in the Maintenance records. Can you search for all the reserved rooms on Crossroads, then cross-reference those to the lists maintained by the various departments, and find the orphans?"

"By orphans, you mean the reserved rooms no department lists."

"Right."

"There's an idea. Yes, Bert, I can probably do that."

"Why don't we get that started, then? See how big this whole thing is."

Stavros worked all afternoon on this new project, while Mangum sent in another report to the Agency. He brought them up to speed on both what he knew and what he conjectured to be true or possible. He also warned them about the RDT sample that should be on its way.

Phillip Marstock, Mangum's contact at the headquarters of the Agency for Interstellar Trade of the Association of Planets – also known as the Association Intelligence Agency, the AIA, or simply the Agency – read Mangum's current report with interest.

He made an appointment with his boss, Frank Latham, the head of operations for the Agency.

"So what do you have, Phil?" Latham asked.

"Mangum's got a hold of something on Crossroads, and it keeps getting bigger. I think he could really be on to something serious," Marstock said.

Latham raised an eyebrow. Marstock was a senior guy – anybody who was going to hold the leash on people like Bert Mangum and Claude Portnoy had to be – and he was not prone to overstatement.

"Really?"

"Yes, sir. It started out as something of a lark. A favor for a police detective on Crossroads. It grew out of their, um, friendship."

"A friendship with a police detective? That doesn't sound like Mangum's style, Phil."

"You would have to see her picture, sir. She's definitely Mangum's style."

"Ah. Got it. So they're involved in other affairs, as it were, and she asked him a favor."

"Yes. Where is the RDT on Crossroads coming from? They see it all the time, and can't get on top of it. You know, they don't do any surveillance on the transient crew spaces – that's something of a selling point for refueling stops – and they couldn't track it down."

"But Mangum isn't limited in that sense. In most senses, actually."

"Yes, sir. Exactly. And they found that RDT was being sold on the station pretty openly. From a room reserved to Maintenance, though Maintenance doesn't know anything about it."

"Which implies that whoever is in charge of room assignments on Crossroads, at least, is involved."

"Yes, sir, but Mangum thinks it may go beyond that. The salesmen in this store are on Crossroads' payroll. In their sales role."

"Station management could be involved, top to bottom, then."

"Yes, sir. The RDT may even be being manufactured on Crossroads. All the RDT, everywhere. Mangum says it's a possibility, if not a likelihood."

"Remarkable. Well, that would certainly be something to get on top of, Phil. We were sort of reserving Mangum for this Wilbourne affair, though, weren't we?"

"Yes, sir. We think Gloria Dent of the BIE is likely going to get herself in trouble over there. Not that she isn't on top of tracking down the problem, but she's not the person to ultimately deal with it. And we and Gaston's BIE have been cooperating pretty well lately."

Latham nodded.

"What's Portnoy's status, Phil?"

"He had a quick courier run after that Abelon clean-up, and is actually in Villacqua, sir. And he still has the courier ship with him."

"Could he work with Dent on the Wilbourne business?"

"Yes, sir. They met in Abelon, so I think we're good there. She already knows who he is, and he knows her. No trust issue."

"All right. Let's assign Mangum to this Crossroads question, and let Portnoy back up Dent on the Wilbourne business."

"Yes, sir."

The call came through, as they always did, with no video. Neither party used any term of address.

"Yeah," Mangum said.

"You have a new assignment," Marstock said.

"I'm listening."

"Assisting Detective Stavros in tracking down the RDT source on Crossroads is now an official assignment."

"Methods available?"

"Any and all."

"And the solution?"

"Contact for further direction before using extreme

measures."

"Got it."

The connection dropped.

The call came through, as they always did, with no video. Neither party used any term of address.

"Yes?" Portnoy asked,

"You have a new assignment," Marstock said.

"Go ahead."

"Travel to Wilbourne. Make contact with Gloria Dent of the BIE at the Somerset Plaza Hotel in Somerset. Assist Dent in her current assignment. Rectify the issue she's uncovered."

"Methods available?"

"Any and all."

"Rectify the issue?"

"Yes. Use extreme prejudice."

"Understood."

The connection dropped. Portnoy signaled the captain of *Silverheel*.

"Langdon here."

"Recall the crew from planet leave, Captain. And let me know where to meet the shuttle. We leave for Wilbourne at your earliest convenience."

"Very well, Mr. Portnoy."

Portnoy cut the connection and sat back in his chair.

Gloria Dent, eh?

Now that was interesting.

He started packing to leave Villacqua.

Mangum gave Stavros the news over supper. The dogs had been fed and were on the sofa.

"I got a call this afternoon, Elina. I have a new assignment."

"Oh, no. When are you leaving?"

"I'm not leaving. I let headquarters know what we were finding here, and what I suspected. My new assignment is to continue to help you with tracking this down."

Stavros brightened right up and clapped her hands.

"Oh, good. I've been so worried that you would get pulled out just as we were closing in on something."

Mangum nodded.

"Me, too. But they're curious, I think. They want to know where this investigation leads."

"And when we find out?"

"I don't yet have any instructions in that regard."

Stavros nodded.

"So where did you get this afternoon with the reserved rooms problem?"

"I had the system collect all the reserved rooms by walking the station. You know, Bert. Querying every map location. Now it's comparing all of those to the reserved lists of the various departments. That's a bigger problem, but there should be an answer soon."

"All right. And the previous problem? Finding any unassigned volume within Crossroads that's big enough for an RDT lab?"

"Still in progress. That's a much bigger problem. A lot of those spaces aren't kept in an inventory, since they're not rooms that could be leased out. I'm having to go through the volume of the space station one bit of cubic at a time."

"Understood. But you're still on that."

"Oh, yes."

"Good. Excellent."

Stavros had not missed the slight change in emphasis from Mangum with regard to the RDT project. It was now an official assignment from the Agency he claimed didn't exist. It was now not just a favor for her, it was his job.

Stavros wondered what the implications of that might be. She herself was a citizen of the Association of Planets. She had come to Crossroads from Mardouk, the Association's capital planet, and, like all Crossroads residents, retained her home-planet citizenship.

For the first time, she wondered if it was time to go back.

To go home.

Gloria Dent, in a penthouse suite of the Somerset Plaza Hotel in Somerset, the capital of Wilbourne, got a message from BIE headquarters in response to her request for direct-action assistance.

The Agency was dispatching Claude Portnoy. Actually, the message said they were dispatching Chuck Pendergast, but Dent knew that was one of Portnoy's common aliases. He would arrive in about two weeks.

Claude Portnoy, eh?

Now that was interesting.

The next day, Stavros had results from the reserved room cross-reference. They were not encouraging.

"The results don't look good?" Mangum asked.

"The problem is there are dozens of them and they all look good."

"Dozens of RDT stores?"

"Not hardly, Bert. The problem with big database searches and cross-references is that mistakes creep into databases. This gets updated and that over there doesn't. So which one is right? Which one is closest to the golden copy?"

"The golden copy?"

"The one that's operationally correct. For instance, we have over a hundred thousand people on Crossroads. Residents and transients. We have a list of them all. What's the golden copy?"

"The immigration listing?"

"No, Bert. The golden copy is the people themselves. If you find someone on Crossroads who isn't in the listing, you don't just space them, just as if there is someone who is listed and they aren't here, you can't create them. The people themselves are the golden copy. Any discrepancy with the actual people in the database means the database is wrong."

"OK, so the golden copy for the rooms listing has to be the rooms themselves, right?"

"Right. So do we go check them all? How do we figure out these discrepancies?"

"Some of the discrepancies may be manufactured, Elina."

"Almost certainly. So how do we figure it out without going to every single one of them and looking?"

"Ah. I see now. We have a candidates list, but almost all of them are likely database errors. Somebody, say, didn't need a reserved space, and surrendered it back, marking their database, but the update never got to the other database. The occupancy listing."

"Right. Short of going and looking, how would we know?"

"So what do we do now, Elina?"

"Let me think about it, Bert. Play with the data some more. If I can find a third listing for some of these rooms, then I can see if two of them agree. That's more likely to be right."

Mangum sat back in the big armchair and stared at the ceiling. Something was twitching. What was it? How else to solve this? Got it!

"Elina, why don't we let Maintenance do it?"

"What?"

"Tell Maintenance you found problems in the reserved rooms listings – databases that don't agree – and let them fix it."

"Why would they fix it, Bert?"

"Maintenance types on a space station tend to be fussy. Obsessive-compulsive types. Because if something isn't right, things can go very badly very quickly."

"OK. I get that. But why am I requesting it?"

"A police detective? Correct information is essential to police investigations. Besides, you're not requesting it, per se. You're just letting them know there's a problem."

"Do you expect that they will go to the RDT stores and check on them, Bert?"

"No, Elina. I expect that they won't. But let's say someone cleans some of these discrepancies up. Will you be able to see who made the database changes?"

"Not normally, but with police access, yes."

"And the fellow changes this one and this one and not this other one. Turns out that's an RDT store...."

"But then we know who in Maintenance is bent. Brilliant."

Stavros thought about it.

"But then aren't they going to know I'm nosing about the reserved rooms, Bert? Won't I attract attention?

"At some point we're going to attract attention, Elina. No doubt about it. Which will likely also surface some rats."

"OK, Bert. I see. Let me send them a note about the discrepancies and the room listing, and we can see what happens."

With the note sent off to Maintenance, Stavros put those rooms on an alarm so she would see when any of the data changed. That done, she turned back to the problem of finding a big enough space for an RDT lab on the station.

She still didn't think they would find one – that the RDT was being brought in, somehow – but, if it was here, she meant to find it.

Lots Of Things, All At Once

Several more days went by before anything happened, then everything seemed to happen at once.

Someone in Maintenance was making database changes in the reserved room listings. Most were what Stavros had hypothesized: a room was no longer needed, but the occupancy database had not been updated. Some sloppy record-keeping there.

Then the database changes stopped. There were a dozen or so discrepancies left. Not an impossible number to check out.

Stavros looked up who had been making the changes, and thought to track him down.

She found him.

In the obituaries.

"So the database corrections were being made by this guy – this Clark Jones – and now he's turned up dead?"

"Yeah. Of an RDT overdose."

"Any prior record with RDT, Elina?"

"No."

"OK, so he wasn't on the inside, and he tripped over something they didn't want him to know."

"Yes. And I set him up."

"Don't go there, Elina. You didn't kill him, someone else did. That's not your fault. We can't tiptoe around these guys just in case someone gets in their way."

"Oh, I know. It still bothers me."

"Oh, sure. And we'll get our licks in, too, before it's over. No worries there."

"Anyway, Jones whittled the discrepancies down to a dozen rooms or so before they offed him."

"OK. That's my job. I'll check them out."

"You going to just go knock on the door, Bert?"

"No. I'm going to do it from here."

Stavros raised an eyebrow.

"I have mobile surveillance assets as well. Do you have that room list for me?"

"Let me send it to you."

Stavros went over to her display and typed.

"You should have it now."

"All right. Catch you in a bit."

Mangum left the living room for the kids' bedroom, and Sam and Jules followed him.

With the kids' bedroom door closed, Sam and Jules both took on their utility personae. Jules looked to be about ten or twelve years old in size, before the big growth spurt hit. He just didn't have enough mass yet to impersonate a full-sized human.

"Can you do the ventilator thing for me again, Sam?"

"Sure, Bert. You have a map for me?"

"Yeah. Let me pull it up."

Mangum pulled up the room list on his roll-up display, then tracked down the first room in the engineering drawings. Even better, the rooms, once sorted into proximity within the station, could be done in six groupings of three, two, or one.

"This is the first group of three, Sam. Down this main trunk, then this branch, this one, and this one. All you need to do is stick an eyeball around the corner for each, and see what's in there."

"All right, Bert."

"What about me?" Jules asked.

"You stay here for now," Sam said.

"Oh, all right."

Sam walked over to the ventilator grille in the wall, and started to ooze through it.

"See you in a bit."

He eased the rest of the way through the ventilator grille and was gone.

The grille ahead should be the first of the target rooms. Sam eased an eyestalk forward to look around the corner.

Huh. Empty and dark. Sam could see little from the dim nightlight built into every electrical outlet on Crossroads. The room looked dusty, like it hadn't been used in years. Hadn't even been opened in years.

OK. That was one off his list.

As Sam approached the second room on his list, he heard voices and saw light coming through the ventilator grille. He crept up to the ventilator grille and snuck an eyestalk to the edge, making sure to keep in the dark well back from the grille.

This looked a lot like the room Mangum had described. A supply cabinet. A table and chairs. Three fellows sat in the room talking. While Sam watched, there was a buzz at the door. A fellow came in and bought an ampoule of something, presumably RDT, then left.

Sam pulled back from the grille and crept back down the ventilation duct.

The second room was an RDT store.

The third room was also dark, like the first one. This one, though was stacked with boxes. He couldn't see all of the room with all the boxes in the way, but it looked like static storage of equipment of various sorts.

OK. Back to the suite and get some more room numbers and ventilation system routes to get there.

Sam had been gone over an hour before he oozed back through the ventilator grille into the kids' bedroom in the suite.

"Hi, Bert."

"Hi, Sam. Whatcha got?"

Sam walked over to the display on the table. He pointed to the first room on his itinerary.

"This room was almost surely released and just didn't get back into inventory. It's empty and dark, and dusty, like it hasn't been used in months. Maybe years."

Sam pointed to the third room.

"This room I think fell off the reserved list in occupancy, but looks like it is being used for the storage of equipment."

"Maintenance, do you think?"

"It was hard to make out just with the outlet lights, but I would expect the boxes to be bigger for maintenance equipment. Perhaps it's kitchen or cafeteria storage. You know. Pots, pans, dishes. That sort of thing. The boxes are on the small side."

"And this room?" Mangum asked, pointing to the second room Sam had visited.

"Oh, that's an RDT store."

"You're sure?"

"Oh, yes. It looks just as you described. And a customer came and bought an ampoule while I watched."

"Pretty definite then."

Mangum looked down at the map.

"You ready for another three?"

"Sure, Bert."

When all was said and done, there were another five RDT stores among the remaining discrepancies. The rest of the rooms were either empty or in normal storage use.

When Mangum told Stavros, she was not pleased.

"How do you know, Bert?"

"As I said, Elena, I have remote surveillance assets. I sent them around in the ventilators and looked."

"And you're sure."

"Yes, I'm sure."

"You're telling me there's a retail chain operating here selling RDT? How is that even possible?"

"Someone – several someones – are covering for them."

"Including in Crossroads P.D."

"I would think so, yes. Elina, was there a department charged with investigating all RDT cases?"

"Yes. Of course."

"Wanna bet they never came up with anything? Wanna bet I know why?"

"Yes, because they were all on the take. That department was where you sent RDT cases to die."

"Yup. Betcha they're very secretive, too. Oh, we can't tell you what we're looking into. Or our progress. Very secret. Am I right, Elina?"

Stavros replied through gritted teeth.

"Yes."

"See? Nice operation. Very secure, when you can hire the cops themselves to protect you."

"O-o-o-oh. I'm going to kill somebody."

"Very likely, in due time. In the meantime, Elina, why don't we take a walk and you can cool off a bit."

THE FAVOR

By this time, it was late in the afternoon. Mangum, Stavros, and the dogs went to an entrance they seldom used, because it would be light there now. This was the entrance by the large hill and the climbing wall.

As they walked along the path, they were both deep in thought about the investigation. When one of the climbers on the climbing wall slipped and fell, caught by the belaying rope his partner held, he called out.

Mangum looked up at the climbing wall and the hill behind it. His eyes grew wide and he stopped. He walked back along the path.

Stavros stopped, too, and looked back at him.

"Bert?"

Mangum walked back a little further along the path and stopped. He beckoned Stavros to join him. When she got there, he pointed.

"What do you think that hill is made of, Elina?"

"Rocks?"

"I doubt it. That big of an eccentric mass on the station has to be compensated somewhere. Every big, heavy installation on Crossroads has a large installation on the other side to balance. It has to, with something rotating like this. Is there a hill this big on the other side of the gardens?"

"No. This is the only one."

Mangum nodded.

"So I think it's hollow. How big would you say it is?"

"Looks like maybe twenty feet high by forty feet wide by a hundred feet long."

"Eighty thousand cubic feet. Is that big enough, Elina?"

Stavros gaped at him.

"It sure is."

She looked back at the hill.

"Fuck me," she whispered. "Right out in the open."

Mangum chuckled.

"The invitation to conjugal relations will have to wait. But yeah. Right out in the open in front of God and everybody."

Mangum took one last look. Now he was triggered to it, he could almost see the regular rectangle underneath the hill's artificially rounded shape. He took Stavros' elbow.

"Come along, Elina. We just stopped to make sure that climber was OK."

Stavros tore her gaze away and accompanied Mangum down the path, the dogs scouting ahead at the end of their leashes.

It was sometime later that Stavros spoke in a low voice.

"I want them, Bert. I want these bastards."

"We'll get 'em, Elina. But we need to get the boss first, lest he get away."

When they got back to the suite, Mangum ordered dinner. Stavros dove into her roll-up display. She only re-emerged when dinner showed up.

There were three hamburgers at the extra place now. Mangum cut one in eighths and set the plate on the floor for Jules. Then he set down the other plate with two full hamburgers on it. Plus a couple dishes of guacamole.

That done, Mangum turned to Stavros.

"So what have you been into so deep since we got back?"

"Looking up some things on the gardens. First, there is no space under the hill in the station layout."

"None?"

"None. Nothing. Like it's all rocks. It's just a big open space that says 'Gardens.' That's it."

"Well, physics won't let that be true, Elina. We know that.

What's on the other side from that wall at that point? Next to the gardens?"

"The distribution center, with an airlock and container lift down from space. The interior surface of the cylinder."

"OK. That's how they get everything in and out. The precursors, the ampoules, everything coming in, and product and waste materials going out. It's just mixed up with all the other station traffic."

Stavros nodded.

"What do they do with the waste materials, Bert?"

"Put them in the waste stream from the station. They probably just push them toward the sun. Get 'em going a little bit and cut 'em loose. You're in no hurry. They'll get there eventually."

"All right. That explains that. What do we do now, Bert?"

"Let's see if our conjecture pans out. Do some reconnaissance on that wall. See if there's a door there."

Stavros raised an eyebrow.

"I'll take care of it, Elina."

"How did I know you were going to say that?"

"Good guesser?"

"The second thing I found out is that that hill has been in the gardens since the station was built twenty years ago. It's actually bragged about in the literature that they have a climbing wall in the gardens."

"How do you know it's the same climbing wall on that hill?"

"There are pictures, Bert. The hill is in the picture."

"OK, so that's pretty cut and dried. Long-term plan, then. By the way, when did RDT become a thing?"

"Eighteen, nineteen years ago."

"Nothing before that?"

"No. Nothing. It was a new thing."

"Wow."

"Yeah, Bert. Wow. Crossroads doesn't just *have* an RDT problem. Crossroads *is* the RDT problem. It was built to manufacture RDT and distribute it all over the cluster, from the very start."

Stavros threw her napkin down on the table in disgust.

"And I work for these assholes. As a cop. Fuck."

Mangum sympathized. What if everything you thought you knew was wrong, and you were, after all, on the wrong side?

"Elina, have you ever heard of something called malicious compliance?"

"No. What's that?"

"Well, your job is to enforce the law, right?"

"Yeah?"

"OK. So let's do that."

"All right, Sam. You know what I need you to do, right?"

"Yes, Bert. Proceed through the ventilation system to this distribution center, getting to this grille here."

Sam pointed to a spot on the engineering plans projected by Mangum's roll-up display.

"Right. Take this tiny camera, and I want footage of this wall. I'm looking for doors or pass-throughs of any kind, from the distribution center to this space marked 'Gardens.' Man doors. Roll-up doors. Any way through that wall."

"I got it, Bert."

"What about me?" Jules asked.

"You stay here," Sam said.

"Again?"

"Your time will come soon enough."

Sam walked to the ventilation grille in the kids' bedroom and started to ease through. The tiny surveillance camera fit between the louvers.

"See you in a bit."

Sam eased the rest of the way through the grille and was gone.

Sam looked out through the ventilation grille at the distribution facility. Taking up the entire inside of the cylinder of Crossroads, it was a huge facility. This was the point through which all the material shipping into and out of Crossroads passed.

The space Sam looked out on was thirty feet high and disappeared into the distance. Even though it was evening, the center was abuzz with activity. It was clearly a twenty-four-hour-a-day operation. He couldn't begin to estimate the size of the space. Perhaps it was shown on the plans.

Sam wasn't at the correct ventilator grille yet. He had several more grilles to go down this duct. He moved along until he got to the end grille, the closest to the end wall of the huge space.

Looking out from this grille, Sam could see the end wall to his right. This was the wall Mangum was interested in. The gardens should be on the other side of that wall, the last enclosed space at this end of the cylinder.

Nothing. A completely blank wall. OK, that was what the plans said, and was what Mangum had expected in this direction. No connection from the distribution center into this portion of the gardens. Sam held the camera up and made sure to get video feed of this view.

Sam moved across the duct to the grille on the other side. The end wall of the cylinder was now to his left.

But this wall was different.

Below him and thirty feet away was a roll-up door from the distribution center through the gardens wall. About eighty feet along was another one. In between these two roll-up doors was a man door. It looked like it had a special locking mechanism, along with some signs, which Sam could not read from this angle.

The containers on the floor near these doors looked different as well. They all had the same shipping company insignia on them. The containers in the distribution center were a mixed bag, as one would expect, displaying the insignias of the dozens of companies one would expect to be transporting containers to and from a hub and spoke distribution center like Crossroads.

But the containers near these doors were all the same shipping company. Griffin Interstellar.

Sam held the camera up to the grille and caught video feed on the doors and the containers nearby.

Job done, Sam headed back to the suite.

Mangum was waiting for Sam to return when Stavros pounded on the locked kids' bedroom door. Mangum looked over to Jules, who switched to his puppy persona, then went over and opened the door.

"Bert! I received an alarm. Someone is restocking the RDT store."

Mangum looked over at Jules, laying on the bed. Jules nodded back, and Mangum followed Stavros out into the living room of the suite.

The Pieces Come Together

Sam oozed through the ventilation grille into the kids' bedroom of the suite. Mangum was not there, but Jules was.

Jules looked up and switched to his utility persona.

"Elina came and told Bert someone was restocking the RDT store. They're out working on that."

"We should probably go out into the living room and listen in so we stay up on what's going on."

"All right."

They both switched to their golden doodle personas and went out into the living room. Sam jumped up onto the sofa and lay down, and Jules curled up next to him.

Mangum and Stavros were huddled around her roll-up display. Mangum looked over at Sam and raised an eyebrow. Sam looked up, nodded, and put his head back down.

Stavros didn't notice. Mangum turned back to her.

"OK, run it past me again from the beginning," Mangum said.

Stavros started the replay of the feed from the door opening. Two men came in, one carrying a large briefcase, which he set on the table and opened. The other sat and waited while the first opened the supply cabinet and started restocking drawers from the briefcase.

When the first man was done restocking the drawers, he made notations on an inventory sheet in the briefcase. He then pulled the money box out of the bottom of the cabinet and opened it on the table.

He pulled out the cash, counted out the smaller bills to some amount, and put it back in the cash box, replacing the box in the bottom of the cabinet. He counted out the rest of the money, put it in a cash bag in the briefcase, and made another notation on the inventory sheet. The inventory sheet and the cash bag both went back in the briefcase. He turned to the second man.

"All set."

The second man nodded and got up, and they both left the room.

"Nice efficient operation," Mangum said.

"Why the second man, though?"

"Bodyguard. Carrying all that cash and RDT around needs security. Did you get face captures?"

"Yeah. Couple good ones of each."

"Run them, Elina."

Stavros set up the facial match problem and started it.

"This should be fast. Yep. Here we are. First guy is Klaus Weber. He's a Crossroads employee out of the Supplies department."

"That makes sense."

"Yeah, and get this, Bert. The second guy is Ian Walsh. He's in Crossroads P.D., though I've never seen him before."

"That makes sense, too. What department is he in?"

"RDT control unit. Twenty-year veteran. He's been here since the beginning, Bert."

"That makes sense, too. Wanna bet he never collects any of his retirement, Elina? Terrible accident. Just terrible."

"Yeah. They'll throw him away like a dirty dishrag when he tries to leave."

Stavros shook her head, then looked at Mangum.

"You're right, Bert. Busting these guys doesn't accomplish anything. They're all victims in their own way. I want the boss. The guy who put this whole thing together."

THE FAVOR

"Track down the ownership of Crossroads, Elina. That's where you'll find your answer. But I may be able to help with that. Pull up the new feed I just got."

Stavros found the video recording and ran it.

"Where is this?" she asked.

"The distribution center next to the garden wall."

"No doors or anything in that wall, Bert."

"Right. But I think this is looking in the other direction. From that location, the garden wall should be on the left, not the right, to see the portion where the hill is."

The view shifted to the other view.

"Ah. Here we go."

"Bert, look at those doors. The roll-up doors and the man door. Those are in the garden wall."

"Yes, Elina. And they aren't on the engineering diagrams of the station."

"And this location?"

"That's where the hill in the gardens is."

The feed hit the end of the recording, and Stavros backed it up and froze it.

"Look at all these containers, Bert. All close in to the facility. All the same outfit. Griffin Interstellar. Never heard of 'em."

"Me either, Elina. But find out who owns Griffin Interstellar while you're at it."

Stavros looked at the time.

"First thing tomorrow. It's too late to work effectively tonight. But I do need to work off some anger and tension."

Stavros lifted an eyebrow to Mangum.

"I live to serve, madam."

Mangum sat with Sam and Jules after Stavros was asleep.

"Nice job on that surveillance, Sam. That was perfect."

"Thanks, Bert. It wasn't particularly hard, but it was a long way from here, and I couldn't use a transit pod."

"Sorry, Sam. I didn't think of that. I could have taken you in closer in a transit pod, then let you go on into the ventilation system from there."

"Not a problem, Bert. It just took a while. Next time, if you're in a hurry, that may be a better plan."

Mangum nodded.

"And how are you guys doing?"

Sam and Jules looked at each other, then back to Mangum.

"Good, Bert. I think it's interesting you found this drug lab, and it was built into the station twenty years ago. That's pretty interesting."

"Yeah. We should have some leads now to the big boss. I suspect, though, that he's not on the station."

"He's not?"

"No, Sam. The station is a means to an end for him, not a place to live. So what's the purpose? Why did he do it?"

"Why is always tough. Let me think about that one, Bert."

"Sure, Sam. That's my big question, though."

Mangum sat and nursed his drink. Sam went off into whatever mental space he occupied when they sat silently.

Jules looked back and forth between them, and finally couldn't help himself.

"But what will you do? I mean, if you find the boss?"

"Kill him, most likely."

"Really?"

"Depending on orders, yes. The one big question is, What happens to all the RDT addicts when we do that? Because if we shut it all down, they are in deep trouble."

"Gosh."

THE FAVOR

The next morning, Mangum woke alone. He took a shower and dressed, emerging into the living room to find Stavros hard at work.

"Anything for breakfast?" he asked.

"Sure. Anything," she said without looking up.

Mangum called in breakfast and then sat down in one of the armchairs to wait. Sam and Jules came out of the kids' bedroom and jumped up to lie down on the sofa.

When the server came, Stavros sighed and set aside her roll-up display so he could set the table. Sam and Jules came over, and Mangum fed them while Stavros watched.

"He really is the cutest little thing," she said.

"Though he's already growing. He's going to be big as Sam, and it's not going to take long."

"That's OK. Sam's cute, too."

"So how's your research going?" Mangum asked.

"Not well. Tell me, Who owns Crossroads?"

Mangum shrugged.

"Crossroads Corporation."

"Correct. Now who owns Crossroads Corporation?"

"I don't know. It's gotta be listed somewhere, though, right?"

"Answer another question first. Where is Crossroads Corporation incorporated?"

"I don't know. Gaston?"

"No. Crossroads Corporation is incorporated on Crossroads. And guess what Crossroads' laws say about corporation ownership?"

"Let me guess. That it's a private matter and is not published."

"Got it in one."

"No shit. Well, that's convenient, isn't it?"

"Yeah. So that's a dead end. At least for the moment."

"You can't penetrate it with your police credentials?"

"Nope. Complete dead end."

"Huh. What about Griffin Interstellar?"

"That's a little easier, but not much. Privately owned company, so they don't have to publish accounting records and the like. Or ownership. They do have a registered agent, however."

"Where are they listed?"

"On Mardouk."

"In the Association?"

"Yeah. Back home. In Ashur, actually."

"Back home? You're from the Association of Planets, Elina?"

"Yes, Bert. I'm from Ashur, the capital. I'm actually still an Association citizen, because Crossroads Corporation doesn't grant citizenship. At its basic, we're all transients here. Or ex-pats. However you want to say it."

"Huh. I didn't know that."

"Yeah. That was at least part of your attraction, Bert. You're from back home."

That was the second time Stavros had called Ashur 'back home,' after having not mentioned her origins once in the last month. Mangum got the impression her allegiance to Crossroads, to whatever extent she had had it, had dissipated.

"But that's just where the corporate agent is located. We still don't know who owns it, or where they are."

"Wouldn't they be in the Association, Elina?"

"Not necessarily, Bert. They could even be outside the cluster."

"But you don't know."

"No. And, so far at least, I can't find out."

"Hmm. Maybe I can help out there."

THE FAVOR

"How can you help, Bert?"

"I'll ask some people back home to look into it for me."

Stavros' eyes widened, then narrowed, and she nodded.

Phillip Marstock, the Agency's operations contact for its direct-action operatives, was an old hand in the Agency. Once a direct-action operative himself – and a legendary one – the Agency had made him the contact with its most effective field agents when he wanted to settle down.

Marstock read Mangum's latest report and put in a meeting request with Frank Latham, the Agency's head of operations.

"Whatcha got, Phil? Is this about Mangum's latest report?"

"Yes, sir. We need to try to track down the ownership of Griffin Interstellar and the Crossroads Corporation."

"Yes. That was his request. Pretty amazing find there, that Crossroads was built from the start as an RDT manufacturing and distribution center."

"Absolutely, sir. And the RDT sample Mangum sent us has been analyzed as well. It's the purest sample we've ever seen. Pharmaceutically pure."

"The question that arises then is why? What is the goal of this whole operation? Could it be as simple as money?"

"Maybe we need to look into the finances of the Crossroads station as well, sir. Find out where the money comes from and where it goes."

"That would be easier if those transactions were based here. Why do I think they're not? I think having the registered agent for Griffin and the financial center for Crossroads in different star nations would be an obvious isolation play."

"Yes, sir, but then it depends on who the other star nation is. If it were Gaston – or Abelon, at this point – we would likely get a lot of cooperation tracking it down."

Latham nodded.

"All right, Phil. I'll bring it up with Henry and see what he says. He may need to talk to Febo about this one."

Isabela Febo was the Chairman of the Association's Council of Planets, the chief executive of the interstellar government. Marstock's eyebrows rose, and Latham nodded.

"For something as important as this, it would be good to get her in the know sooner anyway. This could all blow up pretty spectacularly."

Latham thought about it a moment before continuing.

"And Isabela Febo does not like to be surprised by things her subordinates should have damn well kept her informed about."

Henry Grant was the head of the Agency, but to talk to Febo, he did not go to see her. Nor did she come to see him. Her schedule, and particularly her travel schedule, were too public to accommodate a meeting with the head of an agency which, in the government's official position, did not exist.

But Isabela Febo took a one- to two-hour nap each day. On her schedule, it just said 'Nap.' This gave her one to two hours every day in which she was 'off the schedule.' So Isabela Febo took Henry Grant's call that afternoon.

"Good day, Mr. Grant."

"Good day, Madam Chairman. Thank you for taking this meeting."

Febo waved a hand.

"Of course, Mr. Grant. And I understand this meeting will involve confidential matters, of which you can trust me to maintain the confidence."

"Thank you, Madam Chairman."

THE FAVOR

Grant took a moment to get his thoughts together, and Febo was content to wait.

"One of our operatives has uncovered something of which I think you need to be kept apprised. We also may need special permission for some actions I think would be warranted under the circumstances."

Febo raised an eyebrow at that last.

"Go ahead, Mr. Grant."

"Yes, ma'am. Our operative was between assignments, awaiting new orders on the Crossroads station. He was asked by a police detective there if he could assist her with a problem. She was aware he was more than he seemed due to her involvement with him at the beginning of the Evelyn Barnes affair some months back."

"This operative of yours was the one involved in the Evelyn Barnes affair, Mr. Grant?"

"Yes, ma'am. He is one of our most capable field people."

"Very well, Mr. Grant. Please continue."

"Yes, ma'am. The Crossroads' detective's problem was that they see a pretty large RDT problem on Crossroads, and they don't know how the drug is getting onto the station."

"Smuggling RDT is a pretty simple matter, though, isn't it, Mr. Grant?"

"Onto a planet, yes, ma'am. This is onto a space station, though. Much easier to control, and they have pretty stringent controls in place."

Febo nodded and signaled Grant to continue.

"Our operative, figuring it never hurt to have people owe us one, began looking into the RDT problem on the station. What they have turned up is pretty shocking, ma'am.

"They have discovered an RDT manufacturing facility on the station. This facility is large enough to make all the RDT we see in the entire cluster, and our operative surmises that this facility is in fact the source of all RDT in the cluster.

"Second, this facility was built into the station when the station was built twenty years ago. It is not some fly-by-night amateur operation or makeshift affair. That means it is being actively maintained with the collusion of Crossroads management.

"Third, we know that RDT only became a problem within the last twenty years. This facility on the Crossroads station may be why it became a problem at all."

Febo stared at Grant for long seconds, but he merely nodded.

"And how much credibility do you give to this information, Mr. Grant?"

"Our operative sent various evidence along in his reports, ma'am. RDT stores operating on the Crossroads station. Retail operations. The restocking of these stores is being done by Crossroads personnel, including police personnel.

"The factory operation is concealed in a hidden space on the station. They have done reconnaissance of this location, which is not shown on station maps.

"And he sent us an RDT sample he purchased at one of those retail outlets. Our testing shows it is pharmaceutically pure. That is very unusual in street drugs, ma'am, and usually indicates you are very close to the manufacturing site."

"He sent evidence, Mr. Grant?"

"Yes, ma'am. We have video surveillance recordings of retail sales, restocking of the retail stores and the personnel involved, and even video footage of doors into the facility, which doors are not on the station maps.

"That plus this particular operative is not prone to flights of fancy, Madam Chairman. He was our sole asset on scene in the

Evelyn Barnes affair, which he successfully carried through to a very nice conclusion, including his recommendations for resolving the outstanding issues, which the six star nations carried out."

Febo nodded. That would be the disposition of the warships Barnes' company had made for Villacqua and Wilbourne, including the joint flagships the six nations now maintained to coordinate their navies in cluster defense against any outside threat.

A capable operative, indeed.

"This situation is fraught with problems, though, Mr. Grant. Were we to shut down this facility, RDT addicts across six star nations would either die or be mentally incapacitated for life."

"Yes, ma'am. It makes one wonder what the underlying motivations of the primary players are. But we can't get at the primary players. Crossroads Corporation is incorporated on the Crossroads station, and such records are private and well hidden.

"Griffin Interstellar, a shipping company, is also involved, based on the shipping containers adjacent to the facility, on which we also have video surveillance. That is a privately held company, with all that implies about their records.

"They do list their registered agent as an attorney here in Ashur, though, ma'am. And their banking records must be traceable, though perhaps by extraordinary means."

"And here we get to permissions, Mr. Grant? You need my OK to go after the registered agent and all the banking records here in Association space, don't you?"

"Yes, Madam Chairman. For records elsewhere, we do not need permission to obtain those extralegally. That is, in some sense, what we do. For domestic activities, however, we cannot act without your direct approval."

Febo nodded.

"Very well, Mr. Grant. You have approval for domestic activities insofar as it relates to this situation. Crossroads and its involvement in RDT, including this Griffin company. You do not need to seek extra permissions to follow that trail where it leads. At the same time, this permission does not apply to any other cases you are working on."

"I understand, Madam Chairman. Thank you."

"And please keep me informed on this situation, Mr. Grant. Much like the Evelyn Barnes affair, I believe I will likely need to be involved before the end of it."

"Of course, ma'am. And I agree with you on your ultimate involvement. I think several decisions will have to be made that are well above my pay grade."

Febo nodded, and cut the channel.

Sven Norden, the Agency's chief of analysis, called in Jin Juhua, the group lead on financial systems penetration.

"New assignment. Track down everything about Crossroads Corporation and Griffin Interstellar. Where the money comes from, where it goes."

"And if it leads back here, sir?"

"Follow it. We have the Chairman's permission."

"We're on it, sir."

Frank Latham, the Agency's head of operations, called Phillip Marstock to his office.

"Griffin Interstellar's registered agent? Interrogate him. Find out all you can."

"In downtown Ashur, sir?"

"Yes. We have the Chairman's permission."

"Yes, sir."

THE FAVOR

Investigation On Mardouk

Samuel Broder was walking on the sidewalk in downtown Ashur, on his way back to the office from lunch. While junior partners and associates normally ate in the office, as a senior partner in Alpert, Broder, & Cahill, Broder was free to come and go as he pleased, and he enjoyed his walk and lunch out every day.

As he was approaching the office, a bee stung him on the neck.

"Ow!"

He brushed the offending creature away in annoyance and continued walking. About a hundred feet further on, however, he stopped, confused. Where had he been going?

A man got out of the side of a van ahead of him on the sidewalk.

"Hello, Mr. Broder. I'm Jared Clifton. Join me here for a few minutes and we can chat."

"Oh, all right."

Clifton waved Broder ahead of him into the van. There was a nice conversation grouping in the rear compartment.

"This is nice," Broder said, taking a seat.

"Well, we wouldn't want to inconvenience you, Mr. Broder."

"Oh, no trouble at all, Mr. Clifton."

"I wanted to ask you some questions about certain clients."

"Well, you know we're not supposed to talk about client matters with others."

"This would just remain between us, Mr. Broder."

"Oh. All right."

"Is Griffin Interstellar one of your clients?"

"Oh, yes. Very good client. For many years now. And a timely pay, as well."

"What kind of work do you do for them?"

"We're just their registered agent on Mardouk. We mostly just forward communications to them."

"Are they located here in the Association of Planets, then?"

"Oh, no. This is just their incorporation address. Their physical address is in Wilbourne. Outside Somerset, I believe."

"That's very interesting, Mr. Broder. Is that unusual?"

"To be located somewhere else and have an incorporation address in the Association of Planets, you mean?"

"Yes."

"No, not at all. We have a number of clients who do that. The Association has lower corporation franchise fees and better corporate law. Choosing to pay Association franchise fees and work under Association law is much more favorable than to operate under Wilbourne's fees and laws."

"Do you have an address you submit billings to, Mr. Broder?"

"Just a bank account here, I think."

"Could you send me that account number?"

"Oh, sure."

Broder pulled a mini roll-up display – a nice one – out of his pocket and made an entry.

"And the address?"

Clifton gave him a dead-end burner dropbox.

"There. All done."

Broder rolled the display up and put it back in his pocket.

"Thank you for that, Mr. Broder."

"Oh, sure. No problem."

"So how did you get Griffin's business in the first place? And how long ago was that?"

"Oh, it's twenty years or more, Mr. Clifton. I think I had just made partner. You know, the firm puts out an announcement about new partners, and the legal press picks it up. So I was in some of the legal newsfeeds. That sometimes gets you new business."

"Did the client come in to meet with you?"

"No, I don't think so. As I remember – and it has been twenty years – they contacted me from Wilbourne about incorporating here. I handled the paperwork, and became the registered agent."

"Did they transfer their incorporation from Wilbourne, then?"

"No. It was a new company. Just getting started. As I understand it, they've done quite well. They certainly have no trouble paying my fees, and did not ask me to hand the business off to a junior partner when I became a senior partner and my fees increased."

"I see. Anything else about them, Mr. Broder? Anything unusual?"

"Not really. There hasn't been any litigation in the past twenty years involving them. I would have received the notice of that as their registered agent. I guess one could call that unusual. Most corporations get involved in litigation sooner or later."

"All right. Well, I've enjoyed talking to you today, Mr. Broder."

"Me, too, Mr. Clifton. An interesting break from the normal day's activities."

"At the same time, we should probably keep our conversation to ourselves. Some people might not understand."

"Oh, yes. I see that. Very well. One thing attorneys are good at is keeping secrets."

"And now, why don't you go back to your office, let your secretary know you wish not to be disturbed for an hour or so, and catch up on that reading you keep putting off."

"That sounds like a good idea. Thank you, Mr. Clifton."

"Oh, thank you, Mr. Broder."

Clifton let Broder out of the van and waved goodbye as Broder headed off to the office to sequester himself until the Com-Ply wore off.

Clifton got back into the van and closed the door. The unmarked van pulled away from the curb and merged into the downtown traffic.

The bank account number for Griffin Interstellar's payments to Alpert, Broder, & Cahill and the bank account number for Elina Stavros' paycheck from Crossroads Corporation went into the hopper of Jin Juhua's financial systems penetration group at the Agency.

In – and under – the unassuming office building in suburban Ashur, financial analysts and hackers were grinding away at the problem.

The problem of finding the cash flows, following them to their end, and identifying to whose benefit the massive effort accrued.

It was several days later that Jin Juhua reported in to Sven Norden.

"So what have we got so far?" Norden asked.

"Well, someone is making a great deal of money, but it's not from the Crossroads station."

"Really?"

"Yes, sir. Crossroads Corporation loses money. The hub-and-spoke freight traffic doesn't cover the extraordinary costs of operating the station itself. It's a money loser."

"Really? That's counterintuitive, Juhua. I thought it did well."

"So does everyone. But it doesn't. Operating a huge space station with that many people aboard is stupidly expensive."

"Then why build it?"

"The Crossroads station is extraterritorial. Independent. We have no jurisdiction over it, and neither does anyone else. The people manufacturing RDT on the station and shipping it off aren't even breaking the law. Anybody's law. Only the people bringing it into one of the six star nations are breaking the law, and the freighter captains and their crews don't know what's in the containers they ship. They're common carriers."

"Oh, wow. So the first person you could actually complain about, from a legal point of view, is the knowing receiver."

"Yes, sir. Everything else is completely legal. Somebody sidestepped a lot of criminal liability there. That may actually be the whole purpose of building the station."

"Unbelievable."

"Oh, it gets worse. The actual profits are from the receivers paying for the RDT shipment. Those aren't done through the banking system. Who do you know who pays for illegal drugs with a bank transfer? No. It's all cash, by mail."

"And that's where the profits come in, but we can't track them."

"Right. That's why the as-yet-unnamed owner of Crossroads Corporation is willing to lose money on the station. He's got mailbox money coming in from the drug receivers.

"Now, consider a moment, sir. Let's say we shut down the whole RDT operation. What happens?"

"Well, a lot of people addicted to RDT get sick or die. Permanent brain damage. We end up with a lot of people who need assisted living arrangements. Forever."

"Yes, sir, but that's not all. The Crossroads station doesn't support itself, so Crossroads goes under and ends up abandoned. The hub-and-spoke freight system of the six star nations collapses. The entire free-trade system in the cluster collapses."

"And you get a massive recession."

"Oh, yes. Without the export markets, a lot of people currently employed in the export industries end up unemployed, and without the imports some industries now depend on, those industries lay off people as well. It stabilizes at some point, when the economy works through how to be more independent of interstellar trade, but that will take time."

"And it's worse because it doesn't wind down, it implodes. There's no time to acclimatize to a new supply regime."

"Oh my God, Juhua. It will take years."

"As it took years to get into this mess. Yes, absolutely. And you're going to get political upheaval as well. One thing that you can count on with economic collapse is political turnover. People won't put up with the current powers-that-be any longer than they have to."

"Even though it's not their fault."

"Actual fault doesn't enter into it, sir. But if you're holding the ball when the music stops, in the public's mind it's your fault."

"Shit. I need to tell Henry. Ms. Febo will not be amused."

"Good day, Mr. Grant."

"Good day, Madam Chairman. Thank you for taking this meeting."

"Twice in the same week, Mr. Grant? You have results so fast, then?"

"Some results, ma'am."

Grant brought Febo up to date on what they had discovered so far, including the possible economic and political implications. When he finished, Febo was not happy.

"What a mess. We have flagrant lawbreaking going on, and millions of victims, but the person most responsible is acting outside jurisdictional boundaries. Oh, and if we take him down anyway, we poison our own economies and politics."

"Yes, ma'am. That's what it looks like so far. Not a good situation."

"You have a gift for understatement, Mr. Grant. So what are we to do?"

"Often the operatives involved have the best ideas, ma'am. They're in the thick of it and have been thinking about it a lot, and we don't hire stupid people. My gut instinct is to bring them fully up to speed and see what advice they can offer."

"And in the Evelyn Barnes affair, that approach worked really well."

"Yes, ma'am."

"Very well, Mr. Grant. Proceed in that way. And ask them not to break anything until we have some sort of plan in place. This will likely take a coordinated effort across multiple star nations, and I would just as soon not get blindsided by one of your worst-case scenarios."

"Of course, ma'am."

Philip Marstock stopped by Frank Latham's office.

"You wanted to see me, sir."

"Yes, Phil. Come in. Close the door."

"Yes, sir."

"The financial people have been following up all these leads, and they paint a truly disturbing picture."

Latham brought Marstock up to speed on the financial systems penetration group findings.

"That's rather incredible, sir."

"Yes, and I'm told Ms. Febo is not happy. So we need to find a path out of this mess. To that end, I want you to bring Mangum up to speed and see if he and that detective can come up with a way forward that doesn't result in economic and political chaos."

"Very well, sir. He pretty much nailed it with the solution to the Evelyn Barnes affair."

"Yes, he did, Phil. So let's get them thinking about it. Where's Portnoy now?"

"He should just be getting to Wilbourne, sir. Next day or so."

"All right. Bring him up to speed, too. See what he and Gloria Dent can come up with. And as a secondary priority to his assistance to Dent, see if he can do some discreet poking around about Griffin Interstellar."

"Yes, sir.

"And discreet there is not a euphemism for direct action. We need to not precipitate a worst-case scenario before Chairman Febo has a plan in place."

"I understand, sir. I'll make sure he understands."

"Good. This may come down to direct action sooner or later, but now is not yet the time."

In fact, Portnoy's ship was still en route to the planet from its reentry into normal space when Portnoy got the update from Marstock.

"So poke around, but don't set anything off," Portnoy said.

"Exactly correct. We don't want to precipitate events, but more information may allow a better solution to be crafted."

"Got it."

"And bring Dent up to speed. She was involved in the resolution of that Evelyn Barnes thing, so she may have some good ideas as well."

"All right. I'm on it."

Marstock cut the channel, and Portnoy stared sightlessly at the image of the planet approaching in the display in his first-class cabin.

Bert Mangum had really turned up a mess this time. Not Mangum's fault at all, he just had a knack for finding big problems. He hadn't caused it, the problem had been there all along.

Portnoy respected Mangum, and he knew that respect was reciprocated. They were both at the top of the game they both played. Take whatever action was necessary to fix the problem. That could be damn near anything, from assassination to explosives.

But they could also be subtle, as Mangum had been so far. The gathering of information without disturbing the status quo.

Portnoy nodded. He could do that.

When he got to the planet, Portnoy took an autocab into Somerset, to the Somerset Plaza Hotel downtown. It was late afternoon. When he tried to check in, however, the desk clerk had a note for him.

"Ah. Mr. Pendergast. I have a note for you here."

The clerk handed the envelope to Portnoy and he tore it open. It was in a precise, feminine hand. 'Am in Penthouse 1. Plenty of room. Come on up. Dent.' There was also a room tag in the envelope.

"Very good. Thank you," Portnoy said to the clerk.

"Of course, sir."

Pendergast waved to the two crewmen from *Silverheel* who had his luggage, and they headed to the elevator.

"Ah, Mr. Pendergast. How nice to see you again. Come in."

Portnoy entered the suite, and Dent waved to a room off the living room.

"In that bedroom with Mr. Pendergast's luggage, please."

"Yes, ma'am."

The crewmen took Portnoy's luggage into the bedroom and came back out to salute Portnoy. He nodded and they left.

Portnoy looked Dent up and down. The black-haired field operative for the BIE was as beautiful as he remembered.

"It's very good to see you again as well, Gloria. You're even more beautiful than I remembered."

Dent chuckled.

"Save it, lover-boy. That bedroom is yours, and this one is mine. No nookie until the assignment is complete. We need to keep our edge, not be all fat, dumb, and contented."

"Ah, but I think you will shortly find you have a second assignment here, Gloria."

"Is that so, Claude?"

"Yes. I just received an additional assignment here on Wilbourne, and was told to brief you in. Yours is the priority, but then we have another. Do we need wait until we complete both?"

Dent looked him up and down.

"Perhaps we can have a palate cleanser between courses. As a reward for completing the first assignment."

"And then dessert later. That works for me."

Dent waved him to one of the armchairs, while she walked over to the bar and prepared drinks for them both.

Sitting in the other armchair and handing him his drink –

she recalled his preference from Abelon – she waved to him to start.

"Now, Claude dear, brief me in on this new assignment."

When Portnoy had finished, Dent let out a low whistle.

"Looks like Bert really tripped over a hot one this time."

"Oh, yes."

"And what are we to do then?"

"Be discreet, I was told. Gather information, but don't do anything to turn over the applecart. And to see if we couldn't think of a solution that allows the cluster to get out of this one economically and politically intact."

"That may be a tall order of business."

"Yes. But the big thing is not to precipitate events until some plan is in place."

Dent nodded.

"Yes, I'm definitely going to want a palate cleanser before taking on the entree, Claude. If you're willing, of course."

"I am at your service, madam."

Dent produced a deep chuckle that held the promise of great times ahead.

RICHARD F. WEYAND

Problems And Solutions

Marstock also called Mangum and briefed him on what the Agency's analysts had found out about Crossroads and Griffin. It was late morning several days after Mangum's last report when Marstock called.

Mangum and Stavros talked about it over lunch.

"I heard back from headquarters today, Elina."

"That was fast. What's going on?"

"It's a little surprising. As it turns out, Crossroads is a money loser."

"What?"

"Yup. Crossroads Corporation loses money every year. The owner, whoever that is, actually puts money into keeping the operation going. Oh, it's not by a lot, compared to the cash flow of the place, but they have never made a profit on the station. Running this place is a huge expense."

"Then why do they continue to run the station? Oh, wait. Of course. They're making a ton of money on the drug trade, which isn't part of Crossroads' accounting."

"Got it in one. And they're not even breaking the law."

"Wait. Explain that one to me, Bert."

"Sure. Ask yourself, is it illegal to manufacture RDT?"

"Of course."

"On Crossroads? Are you sure?"

Stavros thought back through the Crossroads regulations, running through them in her mind.

"Actually, Bert, it's not."

Mangum nodded.

"And shipping RDT from Crossroads?"

110

"No. That's not illegal, either. But it is illegal to import it into any of the six star nations. I know that for a fact. I was a cop in Ashur before I came here."

"Right you are. But the transfer of title to freight normally occurs at the loading dock. That's why prices are specified as FOB - Freight On Board. So once the carrier has it, is it a crime to ship RDT as a common carrier?"

"No. The freight line doesn't know what's in the container."

"Right, so the first illegality that occurs is the receiver of the shipment knowingly specifying a delivery address for an illegal shipment. But the guy who made the RDT and puts it on the freighter has not committed a crime."

"But that's crazy, Bert."

"Perhaps. It's also true. And the income from the RDT business is why they're willing to run Crossroads at a loss."

"So RDT addicts are funding the hub-and-spoke trading system of the whole cluster. That's weird."

"But the implications are staggering, Elina. What happens if we – illegally, mind you – shut down the RDT factory?"

"Millions of functional addicts – people who go to work every day, have families, whatever – suddenly die or end up with mental problems. Those with severe mental issues end up being wards of the state, in assisted living or the like. Which could be millions of people. It's a huge social and economic disaster. We've talked about this, Bert."

"Yes, Elina. But what happens to the economies of the six local star nations if we shut down the RDT facility? All of a sudden you no longer have someone willing to fund the station's losses."

"And the hub-and-spoke trading system shuts down. Ouch."

"Ouch, indeed. Trade becomes more expensive. The costs of

imports become much higher. Companies which depend on an export market suddenly have lower revenues and lay off employees. Companies dependent on imported components are facing much higher parts costs, raise prices, and lose sales and revenue, which means they lay off people, too."

"You get a cluster-wide recession."

"Or worse."

"But what about before Crossroads, Bert? How did it work then?"

"There were a bunch of border planets that hosted smaller refueling and freight transfer operations. But those facilities have all been mothballed for twenty years. They're outdated, or non-functional, or have been repurposed. They weren't big enough to handle the current traffic anyway. Crossroads shutting down would be a huge disruption."

"Can't things adjust and adapt? Won't other facilities come on-line to take up the business? It seems it would be a huge opportunity."

"Yes and no. First, there would probably be a time lag of five years or so. Orbital facilities and shuttleports and all that don't just pop into existence when you want them."

"Five years of recession?"

"Yes, Elina. Probably. The other part of it, though, is tougher. How much of an opportunity is it? If Crossroads, which has economies of scale in having consolidated the transfer trade into a huge central facility, can't make a financial go of it, how will smaller facilities make money? Will investors even be interested in the attempt?"

"They'd have to charge higher refueling and transfer rates to make a profit."

"Which increases shipping costs, which increases the cost of imports, which maintains the problem, though at a lower level."

"So RDT has been enabling the economic boom in the cluster."

"Yup. Now, ask yourself the next question, Elina. What happens in hard economic times, from a political point of view?"

"People blame the hard times on whoever is in power."

"Right. And Chairman Febo, among others, won't be pleased to lose her nice cushy job because of a collapse of Crossroads."

"Same with the other five governments, too. Even the hereditary leaders would be in trouble. Maybe even more so, because such an entrenched executive would take more to dislodge it and fall harder. You could have revolutions. What a mess."

"Oh, yes."

"So what's your assignment now, Bert?"

"Try to figure out a solution."

"A field operative? Out here? Compared to all the resources you must have on Mardouk?"

"Yes, Elina. My boss thinks field operatives have a unique view, from the inside of the mess, which sometimes allows them to see a solution others can't see from outside. It worked in Abelon."

"It did?"

"Oh, yes. I don't know how much you watched the news on that situation, but that solution of dividing up all the warships among the six star nations and having two flagships run by a consortium to coordinate cluster defense came from Gloria Dent and me."

"OK, Bert. So you and I, from here, literally in the belly of the beast, try to come up with a macroeconomic solution to a potential cluster collapse? Why am I not hopeful?"

Mangum shrugged.

"There are other people looking into it, too, Elina. But if we can come up with something, or some set of somethings, that would be very much worthwhile."

Stavros nodded.

"All right. I'll give it some thought. And what do we do in the meantime?"

"Try not to rock the boat. We don't want to do anything that would get that whole disaster started. So we just sit tight."

They took a walk in the gardens that afternoon, but they didn't go anywhere near the hill that concealed the RDT facility. They treated it like an unstable explosive that could destroy the economy and politics of the whole cluster.

They were unusually quiet on their walk, as both were lost in their thoughts as to how to resolve the pending crisis.

That evening over dinner, they discussed it again. Sam and Jules, having gobbled down their own dinner, lay on the sofa and overheard the conversation, as they had at lunch.

"I just don't see any other way, Elina. The government – some government, maybe the consortium – has to take over Crossroads."

"Oh, yeah. That'll work great," Stavros said with sarcasm.

Mangum looked up at her and raised an eyebrow.

"Bert, you don't work at your headquarters, but I do. You know what would happen if the government – any government – took over Crossroads? It would operate at half the capacity it does now, have twice the staff, and cost four times as much."

"Why, Elina? Why couldn't they just operate it the same way?"

THE FAVOR

"But they wouldn't, Bert. They'd want to make it better."

"OK. So they make it better. What's wrong with that?"

"A bureaucrat's idea of better is to have more direct reports, Bert. That's how he gets promoted to the next grade level. 'Lessee, a grade ten has fifteen to twenty direct reports, and I have sixteen now. So I need to hire four or five more people. What can I have them do?'

"Do that a couple of iterations, and there would be a quarter-million employees on Crossroads, and they would have to offer higher salaries to get people to come here and put up with the overcrowding. Oh, and full retirement after twenty years at half or three-quarters salary.

"Meanwhile, the costs keep going up, and we're just in the slow boil version of the sudden disaster we're looking at now.

"Having the government take it over is a recipe for disaster."

"Huh. I guess you're right. I just don't see another way."

"Well, there is another way, Bert. There has to be."

She looked up from her dinner.

"What about the military, Bert? Make it a military installation and have the navies run it."

"No, that's just the same problem, Elina. The military's primary role is to kill people and break things. It's the ultimate threat. 'You behave or we'll send several thousand young people to your country and tell them we don't care what they break.' That's the combat people. But the logistics and supply operations are as encysted and bureaucratic as the civilian sector. Maybe even more so. It's still the same problem. And those are the people who would run something like Crossroads."

"Ah. Yeah, you're probably right. Dammit, Bert, there has to be a way to do this."

Stavros sighed.

"But I don't see it either. Not yet, at least."

That night, with Stavros asleep, Mangum poured himself a nightcap and joined Sam and Jules in the kids' bedroom of the suite. Both Sam and Jules were in their utility personas.

"That's some problem you've got on your hands, Bert."

"Oh, yes. We started pulling on a thread and unraveled the whole economic and political stability of the cluster."

"Not yet, though, right? Everything is still going along as it was before you found it."

"Yes, Sam. So far. But now Chairman Febo knows about it, and she won't sit still and let people continue to get addicted to RDT and have their lives be subject to the threat of withdrawing it."

"But if she tears it all down, she probably loses her position as well, Bert."

"Yep. But her sworn duty is to protect the people of the Association, not just ensure her term in office. Which way does she go, Sam?"

"A career politician, Bert? I could offer a likelihood."

"Understood. But bear in mind she would most like to do both. So how does she do it?"

"I heard your and Elina's argument about the government and the military. I don't think I see a path there, either."

"Wait a minute," Jules said, after having been quiet throughout this discussion. "I don't understand the problem."

"What don't you understand, Jules? You've been present in all the discussions."

"Well, everything is going along fine right now, right? Isn't that what you said? So why not leave it that way?"

Mangum and Sam looked at each other, then back to Jules.

"Leave the RDT system in place, and the drug dealers on the

planets in place, and the big boss continuing to make tons of money off of the recruitment of more and more addicts?"

"No, not all of it," Jules said. "But what if you took over Crossroads, and then let the same guy run it? You said he didn't break the law on Crossroads, right? Confiscate a lot of his ill-gotten gains from the planetary drug dealers, and make him earn it back by running Crossroads. If you only give him so much money a year, he'll continue to operate it efficiently."

Mangum opened his mouth, then closed it.

"How would we deal with the RDT facility?" he asked.

"Well, you have to keep running that, too, or the addicts all have problems. But you don't want to be creating more addicts. That one's hard."

Sam shook himself and turned to Mangum.

"Arrest and charge the planetary dealers, Bert. They're unequivocally breaking the law. Then sell RDT to people who are already addicted in government stores. There won't be any incentive to push the drug to new addicts. Who knows? Maybe someone can come up with a cure or something."

"The problem with cures is that most drug addicts don't want to be off the drug, Sam. They like it. For the addictions for which we have cures, the hardest part is getting the addict to accept the cure. They don't want the cure. They want the drug."

"For them, I guess you keep selling them the drug, Bert. Better than having them deteriorate into becoming a public burden. And right now you don't have a cure anyway."

Mangum nodded. As crazy as it first sounded, the scheme might work. RDT as a maintenance drug for those already addicted, but get the dealers out of the business.

And let the one person who knew how to run Crossroads continue to run it.

"I'll have to think about that one, Jules, but you may have the core of a solution there."

Stavros got up and Mangum wasn't there. His usual nightcap, she knew. She couldn't get back to sleep, so she got up, put on the bathrobe in the bathroom, and padded out into the living room looking for him.

Mangum wasn't in the living room, though, and the door to the kids' bedroom was closed. She padded over to the kids' bedroom door, and put her ear up to the door.

She dimly heard voices. Two *different* voices. No, *three*.

One of them was Mangum, but who were the other two?

She hurriedly crossed the living room back to the bedroom and crawled back into bed.

The next morning over breakfast, Mangum explained Jules' solution to Stavros. He didn't credit Jules, of course.

And Stavros didn't say anything about her eavesdropping the night before. At this point, she wasn't even sure it really happened.

"Elina, I was thinking last night. The big problem is if we break up what's currently going on, right?"

"Right, Bert. Everything blows up. The current addicts. The hub-and-spoke trading system. Huge social, economic, and political implications."

"OK, so what if we left almost everything in place?"

"Almost everything?"

"Yeah. Crossroads and its management. The RDT facility and RDT shipping. Just leave them in place."

"What do you not leave in place?"

"The dealers on the planets, for one. They have an incentive to increase addiction. To get more people hooked. They have to go. The nice bit there is they are in fact breaking the law. So we take them out."

"How do we distribute the RDT to the current addicts, then?"

"Government stores. Government-licensed stores, anyway. Like liquor stores or something."

"And the big boss?"

"Leave him in place."

"What?"

"Yeah. Leave him in place. First, he's already running Crossroads, and doing a better job of it than the government would. Right? Second, he's not doing anything illegal. You gonna claim huge support of the rule of law and then act against him extralegally?"

"That one burns, Burt. He's the cause of all this."

"Yes, and the cause of all this cheap trade and economic boom, as well."

"What about all the money he's been getting paid by the dealers?"

"OK, say we stipulate that is tainted money. We confiscate the money and then make the big boss earn it back by running Crossroads. Pay him so much a year to cover his losses and make a profit. We know he already knows how to do that, and how to keep the operation lean and efficient."

"All of which avoids the addict problem and the trade problem. So you think this is a solution?"

Mangum shrugged. Stavros looked at him a long time.

"I hate to say this, but I kind of like it. All except letting the big boss get away."

"Get away with what, Elina? Not committing a crime?"

Mangum wrote up the potential solution that morning and

asked Stavros to look it over.

"One more thing, Bert. I think the government stores could check if someone is an RDT user already. That chemical test we use in immigration control would work. No new addicts, just supply existing users."

Mangum added that detail, and shipped his write-up off to Agency headquarters.

Consternation All Around

"Did you see Mangum's latest?" Phillip Marstock asked.

"Yeah," Frank Latham said. "Outside the box, that's for sure."

"I don't think anyone ever told Mangum there's a box."

"He'd probably be disappointed to find out."

"So what do you think?" Marstock asked.

"It seems to solve all the big issues, if we can see ourselves clear to letting the big boss, whoever he is, off the hook."

"Yeah, that's going to stick in some people's craw, sir. Mangum's point that he didn't actually break the law is on point there, I think."

"Other than receiving payment for contraband, Phil."

"But it wasn't contraband leaving the dock on Crossroads, sir. After that, it's actually the dealer's product, and they're the importer. They bought it off the dock. The payment was legit, for a product that was legal at the point of sale."

"Yes, I know. If we tried to prosecute him, it would probably be thrown out of court on that basis."

"So now what do we do, sir?"

"What do I do? I'm taking it to Henry, Phil. This is way above my pay grade."

Henry Grant read Mangum's write-up of a potential solution with interest. It was Mangum – and Gloria Dent, he supposed – who came up with the solution to the Abelon crisis, and that had worked out very well.

And everyone involved – Coordinator Jacques Martin of Abelon, President Randall Paxton of Villacqua, and King

Ferdinand IV of Wilbourne – felt like they owed Association of Planets Chairman Isabela Febo one for surfacing and then solving the problem. Not a bad thing, all in all.

This problem had similar import. Instead of the cluster descending into war, it would descend into social, economic, and political chaos. Fixing it was absolutely imperative.

Mangum's solution, though effective, would probably be objectionable, at least if presented haphazardly. Letting the single person most responsible for the flood of RDT into the six star nations skate?

Grant stared out the window while he considered. He supposed the first thing to do is to find out if Mangum's solution could actually work.

Grant called Sven Norden to his office.

"You wanted to see me, sir?"

"Yes, Sven. Come on in. Catch the door."

Norden came in and closed the door to Grant's office. Grant waved him to a seat.

"Did you take a look at Mangum's proposal?"

"Yes, sir. That's quite a bit outside the bounds of the things we were thinking about. Then again, we haven't come up with anything that would avoid all the problems we discussed."

"Would Mangum's solution avoid all the problems?"

"It may, sir. All the big ones, I think. We have to take a look at it. It sounds like a good start, but I'm not sure there aren't tweaks we could make to it."

"All right, Sven. Work on it for me. I need analysis and recommendations. I'm not taking this to Chairman Febo before I'm better prepared."

"Yes, sir. We're on it."

THE FAVOR

It was several days before Henry Grant felt comfortable taking such a radical proposal to Chairman Febo. Sven Norden's group's analysis and write-up was instrumental in that.

Mangum was on the right track.

Oh, they had some tweaks to his plan. Government monitors on Crossroads, probably reporting to the consortium the six star nations of the cluster had come up with in the wake of the Evelyn Barnes affair. Some additional constraints on whoever the hell was behind all this, and whom they had still not found.

But it was basically Mangum's plan, with numbers to back it up. Financials, mostly.

Grant sighed and put in a meeting request to Isabela Febo.

Well, here goes nothing.

"Good day, Mr. Grant."

"Good day, Madam Chairman. Thank you for taking this meeting."

"You've made some progress on this problem, then, Mr. Grant? Because I've been thinking about it since last we talked, and I'm at a loss."

"Yes, ma'am. We received the bones of a solution from our operative on the scene, and we've worked it up into a complete package."

"This is the operative from the Evelyn Barnes affair, Mr. Grant?"

"Yes, ma'am. I have to warn you, though, it is not a conventional solution. In some ways, at least, it is counter-intuitive."

"Some of the best solutions are, Mr. Grant. Proceed."

"Yes, ma'am."

Grant explained Mangum's solution to Febo. Leaving the big

boss in place, to continue operating Crossroads as before, to continue making RDT and shipping it to the planets. Taking down the dealers in whose best interest it was to expand the use of RDT to more people and replace them with government retail outlets. Seizing the ill-gotten gains of the big boss and using them to fund the Crossroads operation going forward, while spending significant funds researching either a cure or a less harmful drug that would wean users from RDT while maintaining their cognitive function.

"That's the gist of it, ma'am," Grant said when he concluded.

"Well, you said it was counter-intuitive, Mr. Grant. You have once again demonstrated your gift for understatement."

"Yes, ma'am."

"I think the hardest part – the part that rankles me – is leaving the mastermind of the RDT problem in place. That's a hard sell, Mr. Grant."

"Understood, Madam Chairman. Yet it is the key to the whole plan. The government – any government, really – has well demonstrated in the past its inability to efficiently run a large shipping facility."

Febo looked at him for a few seconds, then nodded.

"At the same time, ma'am, we have no legal basis on which to go after him. He has not done anything illegal in any of the six star nations. The RDT is all being manufactured and sold on Crossroads, which is extraterritorial and outside of any of our jurisdictions."

Febo sighed.

"Yes, that was likely a mistake, in retrospect. It's led to this whole thing."

"It's also led to an economic boom, ma'am. The station has created real economic benefit for us all."

124

"Yes. That's part of what makes all this so hard. So he is not operating illegally, yet you plan to seize the funds he obtained, or some large part of them. How do you justify that, Mr. Grant?"

"Those funds came from the dealers, ma'am. It is their ill-gotten gains that were transferred to him. We think we can go after them within the law."

"I see. And what's to keep this fellow, whoever it is, from saying, 'No, thank you, I'll just carry on as I am,' Mr. Grant?"

"There is one key card we hold, ma'am. The reason Crossroads operates at a loss is that it was incredibly expensive to build in the first place. The Crossroads Corporation is carrying a large amount of commercial debt on the initial construction. On an operations basis, it's actually making money, but the station has not yet paid itself off."

"How does that help us, Mr. Grant?"

"If it became known Crossroads was being investigated for being involved in RDT trafficking, ma'am, the banks would call the loan. They would then be the creditor in possession."

"Assuming the law of Crossroads would even permit that, Mr. Grant."

"Yes, ma'am. We're trying to research that, but we are, of necessity, doing it quietly."

"I need more details about how Crossroads would be administered on a legal basis going forward in this plan, Mr. Grant. I don't think we can allow it to continue as its own jurisdiction going forward, but that raises a whole other set of issues."

"Yes, ma'am. Under whose jurisdiction would it then be? Having it independent has been a benefit thus far, because no one star nation can control the cluster's shipping system."

"Give it some thought, Mr. Grant. In the meantime, you

have a write-up of this proposal for me?"

"Yes, Madam Chairman. I will send it to you."

"Thank you, Mr. Grant."

Febo cut the connection.

Mangum and Stavros were having lunch in the suite.

"Bert, I have a question."

"Sure, Elina."

"The other night, when you were up for your nightcap, I woke up and couldn't get back to sleep. All the findings about the station, I suppose. I got up thinking I would sit with you for a bit. You were apparently sitting in the kids' bedroom. The door was closed, anyway. I listened at the door, and heard voices."

She looked up at him and caught his eye.

"Bert, who were you talking to?"

"Headquarters. On my roll-up display."

"*Three* voices."

"Yeah. It was a briefing, so there were two headquarters people on the call."

"That's what I thought it must be, but I checked. Ashur and Crossroads are pretty much in sync right now. It was three in the morning in Ashur. That wasn't a headquarters briefing."

Stavros looked down at her plate, then raised her eyes again, looking at Mangum intently.

"Bert. Can your dogs *talk*?"

Mangum was trying to think of a way out of this one when another voice piped up from the sofa.

"I can explain it, Ms. Stavros."

Stavros turned to the sofa and stared as Sam stood up on his hind legs on the floor and morphed into Gloria Dent, as he had on Abelon when he and Mangum confronted the assassin Linas

126

Karvelis.

"You see, we're not really dogs," he said in Dent's voice.

Stavros' eyes rolled up in her head and she tipped over sideways, falling in a dead faint to the floor.

Stavros came to slowly, as if she were walking out of a fog.

"Elina. Elina, are you OK?"

Her head cleared and she found she was lying on the sofa, a pillow under her head and Mangum kneeling on the floor alongside her.

"Yes. Yes, I'm coming out of it."

Stavros blinked her eyes hard, twice, and the world settled down.

"Bert, did that really happen?"

"Yes, Elina. That really happened. It wasn't my secret, and so I couldn't tell you."

Stavros nodded, and struggled to a sitting position, Mangum helping her.

Sitting across from her in the armchairs were two robot-looking creatures, with a plastic-skin look and the gross features of humans but without specific details. One was larger than the other.

"My name is Sam, Ms. Stavros," the larger one said.

"And I'm Jules," the smaller said.

"But who – *what?* – are you?"

Mangum sat on the couch alongside her.

"Shape-shifting aliens," he said.

"*Sentient* aliens?"

"Yes," Mangum said. "And you are now the second human to even know they exist."

"We would rather our existence not be known, Ms. Stavros. Humans being who and what they are, some would immediately start to think of ways to use us to further their own ends. Perhaps even try to conquer or enslave us."

Sam looked to Jules, then turned back to Stavros.

"We're not interested."

"As a cop, given what I know of human nature, I shouldn't wonder."

Stavros turned to Mangum.

"How the hell did you find sentient aliens?"

"I was on an assignment. I got in trouble. The aliens helped me out rather than let me die. A rescue ship came in response to the call for help, and Sam decided to go along with me for the hell of it."

"It sounded interesting," Sam said, nodding.

"How did you get Sam aboard the rescue ship?"

"Their shape-shifting can take many forms, Elina. Allow us to demonstrate."

Mangum stood up. Sam oozed off the chair and to Mangum's foot, then up his leg, eventually covering him in what looked like an anti-radiation suit.

Mangum shrugged.

"I just wore him aboard when they brought me onto the ship."

"That's incredible."

"And very useful. Together we can impersonate people, too, as long as they're bigger than me."

Sam morphed again, while staying on Mangum, into the appearance of Jeremy Faust, Evelyn Barnes' assistant in her offices on Mystik.

"Wow. You could walk right past most security setups in a getup like that."

"Indeed we did, Elina."

Sam oozed back down across the floor and back up into the

chair, resuming his utility persona.

"And you came along because it sounded interesting?" Stavros asked Sam.

"Indeed, Ms. Stavros. And it has proven so."

"Please, call me Elina."

Sam nodded.

"So where did Jules come from?" Stavros asked.

"Jules is my actual child, Elina, though not conceived or born in the human fashion."

"Which is why all the secrecy around the birth."

"Correct," Mangum said. "We had to hide Jules until he could impersonate a puppy. We were trying to maintain the ruse. For the protection of this entire race of aliens. Why Sam chose to come out to you now, though, I don't understand."

Mangum turned to Sam, and the alien turned from Stavros to Mangum.

"Two reasons, Bert. One is that there are now two of us, and we can assist the two of you going forward if Elina also knows our secret. The other reason is that we now know Ms. Stavros pretty well, and trust her to keep our secret. Jules may wish to accompany Elina in the same way I accompany you."

"That sounds interesting. Is that what Jules wants, though?" Stavros asked.

"We've talked about it," Sam said, turning to Jules.

"I would be pleased to be your companion, Elina," Jules said.

He morphed into the golden doodle puppy, jumped down off the chair, and jumped up on the sofa to sit next to Stavros.

Stavros scratched Jules behind the ears absently while she stared off into the distance.

"Human-level sentient aliens. Amazing."

"Or smarter, Elina," Mangum said. "Keeping the big boss

man in place to avoid all the dire consequences of shutting down Crossroads was Jules' idea."

"Really?" Stavros said, turning to Mangum.

"Oh, yes. They are not stupid. Not at all. They are likely smarter than most or all humans. For all their natural appearance would suggest otherwise."

"What is your natural appearance?" Stavros asked Sam.

"My understanding is that our natural appearance is not pleasing to most humans, Elina. You need to brace yourself."

"Very well. Go ahead, Sam."

Sam oozed from his utility persona down into an orange-brown, lumpy, irregular mass on the floor.

Stavros took a sharp breath, then let it out.

"Thanks for warning me, Sam."

A mouth on a stalk extended from the mass. It spoke.

"You're very welcome, Elina."

One of the system administrators of the Crossroads police computer facility turned to his colleague as they were going through the monthly usage numbers.

"This is weird," Stanley Wozniak said.

"What's that, Stan?" Alan Grisman asked.

"Isn't Detective Stavros on vacation?"

"Yeah, for a month now. Five weeks. Something like that."

"Then why is she using more computer time than the whole rest of the department?"

"What?"

"That's what I said."

Grisman looked at the numbers.

"OK, now that's weird."

"I wonder what she's up to?"

"Undercover, maybe?" Grisman asked.

"Don't know. Sure is weird, though."

"Should we point it out to our superiors?"

Wozniak thought about it a few seconds before replying.

"Nah. It's in the usage reports. If they want to know that kind of stuff, they can read it themselves."

"Makes sense to me, I guess. Whatever Stavros is up to, we don't want to risk ruining her investigation."

"Yeah. She seems like the sort that would hold a grudge."

Wilbourne Liaison

Wilbourne's capital city of Somerset was abuzz this morning with the news of Hugh Gannet's recent suicide. The successful entertainer had let himself out onto the roof of the downtown Somerset Plaza Hotel and leapt thirty stories to his death on the pavement below.

The big news, though, was what police found investigating his death. Gannet had been involved in a sex trafficking operation, recruiting young, naive small-town girls into a life of prostitution and drugs, servicing the entertainment industry and other celebrities.

Quite a few popular entertainers, politicians, and sports figures had been caught up in the whole thing after police found his appointment book in his computer account.

Gloria Dent and Claude Portnoy were eating breakfast in her penthouse suite in the Somerset Plaza Hotel this morning.

Dent was scanning the news.

"One less scumbag in the world, Claude. That's a good thing."

"Yes. That was a good idea, having him jump off the roof."

"Yeah. Stepan Gorelik jumped off our balcony on Abelon, and the police got all upset about it. They thought maybe we were involved. Imagine."

Portnoy laughed, and Dent smiled, before she continued.

"It was a good idea to dummy up his appointment book and leave it in his computer account, too."

"Well, it seemed a waste not to use all that information you had gathered, Gloria."

Dent chuckled.

"Yeah, you should see what the newsfeeds are making of that little gem. It appears somebody – ahem! – leaked it, and quite a few people are in some serious trouble. Even if there's not enough evidence to prosecute most of them, I predict a sudden downturn in their popularity and careers."

"Good. Taking advantage of children? I have some serious issues with that."

"As opposed to good old-fashioned consensual sex between adults?"

"I have no problem with that at all, Gloria."

"As you have since proved."

"Yes. Speaking of which, I have a question. How do I compare with Bert Mangum?"

"Better. Much better."

"Really?"

"Oh, yes. The man I am with is always much better than the man who isn't here."

"Gloria! I meant in an absolute sense."

"Absolutely, the man I am with is always much better than the man who isn't here."

Dent smiled at him. She had a beautiful smile.

Portnoy gave up that line of questioning, and came up with another.

"So, is there any of that palate cleanser left in the dish, or have we finished it?"

"Oh, I think a little bit. Before we head into the entree. You know."

Having proved once again that neither of them had any problem whatsoever with consensual sex between adults, they were enjoying lunch out on the balcony.

"On to the entree," Dent said. "I did get orders from home, as I mentioned before, so what are we up to with regard to this new assignment?"

"The first thing, I think, is to gather whatever information we can about this Griffin Interstellar, and see where that leads."

"Sounds good. First thing after lunch."

Portnoy nodded. Dent patted his hand on the table.

"By the way, that was very nice, Claude. But now we need to hold off until this assignment is complete."

"I see now the wisdom of your approach, Gloria. This assignment should go much quicker with such motivation."

Dent began her investigation by searching all public sources on Wilbourne as well as the BIE archives on Gaston.

Some of the hits were behind paywalls, subscription services that charged. There were two ways around this. First, since paywall sites did want their results to show up in the various search applications available, one could break in by pretending to be a search routine.

For the sites which had programmed out that little trick, Gaston's BIE maintained a single subscription. One logged into the BIE's computers, and then a BIE bot would hit the service, download the article, and mirror it to her.

The pickings were pretty slim, however. Griffin Interstellar was operating well under the radar. There weren't any sites that quoted the president or anything like that. Nothing to get to the leadership.

On to the next step. Griffin Interstellar was a freight company. All of its shipments would have to be on bills of lading, on customs forms, on landing forms.

Dent added those sources to her search list, both the ones she could hit here and the ones she could hit through Gaston

BIE's database. She started to have more luck with that, but not much. These people were going to be hard to pin down.

Dent looked at the pictures Mangum had submitted with his proposal again. BIE had them in the Agency's request for assistance. There were the Griffin Interstellar containers around the purported RDT lab.

Wait a minute. Dent zoomed in on one of the containers, then zoomed in again. There it was. She added 'GIX' – Griffin Interstellar's container prefix, the first three characters of each of the container's ID markings – to the search terms.

That was looking a little better.

Dent may actually get enough data to analyze.

Later that afternoon, Dent contacted the BIE financial penetration and analysis people to see if they'd made any headway with bank records. It was just the beginning of the work day in Blanchefleur, on Gaston.

Bank records were always hit or miss. Some banks had great security, others had poor security. And it wasn't just based on their size, either. Some large banks' security systems were pathetic, and some small banks were locked up tight.

The question was, which sort of bank did Griffin Interstellar have?

With regard to Griffin Interstellar's bank accounts, two money streams were of potential interest. The incoming cash from RDT dealers was one. Where did that enter the electronic banking system? Did it come in through Griffin?

The other was Griffin Interstellar's payouts. Where did they go? Cui bono? Who profited, and, more to the point, where was he? The company was allegedly located here, but where was the guy making the money?

So Dent called headquarters to find out what they knew, and

got a simple answer.

They didn't know anything.

"You can't find the bank?" Dent asked.

"Oh, we know which bank it is, Ms. Dent. We know where Griffin Interstellar has their accounts. But we haven't been able to penetrate it."

"What about their financing? Someone financed building that space station, and, after only twenty years, those huge loans have to still be out there."

"We understand, Ms. Dent. We're looking for that as well, but have not yet found the money men behind Crossroads."

"So now what do we do?"

"We're working another angle, Ms. Dent."

"I'm listening."

"We believe the dealers are paying for their shipments in cash, Ms. Dent. We don't think they're creating bank records about those payments. But a large amount of specie floating around also leaves tracks. Physical sovereign currency has to be repatriated to have value. So how is all that money coming back into the system? Who is on the other end of those transfers?"

"And you can see that?"

"We are talking about a great deal of money, Ms. Dent. A flow of currency that large we should be able to see, yes."

"But you don't have the results yet."

"No, Ms. Dent. Not yet. In this case there is almost too much data. We are trying to make heads or tails of it all, but no pattern has emerged yet."

"All right. Well, keep me informed."

"Of course, Ms. Dent."

THE FAVOR

Dent complained about it to Portnoy over supper.

"They haven't found anything. They are pounding on the problem, but, whoever set this up, they were very careful."

She looked up from her dinner.

"What about you?"

"I checked in with headquarters, and it's much the same story. They have hooks into the financials, but they lead nowhere. Even the banks were chosen with care, to work with those who had the best security."

"So what are we going to do? How do we surface this thing?"

"I suspect it will come down to the tried-and-true method of causing a lot of trouble and seeing who reacts. See if we can't catch them in a mistake."

"Force them to come after us."

"Yes. Either us or Bert and this Detective Stavros. We're in a good spot that way, because we're here and they're on Crossroads. One of us causes trouble, and then we both watch. So it sort of depends on who we think will get the better reaction. Do they cause trouble, or do we?"

"When do we do that?"

"Not until the politicians decide what the plan is, and not before the financial people have exhausted their leads. When we cause trouble, things will move quickly, and we need to be ready."

"So more sit and wait."

"Yep. Just like every other op. Why should this one be any different."

Dent nodded.

"Yeah. That's the part I always hated. Why can't it be simple?"

"If it was simple, Gloria, someone else would have dealt

with it already."

"And then you and I wouldn't have a job."

"There you go. In the meantime, we just keep pounding on it. Keep looking."

Both worked all the next day, and lunch was a quiet affair, with both lost in their own thoughts about their researches.

At dinner, though, Dent had some progress to report.

"I've tracked down most of Griffin's shipping schedules, I think. BIE maintains a database of shipping related things like bills of lading and customs declarations."

"Outstanding, Gloria. What are you finding?"

"First thing is that they ship a lot of small loads – mostly single containers – to planets all over the place."

"That makes sense. You can put a lot of RDT in a shipping container."

"Right, and at that, most would probably be bulkheaded."

"Bulkheaded?"

"Yes, Claude. That's where you have only a quarter of a container to ship, say, so you put it in the container and then put in a bulkhead so the shipment doesn't move around. The rest of the container is empty."

"That sounds expensive."

"It's not so bad. Charges are both by the container and by weight. You get off on the weight part. But there's no interstellar shipping unit smaller than a container."

"OK, Gloria. That makes sense then. So lots of single container shipments, mostly running light."

"Right. Out from Crossroads, that is. Shipments into Crossroads tend to be multi-container shipments from a select few locations."

Portnoy frowned as he puzzled that, then brightened up.

THE FAVOR

"Precursors. For the RDT. Has to be."

"That's what I figure. Chemicals of one kind or another. The ingredients for whatever recipe they're using. And probably ampoules and shipping cartons for the ampoules."

"They're not shipping in bulk, Gloria?"

"I don't think so. Mangum reported that the RDT for sale on the station was all in ampoules, and bottling it in ampoules is a lot cheaper en masse than it is piecemeal on each planet."

Portnoy nodded.

"It also makes dosage much more controllable, I think."

"Right. You wouldn't want people to be dying of overdoses from bad quality control in the packaging. It would tarnish the brand."

"So have you nailed down the suppliers, Gloria?"

"No. Just the planets. I don't have as much visibility into on-planet shipments, and they're being cagey."

Portnoy nodded.

"Well, keep at it."

"What about you, Claude? What are you up to?"

"I'm looking into charitable activities here on Wilbourne."

"Charitable activities?"

"Oh, sure. Very common for big criminals to be very active in charities. Make big donations and such. It leads people to think they're good people and not look too closely at where their money is coming from."

"So what are you doing with that, Claude?"

"Looking closely at where their money is coming from."

"Looking for someone who overspends what he can reasonably be assumed to be making from his legal activities."

"Yep. Our guy has a lot of extra money coming in, Gloria. I'm looking for it. And I'll find it."

View From The Top

Ivan Petrov, the head of the Bureau of Intelligence and Espionage for the Gaston Alliance – and Gloria Dent's ultimate superior – had read Mangum's write-ups and his proposed solution to the Crossroads RDT problem. He had not yet taken them to his superior, Michael Corliss, the Speaker of the Assembly for the Gaston Alliance.

Unlike his counterpart, Henry Grant, the head of the Association Intelligence Agency in the Association of Planets, Corliss could meet openly with the chief executive of the Gaston Alliance, because the Gaston Alliance did not deny the existence of the BIE. Whether it was time yet or not to meet with Speaker Corliss and bring him up to speed was the issue Petrov now considered.

It was a two-pronged issue. With something as explosive as what could happen if the whole Crossroads situation collapsed – or exploded, another term that might be even more appropriate – Petrov was loath to propagate the information any further than he had to.

On the other hand, if Chairman Febo of the Association of Planets brought the situation to Speaker Corliss before Petrov did, Corliss would not be happy. He didn't like to be blindsided.

It wasn't a purely political consideration. Petrov was keenly aware of his responsibilities, and Corliss' trust in him was one of the reasons the BIE was able to operate as independently as it often did. Generally speaking, the BIE was good at what it did, and Corliss understood the need for clandestine operations on sensitive issues to remain as secret as possible.

Which meant it was Petrov's call. Did he bring Speaker Corliss up to speed on the issue now, or wait?

Petrov sighed, then put it on the agenda for his weekly meeting with Corliss.

"So we're on to your last agenda item, Mr. Petrov."

"Yes, Mr. Speaker. It's actually two items. The first part of it is the completion of that nasty sex-trafficking business on Wilbourne."

"Ah, yes. I recall. Remind me why we were involved in that, Mr. Petrov. It was Wilbourne's business, after all."

"Mostly it was, sir. There was some bleed-over into our space – celebrities traveling with their, um, underage companions – which we don't tolerate. But King Ferdinand was getting pushback from his own people on putting a stop to it. We subsequently found out why. A key player was getting payments to look the other way.

"King Ferdinand's foreign minister, the Duke of Blackwater, asked our assistance in cleaning it up. Part of the residual good feelings from the Evelyn Barnes affair, I assume. So we sent an operative to collate all the evidence they had and track it all down. The Association sent one of their direct-action people in to assist.

"That whole thing has now had a satisfactory conclusion, sir. Blackwater is very pleased about it."

"That conclusion was what, Mr. Petrov?"

"The key player, an entertainer named Hugh Gannet, suffered an unfortunate mishap. The subsequent investigation into his death discovered his appointments book, which somehow leaked to the newsfeeds. All of his clients are now outed."

"An unfortunate mishap, Mr. Petrov?"

"Yes, Mr. Speaker. A fall from the roof of a thirty-story building. Security cameras showed no one else present. It's been ruled a suicide."

Corliss nodded. The Agency was very good at certain tasks. That sounded like their work.

"You said there were two items here, Mr. Petrov."

"Yes, sir. The second one is a major developing issue."

Petrov told Corliss of the more-or-less accidental discovery that all the RDT in the cluster was being manufactured on and distributed from Crossroads. That the operation was not, strictly speaking, against the law. That shutting it down would result in catastrophic results for those addicted to the drug, as well as shut down the cluster's hub-and-spoke trading system because Crossroad was not profitable without the drug trade. That the current investigation had led to Wilbourne.

"My God, what a mess."

"Yes, sir. The Association's operative on Crossroads has proposed a potential solution, but it is wildly unconventional. For all that, it is the only solution on the table at the moment."

"Do we know anything about who came up with this potential solution, Mr. Petrov? I respect the Association's capabilities in some areas, such as the recent demise of Mr. Gannet, but this isn't their prime expertise."

"Yes, sir. While we do not share the names of agents, the Association operative who proposed this solution is the same operative who solved the Evelyn Barnes affair and proposed the consortium of the six star nations to resolve the military imbalance. He's working directly with a police detective on Crossroads."

"With a police detective on Crossroads, Mr. Petrov? How do we know he isn't part of the problem if Crossroads is so compromised?"

"The police detective in question is doing this on their own, sir. They've teamed up to work through this situation."

"Wasn't one of our agents involved in the Evelyn Barnes affair as well?"

"Yes, sir. That agent is still on Wilbourne after the sex-trafficking investigation, following up on that end of this situation. The Association operative who assisted in the successful resolution of the sex-trafficking case is staying on as well, so the Association and we are cooperating on the Crossroads investigation as well."

"So we have competent teams at both ends? In your opinion, Mr. Petrov?"

"Yes, sir. I'm very comfortable with where it's at right now."

"And the reason you brief me on this now, Mr. Petrov?"

"With a proposal on the table, and our operatives cooperating once again, I expect that Chairman Febo may be in touch with you on this matter, Mr. Speaker. I would not have you be blindsided by being unaware of what was going on."

Corliss nodded. With their intelligence agencies working together, and a proposal on the table, Febo might well be in touch soon. Which, to Corliss, was a good thing. He liked Isabela Febo. She didn't make big mistakes.

"Very good, Mr. Petrov. And you have a copy of this proposal for me?"

"Yes, sir. As I said, it is wildly unconventional, but our analysis people think it would work. It's the only thing on the table right now that addresses all the issues."

"Let me look at it then, Mr. Petrov. I may have questions for you afterward."

"Of course, Mr. Speaker."

Corliss read the proposal with interest, and then mused on

Ivan Petrov's gift for understatement. Wildly unconventional didn't begin to capture it.

Leave the mastermind of this whole thing in place? Leave his organization in place? Leave RDT manufacturing in place? Pay him to run Crossroads?

Unacceptable on its face.

And yet....

There was no prosecutable crime here. Oh, against the dealers on the planets, sure, but not against the head of the whole thing. The extraterritoriality of Crossroads, which is what had made it acceptable as the hub of the hub-and-spoke trading system that centered on it, had also made it immune to the legal system in any of the six star nations of the local cluster.

That had not been anticipated when the station was constructed. Not by those who had let it proceed, in any case. It had surely been intended by the as-yet-unknown mastermind behind this whole thing.

The proposal also dealt with the existing addicts, who would be debilitated by a lack of RDT. Who would make RDT if not the current manufacturer? Did anyone else even know how?

The collapse of the hub-and-spoke trading system was also avoided by the proposal. Crossroads was a huge facility, and handled millions of containers a year, both in its internal distribution facility and in direct transfers between ships in space.

The operative on the scene was probably right that government control of the facility would be a disaster. Logistics was one of government's weak spots. Everything would be slower, more labor-intensive, and much more expensive with a government takeover.

There was also the question of which government. Any

government which ran Crossroads was in a position to control, throttle, or filter the trade to and from any of the other star nations in the cluster. While the executives of the six star nations were getting along at the moment, that had not always been the case, and would likely not be the case at all future times.

Leaving it under its current management was the one thing that made sense as a solution. Who else?

Damn. He really wanted not to like this proposal.

But they would take out the planetary drug dealers and the uncontrolled trafficking in the drug. They were the ones who had the incentives to increase the number of users, making the problem even worse over time. Instead, the drugs would be dispensed by government stores or licensees to those who were already addicted and dependent on it for their ongoing well-being.

That was something, anyway.

Several days later, Chairman Febo of the Association of Planets did get in touch.

"Hello, Michael. How are you?"

"Good, Isabela. Good. And you?"

"I'm well. And yet I thought we were done with the whole major-threat-to-the-cluster thing months ago. But here we go again."

"Yes. I've read the briefing papers on what your man on Crossroads found, together with this detective."

Of course, Corliss didn't know if it was a man or woman, but, then again, neither did Febo.

"Did you also see their proposed solution, Michael?"

"Oh, yes. It's rather startling."

"Indeed it is. I hate it, but my analysis people tell me it's the only thing on the table that would avoid all the possible disasters while controlling or even walking back the ongoing damage."

"That's my take as well, Isabela, and my analysis people agree with yours. So I suppose we have little choice."

"Little rational choice, I suppose."

Febo sighed before continuing.

"I hate these situations, Michael. Where the only way forward must be a practical one. Where justice and morality must be set aside to pick the best path forward in an imperfect world."

Corliss nodded.

"Yes, that's why we get paid the big credits, Isabela. If it was easy, anyone could do it."

"I suppose."

Febo looked down at her desk for long seconds, then back up to Corliss.

"So what do we do now, Michael? Push this proposal?"

"I think we have to, Isabela, lacking anything better. We must not let this situation blow up as badly as it could."

Febo nodded.

"And we still don't know with whom we will be making this agreement."

"Your people must have a plan for finding that out, though, don't they, Isabela?"

"Oh, yes. Or so I'm told, anyway."

"I would assume so. Some plan that's occurred to them."

"So is it time to start recruiting the other executives, Michael? Randall, Ferdinand, Catherine, and Jacques?"

"I think probably it is. We do not want to have no plan in place when this comes unraveled. Which it could at any time."

"Very well. I will contact Jacques and Catherine. I think I

have the better relationships there."

"Then Ferdinand and Randall are mine. That works, I think, Isabela."

"And the consortium controls the management of the concession on Crossroads?"

"Of course. That is the only solution that gives all of us an equal voice going forward."

"Very well, Michael. Of course, anyone can contact either of us if they want to cross-check our answers."

"Of course. But you and I are of one mind on this, Isabela. It's the worst solution there could possibly be, except, of course, for everything else."

"Very well, Michael. Stay in touch."

"You take care, Isabela."

For as glibly as Febo and Corliss had spoken about it, convincing the other four chief executives in the cluster took some doing. King Ferdinand IV of Wilbourne and Queen Catherine II of Lyon, with greater ruling powers and more job security than President Randall Paxton of Villacqua and Coordinator Jacques Martin of Abelon, were the harder nuts to crack.

Within a week, though, all six of the chief executives in the cluster had been convinced. All six had agreed to pursue the proposal the Association operative had put forward.

They had all signed on to the solution that had first been proposed to Bert Mangum by the shape-shifting alien, Jules.

Researching While Waiting

Elina Stavros was still getting used to the idea that Sam and Jules were actually intelligent, shape-shifting aliens. They still went for their walks every day in the gardens, with both aliens in their golden doodle personas. But at meal times now, they sat as a table for four, with Sam and Jules in their utility personas.

In the evenings, they often sat in the living room working through their thoughts on the current case.

"One question I had, Bert," Sam said.

"Go ahead."

"How was Crossroads constructed in the first place? And how could the company that built it be incorporated on Crossroads before it existed?"

"That's a good question. Do you know the answer to that one, Elina?"

"No. I know how it's been extended. The radius was always the size it is now, but it wasn't always so long in the axial direction. In fact, it's been extended multiple times."

"That's interesting."

"Yes. They build a new piece of cylinder in space, far enough from Crossroads not to interfere with shuttle landings in the center hub. Then they start it spinning with rocket engines until it matches Crossroads' spin. They use the same rocket engines to slowly move it into place and butt it up against the existing station. They latch it in place, then weld it up."

"So they add a chunk to the station while everyone's on board?" Mangum asked. "That sounds tricky."

"The big thing is to have the spin the same. Then they just maneuver it in until it's adjacent to the existing station and pull the station and the new piece together with big winches. They always add on the back end, never on the sun side. The gardens were part of the initial construction."

"As was the RDT lab under the hill in the gardens."

"That's right, Bert. I think they added a mile to Crossroads' length last time. They're building another mile right now, actually. They're pretty much always building a new section or welding up the previous one."

"So there's a permanent space construction crew on board?"

"The Construction department. Yes. They're not real big. It takes them years to build and attach a new section, but they work continuously. Ever since I've been here, at least."

"So what did they start with, Elina?"

"I don't know, Sam. I'll look into it."

"And where are the parts being built?" Mangum asked.

"That's another good question, Bert. I don't think I can figure that one out from here."

"I know someone who can, I think."

"Dent."

"Bert Mangum here, Gloria."

"Bert! How are you? It's good to hear from you."

"I'm good, Gloria. I understand you've been briefed in on this little puzzle we found."

"Oh, yes. We're trying to track down all the income and payment streams. The shipping records of this Griffin outfit. All that stuff."

Mangum nodded. The BIE was better than the Agency at tracking financials through the computer and banking systems of the cluster. They had the better computer and accounting expertise. Everything from bank examiner and auditor types through to full-on hackers. Hackers like Gloria Dent, for example.

The Agency was better at dealing with what they found.

Permanently dealing with it.

"Good. We had a couple of questions come up here, Gloria. They sound like they might be up your line."

"Whatcha got, Bert?"

"First one should be simpler. Turns out they are constantly working on additions to Crossroads. They build a new cylinder portion, then spin it up and move it up against the station and weld it on. They work at it continuously, and add like a mile to the length of the station at a time. Each new chunk takes them years."

"Wow. I didn't know that."

"I didn't either. But that raises a question. Where are the parts coming from? They're not making steel here."

Dent nodded.

"OK. That's a good one. I can probably track that down. What's the other question, Bert?"

"So Crossroads Corporation is incorporated on Crossroads, right? That's what makes them immune to the corporate transparency and reporting rules in the six star nations. That's also why manufacture of RDT on Crossroads isn't against the law."

"Right. That's the key part of the whole immunity problem."

"And Crossroads Corporation built and owns Crossroads, right?"

"That's right, Bert. Oh. I see where you're going."

Mangum nodded.

"How do you incorporate Crossroads Corporation on Crossroads if Crossroads isn't built yet?"

"That is a very good question. Let me look into it, but you might have better access to that from there. The engineering drawings might give some clues, for example."

"All right, Gloria. That's what I had for you today."

"I'm on it, Bert. What are you working on?"

"We're looking into this and that. Mostly we're waiting for word to kick off the party."

Dent nodded.

"'We' is you and this Detective Stavros?"

"Yes. She brought me the problem in the first place."

"Is she pretty?"

"Oh, yes."

"Are you having some fun then? I mean, it's not all work, work, work, is it?"

"No, Gloria. We're having a good time, too."

"Oh, good. I wouldn't want you to be lonely, Bert. It would be such a waste."

Dent winked at him, and Mangum chuckled. Gloria Dent was always Gloria Dent. She was a one-off.

"And you, Gloria? How are you doing?"

"Claude is here, and he's a delightful man. A lot of fun. I don't know where your employer finds all you beautiful men, but I appreciate it. Of course, we're on a bit of a hiatus right now, with the assignment under way."

Mangum nodded. That was Dent's general policy. It had been with him during the Evelyn Barnes affair, anyway. And previously. That had not been their first time working together.

"Well, that just gives you something to look forward to, Gloria."

"Exactly. All right, Bert. We'll talk later."

"Bye, Gloria. Take care."

After the call from Mangum, Dent started tracking down the parts shipments to Crossroads. She had already done one big search across the BIE's shipping records archive for the Griffin Interstellar shipping records. She now initiated a search with Crossroads as destination and cargo as steel, steel parts, steel sheet, steels beams, and steel modules.

Dent set that to running and watched the results coming in. It was currently morning in Somerset, and the search ought to complete this afternoon sometime.

There was only so fast you could search really big databases.

The next morning, Stavros started researching the beginning state of Crossroads. What was the extent of the initial construction?

The engineering drawings were first. They were amended with each addition of a new section to the station. Stavros began walking them back through their revision history. She skipped from major revision to major revision, moving back one big step at a time as each section was added.

Mangum was searching back through newsfeed archives. The Agency kept an archive of every newsfeed article and had for decades. This to ensure that a news archive would not disappear if the newsfeed went out of business, or be edited by a newsfeed that wanted to erase, after publication, any errors it had made.

Sam and Jules sat on the sofa in the living room, in their utility personas, apparently quiet. They did hold hands, though, and Sam had told Bert they could communicate with each other as long as they were touching.

Mangum wondered what they were talking about.

Over lunch, Mangum and Stavros compared notes on what

they were seeing.

"I found the engineering drawings for the first construction, Bert. The first completion of a ring structure. They began with a space construction crew habitat shipped here intact. The construction crew all lived in that while they built the first ring, then spun it all up to one gravity."

"So what happened to the space habitat, Elina?"

"Oh, they built it in as they went. It's now the office for the distribution center. The top deck on the inside of the cylinder."

"And the gardens were built then, Elina?"

"Actually, no. The deck and roof were built, but the windows weren't installed yet, or any of the plants. They were allowed for in the plans, but their completion was after they got the rest of it up and spinning. The glass went in from the inside."

"That makes sense. Easier to install the glass in a spinning structure than trying to do it in zero gravity. And it has to be installed from the inside anyway. The internal air pressure holds it into the frame rather than trying to push it out."

"I think that's right, Bert."

"And was the RDT facility there in the plans?"

"Oh, yes. It came in as a completed module and got welded into the structure. A lot of the structure came as modules, filled with other materials. Those modules became hallways and rooms once the supplies were emptied out.

"But it's interesting to note that the second set of plans don't show the RDT facility at all. It was erased from revision one to revision two."

Mangum nodded.

"OK, so they had to show it in the initial plans so it got placed properly, then it just sort of disappeared."

"That's right, Bert."

"Wow. So it *was* an RDT facility from the very beginning."

"Yeah. So what did you find?"

"Corroboration, I think. The earliest newsfeeds on Crossroads, twenty years ago, noted the placement of the space construction crew habitat in orbit around this star. They called it Crossroads even then, and said they would be expanding it into a full-service space station."

"So the crew habitat was called Crossroads?"

"Yes, Elina. But who paid to put it here I did not find. The articles I found were after the fact, and they noted that Crossroads Corporation would be expanding and then operating the space station."

"So the goal was to hide Crossroad's origins from the very start."

"Looks like."

Stavros sighed.

"Are we ever going to find them, Bert?"

"I think so, Elina. But it won't be easy. After all, they have a twenty-year head start."

They were all sitting in the living room area of the suite after dinner. Sam and Jules were in their utility personas.

"So what have you guys been up to while we've been banging our heads against the wall?" Mangum asked Sam and Jules.

"Practicing," Jules said.

"Jules has been practicing various disguises, to be available to assist Elina when things become more active."

"Like what?" Stavros asked, intrigued.

"Like this," Jules said.

He stood up, and then seemed to melt into the floor, becoming an attractive area rug.

"Oh! Oh, look at that, Bert."

Stavros turned to Mangum.

"I guess I always thought of impersonating another creature. That I didn't expect."

Jules pulled together and became the golden doodle puppy. He jumped up on the arm of Stavros' chair, and a mouth formed at the end of his tail.

"Throw me at the wall, Elina."

"I can't do that. It's like puppy abuse or something."

"Just do it."

Stavros turned to Mangum, and he nodded.

"OK."

Stavros picked up the golden doodle puppy and threw him at the wall. When Jules hit the wall, he changed into a picture, a framed landscape hanging on the wall.

"Oh, that's clever."

"They can just pretend to be part of the wall as well," Mangum said.

Jules turned the color of the wall and spread out. He couldn't spread out as far as Sam, but it was very hard to see him.

"Wow," Stavros said. "That's handy."

Jules pulled himself back into the golden doodle puppy, standing on the wall like it was a floor, and jumped down onto the sofa. He resumed his utility persona.

"We also have ways to infiltrate an unfriendly position," Sam said.

"Like what?"

"Tell me, Elina," Jules said. "Back on Mardouk, did you ever go bowling?"

In Somerset, on Wilbourne, Gloria Dent and Claude Portnoy

were also struggling.

"This is so frustrating, Claude. Every time I get close, I run into a closed door. A bank BIE hasn't penetrated, or a privately held corporation with no transparency, or something. Like all the paths were anticipated, and doors installed on purpose."

Portnoy nodded.

"I'm not having much more luck, Gloria. I thought I had the guy. The perfect person, with the assets and power base twenty years ago to pull this off, and doing a lot of charity work, but with really sketchy sources for his observed cash flow. Wendell Taylor Evans."

"That sounds good. What happened?"

"He died three years ago. In his eighties."

"Shit."

"Yes. Obviously the operation has not ceased, so it's unlikely to have been him."

"Now what do we do, Claude?" Dent asked.

"Wait some more. At some point, we're going to get told to make trouble and see if we can't get some reaction that shows us who it is."

Portnoy got a gleam in his eye.

"That's when the fun starts."

THE FAVOR

Two Men, Each With A Problem

William Taylor Evans had a problem. He knew he had a problem, he just didn't know what it was or how big it was.

His father, Wendell Taylor Evans, had died three years ago, at the age of eighty-four. His mother had actually predeceased his father by five years, though she was three years younger.

William Taylor Evans, age fifty-two, was his parents' only child and their sole heir. This had not prevented multiple false claimants from coming out of the woodwork at the old man's passing.

It had taken over two years to shove all the other claimants aside and fully inherit his father's estate.

That process had completed six months back.

The younger Evans was now in nominal sole possession and control of his father's holdings. He added the 'nominal' himself, as he didn't feel in control.

Oh, some of his father's holdings were indisputably under his control. Evans had managed his father's biggest single company, Evans Machinery, Supply, and Consulting, Ltd., for years. The company manufactured large chemical and refinery complexes to spec or to order, and assisted in the installation and startup of same.

It was very lucrative, and Evans had done a good job with it and the other companies under his direct control.

Others of his father's holdings were more opaque to Evans. Most of those were gathered under the direction of his father's long-time assistant, Tanner Linden. Linden had retained direction of those companies during the probate period, just as

Evans had of the companies under his management.

Linden had worked directly for his father for over twenty years. He had thirty years with the company by this point, and was in his early sixties, ten years older than Evans.

And he was notably unforthcoming about the companies he managed under the Evans umbrella, even since the probate court had released the Wendell Taylor Evans estate to his son.

What Evans was going to do about that, he hadn't yet decided.

His father had not been helpful in that regard. He had told his son that he trusted Tanner Linden implicitly, and the younger Evans should probably just let him continue to manage those assets without interference.

For that matter, that part of the Evans business empire was very profitable. Tanner Linden's generous profit-sharing deal with the Evans business group on the companies he managed had made him a wealthy man, but that was still a fraction of the profits that had accrued to Wendell Evans and now his son.

William Taylor Evans decided it was perhaps best to let sleeping dogs lie, at least for the moment.

For his part, Tanner Linden also had a problem. He had tied up Wendell's estate for over two years, to the point of funding the other claimants to the inheritance. Those efforts had all been dismissed now, and Bill Evans was in control.

Whether and when he would attempt to assert that control was the issue. Linden had argued with the senior Evans that his son should have been brought wholly into the know about what his other companies were up to, but Wendell had disagreed.

The upshot of that was that Bill Evans didn't know about Crossroads, or the RDT business, or about Griffin Interstellar.

And, at age fifty-two, his value system had hardened. Bringing him up to speed on his other businesses without upset now would be very difficult, if not entirely impossible.

What Tanner Linden should do about that, he didn't know.

He hoped extreme measures would not be necessary.

The call came through, as assignment calls always did, with no video. Neither party used any term of address.

"Yeah," Mangum said.

"You have new orders," Marstock said.

"I'm listening."

"Agreement has been reached on your proposal for a solution."

"Agreement by who?"

"The council of six chief executives."

"No shit."

"You are to undertake such activities as may force the players out into the open, then act to pursue the proposal."

"Got it."

The call disconnected.

The call came through, as assignment calls always did, with no video. Neither party used any term of address.

"Yes?" Portnoy asked,

"You have new orders," Marstock said.

"Go ahead."

"Agreement has been reached on the proposal on which you were copied."

"Agreement?"

"By council of six chief executives."

"All right."

"You are to undertake such activities as may force the

players out into the open, then act to pursue the proposal."

"Understood."

The call disconnected.

"Nice," Claude Portnoy said when he got off the call.

"What's up?"

"They accepted Mangum's proposal."

"Who did?" Dent asked.

"The six chief executives."

"No shit."

"Yeah," Portnoy said.

"So now what?"

"We get to cause trouble."

"Oh, good," Dent said. "I was tired of sitting around. What do we do first?"

"Well, I keep thinking about that Wendell Evans guy. The guy who died."

"Yeah?"

"He has a son who inherited everything. Maybe we can pester him a bit, and see what he knows."

"Claude, did I ever tell you how good I am at pestering people?"

Preparations On Crossroads

"I've gotten new orders," Mangum told Stavros over supper. "What are those?"

"To cause trouble. Get our friends to out themselves."

"They have a plan for the aftermath, then?"

"Yes. Our plan. Or rather, Jules' plan."

"Leave everything in place then?" Sam asked.

"Yes, as much as we can. Somebody shoots at me, he's gonna regret it. For a very short period of time. Other than that, we see what kind of reaction we can get going."

Sam nodded.

"We've been practicing some things, Bert. Things you haven't seen before. We should show you. They might come in handy."

"All right, Sam. After supper, then."

"In the meantime," Stavros asked, "what do we do to cause trouble?"

"Well, you could go back into work and ask your boss why the Crossroads Police Department is shielding an RDT manufacturing facility. That would probably lead to trouble."

"Oh, I can pretty much guarantee it."

"Maybe we should just start with that and see where it leads."

After supper, with them all seated in the living room area of the suite, Mangum gave the aliens the go-ahead.

"All right, Sam. Jules. Whatcha got?"

"This for one," Jules said.

He turned into his golden doodle puppy persona and

climbed up on the side table of the sofa. Once there, he turned into a copy of Stavros' purse.

"Oh, my," Stavros said.

She got up and walked over to the table and picked the purse up by the strap.

"It's a little heavy, but not bad."

"Not quite as much storage as the real one either," Sam said, "but enough for necessities."

"Nice," Mangum said. "That allows Jules to stay with Stavros. She could go back to work, for example, and not be alone. Jules could at least escape and come get us."

"Exactly, Bert," Sam said. "We were concerned about her having no back-up. This will work, at least for a while. While Jules is still so small. It wouldn't work for me."

"It's a very good imitation," Stavros said. "It'll definitely pass."

She put the purse back on the side table, and Jules turned back into a puppy, climbed down onto the sofa, and resumed his utility persona.

Stavros looked at the purse a moment longer.

"You know, I usually keep my service pistol in my purse. How good are you with a pistol, Jules?"

"I have no experience with one at all, Elina."

"Well, we need to fix that. I'll take you to the range right away when I go back to the office."

Stavros returned to her armchair as Sam spoke up.

"The other new thing's strong suit is its surprise factor. If you could both close your eyes a moment, please."

Mangum and Stavros closed their eyes. It was just seconds before Sam spoke again.

"OK, you can open them now."

Standing in front of Mangum and Stavros was a copy of

Stavros, in her detective suit, which Sam had seen that first morning when she went back to her apartment to get other clothes.

Jules was nowhere to be seen.

"Heavens. It's like looking in a mirror," Stavros said.

"Oh, that's very good, Sam," Mangum said.

"It has an additional wrinkle," the ersatz Stavros said, with Stavros' voice. "If you would stand up, Bert, and pretend to hold a gun on me, please."

Mangum stood up, and the ersatz Stavros walked about fifteen feet away. The real Stavros remained in her armchair and watched with interest.

"All right. So you have the drop on me and I'm helpless, right?" the ersatz Stavros asked.

"Right," Mangum said.

The fake Stavros reached up to her head, with one hand over each ear, as if in surprise.

Then she hurled her head at Mangum.

"Shit!" Mangum said.

As it reached Mangum, the head turned into a mass that wrapped itself around Mangum's hands and covered them completely, manacling him at the wrists. He could not move his hands.

A new head grew out of the neck of the fake Stavros.

"What do you think?" Stavros' voice asked from the new head.

"Gosh," Stavros said. "Your head came right off."

"That's very good, Sam," Mangum said, "and likely to be effective by freezing the antagonist in place while he tries to figure out what the hell's going on."

A tendril with a mouth on the end extruded from the mass entangling Mangum's hands.

"I thought you'd like it," Jules' voice said.

He released Mangum's hands and dropped to the floor, turning back into the golden doodle puppy on the way down. He jumped up on the sofa and resumed his utility persona.

Sam resumed his utility persona as well, and walked over to resume his seat on the sofa.

"Oh, that's why you can do that," Stavros said. "Because there are two of you."

"Yes. Because there are two of us, we can do a lot of things like that. Things I couldn't do by myself."

Mangum nodded as he sat down.

"Well, that was very effective, Sam. Hopefully we don't need it."

That was Friday night. Saturday morning they went to the gardens. Relieved of the necessity not to upset the apple cart, on this trip to the gardens they reconnoitered the hill carefully.

"Yes, it has a very rectangular shape," Stavros said, looking around. "I mean, given that it follows the curvature of the station in one axis."

Mangum nodded.

"Yes. It's clearly pretty unimaginative in shape. Of course, they were limited in what they could do given they have to worry about the off-center mass."

"We should probably poke around at the edges a bit, and see if we can see the edges of the chamber below."

They did go right up against the wall, looking down at where the surface of the hill met the wall.

"I don't see anything," Stavros said.

"No, the dirt and pebbles fill the gap completely."

"Let's walk the perimeter below, Bert."

"All right."

They walked back down the path, then walked from the wall on one end to the wall on the other, following the edge of the chamber out into the gardens, along the curvature of the station, and back to the wall.

"No, Elina, they've covered it completely."

"We need to see if we can't get to the doors on the other side, Bert."

"OK. There's something we need to do first, though, I think."

Back in the room, Mangum turned to Sam, who was back in his utility persona.

"Sam, do you think you could go back to that ventilator in the distribution facility and plant a permanent surveillance camera on the outside of the ventilator shaft there?"

"Sure, Bert. Just let me look at the station plans once more."

"Your mobile assets?" Stavros asked.

"Of course."

Stavros nodded. The shape-shifting aliens could maneuver around in the station's innards with ease. Another huge benefit for them in the coming effort.

Sam was studying the station plans, following along his path.

"OK, Bert. I remember."

"All right, Sam. Good. Now I want the camera on the underside of the duct, pointing down, to get a good view of the whole area."

Sam nodded.

"OK, Bert. I got it."

Sam went over to the ventilation grille on the wall and oozed through the grating, fitting the camera between the fins on its edge.

"Wow," Stavros said. "That's impressive."

And then he was gone.

When Sam got to what he remembered as the right ventilator grille, he looked out and verified. Yes, there below him were the doors through what should be a blank wall.

Sam reached out between the fins in the grille with the camera, and the tendril curled around under the duct and put the magnetic camera against the bottom surface under him. With it secure, he withdrew the tendril and headed back to the suite.

Mangum was monitoring the camera feed as Sam took it to the distribution center and mounted it.

"So why didn't you have Sam leave a camera in that location when he was there before?" Stavros asked.

"It's visible from the floor if someone looks closely. I didn't want to take a chance on being found out."

"Ah. Of course. And now you don't care."

"Right. Works for me either way. Can we set an alarm on this image for when anything changes?"

"Sure. Let me do that now."

It didn't take Stavros long to set up the alarm. She looked at the time, then turned to Mangum.

"I think I should run over to the police range and bring Jules up to speed on shooting a firearm. It could get real important in a hurry, and the range is mostly abandoned on Saturday. And tomorrow it's closed."

"That makes sense to me, Elina."

Stavros turned to Jules, sitting in the living room area with Sam.

"Hey, Jules. Let's go to the range and I'll show you how to shoot."

"All right, Elina. Sounds like fun."

Jules switched to his puppy persona, climbed up on the side table, and turned into a copy of Stavros' purse.

Stavros took her service pistol – an 8mm semiautomatic – out of her actual purse and put it into the Jules fake purse.

"Now don't mess with it on the way," Stavros cautioned.

"Understood," Jules said.

He was using a pocket on the side of the purse as a mouth.

Stavros slung the purse over her shoulder and headed for the door.

"We should be back within two hours, Bert. If not, send Sam to look for us. I marked a couple spots in the station plans."

"All right, Elina. Have fun, you guys."

They were back in an hour and a half.

"Well, that was interesting."

Stavros put the purse down on the sofa's side table. Jules turned back into a puppy, leaving the pistol on the side table. He jumped to the sofa and resumed his utility persona.

"How'd it go?" Mangum asked.

"Jules shot from inside of the purse. Just opened a hole in himself and shot through it."

"Nice."

"Yeah. And after I explained the sight picture he wanted, he made an eyeball behind the gun that kept the sight picture all the time. He never had to reestablish the sight picture as he moved the gun around."

"Well back from the action, I hope."

"Oh, yes. I warned him about that. Bert, he's a very good shot. And stupid fast. I think they have faster reflexes and muscles than we do."

Mangum thought back to Sam's lunge at Rodney Stephan's arm on Mystik, to move his gun off-line on Mangum.

"Yes, I think that's right. That should help a lot."

"I would say so. Bert, he can empty a fifteen-round clip in under five seconds with a one-inch pattern at fifty feet."

"Criminy."

"Yeah. And I don't even have to take the gun out of my purse."

Stavros thought about it.

"I think part of it is that he doesn't get a lot of kick. The gun's as stable as if it's in a bench vise."

"Yes. Sam is very strong. I've seen that before."

"Well, I think from now on, I'll just let Jules do the shooting. He's amazing."

Jules turned his head at the mention of his name.

"That was fun. And it's surprisingly easy. Loud, though. I had to make new ears."

Sam looked on proudly.

Causing Trouble On Crossroads

On Sunday morning, Elina Stavros, Bert Mangum, and Sam went to the massive distribution facility that wrapped all the way around the upper deck of Crossroads, just below the inner surface of the cylinder.

Sam was currently in a persona mimicking Jack Sturm, the Abelon Intelligence Service agent Sam had met on Mangum's last mission. About ten years older than Mangum and Stavros, he didn't look like somebody one wanted to mess with.

Stavros was dressed in her workaday detective clothes – a business pants suit – and carried Jules as her purse.

Of course, the distribution facility was open on Sunday. It was a seven-days-a-week operation. It had to be, to keep up with Crossroads' heavy transfer traffic. But the everyday management team would not be here today.

They went into the office entrance where a single clerk manned the counter. Stavros walked up to the counter.

"Detective Stavros, Crossroads PD," she said, holding up her badge. "We're going to look around."

"All right, Detective, but stay out of the way of the container transports."

Stavros gave him her 'Of course. Do you think I'm a fool?' look, then Stavros, Mangum, and Sam walked on through the office and out onto the floor.

Sam led them unerringly to the doors in the bulkhead wall that led into the gardens, into the space under the hill, that they considered the RDT manufacturing facility. That was their supposition, still unproven.

It was the equivalent of two city blocks from the office entry across the huge space. Only thirty feet high, the distribution center stretched the entire length of the station and ran all the way around its inner surface. They couldn't see anywhere near all of it, because much of it was full of containers, most stacked two high, but they caught occasional glimpses down corridors between the containers.

"Wow. This is incredible," Mangum said.

"This is really why the station's here, and why it's so important to the cluster," Stavros said. "This and the refueling and container operations that are run with shuttles directly between ships. This whole facility only handles the smaller shipments. A few containers."

When they got to the doors through the bulkhead, the doors were all closed. Now Mangum could read the signs next to the man door.

DANGER!
HAZARDOUS MATERIAL FACILITY
AUTHORIZED PERSONNEL ONLY
RING FOR ENTRY

"I don't think they want us to go in there," Mangum said.

"Apparently not."

Sam walked over to some floor grates that ran across the floor from the nearest row of containers – the Griffin Interstellar containers – across the aisle to the wall of the facility. Mangum could see now that these weren't drains, but were an access for hoses from the containers into the facility.

At the wall of the facility, Sam extended a tendril from his foot down into the grate and into the facility.

"Ketones and other chemical byproducts in the air, Bert. Just looking around, I can see there's some sort of chemical plant thing in there. Tanks and pipes and such. Some people, too. White lab coats and stuff."

"That all checks," Mangum said. "Now what?"

"Why don't I ring the bell and see if we can look around?" Stavros said.

"I can't imagine they're going to allow that."

"Who's going to stop me?"

Mangum nodded to Sam, who took up station alongside the door on the opposite side from the bell.

Bold as brass, Stavros walked up to the door and pushed the bell.

After a minute, the door opened and a big guy appeared in the doorway. Stavros recognized him as a member of the Crossroads P.D. RDT control unit.

"What are you doin' here?" he asked Stavros, and grabbed for a pistol in a shoulder holster.

As he pulled the pistol, Sam grabbed his wrist with his right hand and squeezed hard enough the big guy dropped the weapon. He turned toward Sam, and Sam hit him with a haymaker from his left hand. The big guy went down.

Mangum pulled the small dart gun from his pocket and shot him in the neck.

"Well, that was exciting," Mangum said.

"He's Crossroads P.D.," Stavros said. "RDT control unit. Jimmy Forney."

"Well, he's got control, clearly," Mangum said. "We'll be able to ask him questions when he comes to."

"That I'll enjoy."

When Jimmy Forney came to, he was sitting on the steel

deck next to the door into the RDT facility, leaned back against the wall and his legs out in front of him.

"Oh, man. I feel like I got hit by a truck."

"Sorry about that," Sam, in his Jack Sturm persona, said. "I might have hit you a little hard."

"That's OK. You gotta do what you gotta do, you know?"

"You dropped your pistol," Mangum said. "You might want to holster that so no one gets hurt."

"Good idea," Forney said.

He picked the semiautomatic weapon up from where it had fallen and replaced it in his shoulder holster.

"Hi, Jimmy. What are you doing here?" Stavros asked.

"Hi, Elina," Forney said and shrugged. "It's what I do. Guard the facility. That's my job, basically."

"RDT control unit?"

"Yeah. We guard the RDT lab. Funny, huh?"

"I'm not laughing, Jimmy."

"Yeah, I know. It's a shitty drug. Fucks people up. But nothing I do is gonna stop that, Elina. And I need the job. The money's good, too. You just stand watch and you keep your mouth shut."

Forney looked up at her.

"You're not gonna tell anybody I said anything, are you, Elina?"

"No, Jimmy. You didn't tell us anything. We got here on our own, right?"

"Oh, yeah. Right. Only reason for you to be here is you already knew."

"That's right. But as long as we're here, Jimmy, can you show us around?"

"Oh, sure, Elina. No problem."

Forney scrambled up off the deck and led them into the

facility.

After the tour, Forney was very concerned.

"You're not going to say anything, are you, Elina?"

"No, Jimmy. I got nothing against you. I'm after bigger fish. This never happened, I was never here. You and I can agree on that."

Forney nodded.

"OK. Thanks, Elina. I owe you one."

"You just have to worry about your buddies in there in the lab coats."

"I'll talk to 'em. They won't say anything. They don't need the hassle either."

In the transit pod back to the first-class section, Stavros had a question for Mangum.

"What about when Forney comes out of it, Bert? Does he stay quiet?"

"Oh, yeah. It's like a post-hypnotic suggestion. He'll be convinced he decided to keep it quiet himself, and for good reasons, and he won't rethink it."

"So that visit doesn't really cause any trouble."

"No, Elina. It just confirms all our conclusions. To cause trouble, we're going to have to step it up a notch."

Stavros nodded.

"I can do that."

The next day, Stavros went into the office, returning from seven weeks of vacation. She put in a request to meet with the head of Investigations, Captain Brendan Daley. She got a meeting time back from Daley – ten o'clock, in his office – and caught up on paperwork while she waited.

When she went to Daley's office for the meeting, she was

sure to take her purse with her.

"Hi, Elina. Welcome back. Did you have a good vacation?"

"Wonderful."

Daley waved her to one of his guest chairs. Stavros set her purse on the corner of his desk and took a seat.

"I suppose you want me to bring you up to speed on what all has been going on while you were gone."

"Yes, sir," Stavros answered. "Mostly I want you to tell me why the Crossroads Police Department is concealing an RDT manufacturing facility on Crossroads."

"What? Who told you such nonsense? That's a dangerous accusation to be throwing around."

"It's not an accusation. I've been there. I've seen it. The chemical manufacturing. The packaging into ampoules. The ampoules packed into cases for shipment.

"It's not an accusation, it's a fact. If that fact is dangerous, it's not dangerous to *me*."

"I know of no such thing, Stavros."

She didn't miss his switch to her surname, putting distance between himself and this dangerous woman.

"With all due respect, Captain, that's bullshit. You either knew or you should have known. You're not that stupid."

Stavros tilted her head while she held his eyes.

"Then again, it's probably a fifty-fifty bet."

"I don't need to listen to this, Stavros. Get out. And put yourself on report."

Stavros stood up and picked up her purse from his desk. She hung it on her shoulder.

"For what? For not being a drug dealer like you? Go fuck yourself."

"I'll have to tell my superiors about this, Stavros."

"Good."

THE FAVOR

She turned and walked to the door. She was seething, that the organization for which she had worked for years had, all along, been so corrupted, and it came out now. She turned back to Daley.

"Good day, you drug-dealing scum," with all the loathing she could muster.

Stavros walked out and went back to her office.

Something would happen now, Stavros was sure. She didn't know what, but something.

Sitting in her office, she called Mangum, back in the suite.

"Well, my boss knows I know, though I don't know if he knew or not. Hard to read. He should've, but may not have."

"Head of Investigations? He should have," Mangum said.

"Yeah. He said he had to tell his superiors about our little dustup. I pushed his buttons pretty hard, so I'm sitting in my office now waiting for the other shoe to drop."

"We're on our way."

Mangum cut the connection, and Stavros spoke softly.

"Remember, Jules. Don't kill anybody if you don't have to."

"I understand, Elina," her purse said.

Causing Trouble On Wilbourne

William Taylor Evans was on his way into his office in the morning, in downtown Somerset, when he was accosted by a reporter.

Evans' office was in the Evans Building, right in the middle of downtown. His father's company headquarters occupied the top four floors, and the company leased out the rest of the offices to other companies. It was a prestigious address in Somerset, and in the entire kingdom, for that matter.

Evans' driver had let him off at the curb in front of the building, and a reporter with a cameraman accosted him on the sidewalk. She was an attractive young woman, the sort you see getting into media jobs.

"Gladys Mint, Capital Newsfeed. Mr. Evans, can you tell our viewers why you're running an RDT manufacturing facility on Crossroads space station?"

Evans had not been accosted by reporters often, and he had ignored them when he was. This accusation, though, stopped him in his tracks.

"What? What are you babbling about? I have nothing to do with Crossroads."

"Your companies don't own the Crossroads station, Mr. Evans? Is that on the record?"

Evans thought about how little he knew about what Tanner Linden's side of the company was up to. Did he in fact own Crossroads? Evans had no way of knowing. But he would find out.

"I have no further comment," Evans said.

He passed by the reporter and walked on into the building.

"Well, what do you think?" Dent asked Portnoy later, back in the hotel suite. "Did we get something started there?"

"No way of knowing."

"He reacted like he didn't have anything to do with Crossroads. But he's still your high-runner?"

"Oh, yes. One of the richest people on Wilbourne. And he shouldn't be, not from the actual numbers from the companies he's known to own. He has the biggest hole in his known revenue compared to his observed wealth."

"So do we go pester someone else, or wait for a bit?"

Portnoy thought about it a moment.

"There is one other guy we could poke at for fun."

"Who's that?" Dent asked.

"Tanner Linden. He was Evans' father's right-hand man, and still runs a big chunk of the Evans business empire. Bill Evans could own Crossroads and not even know about it."

"That's amazing to me. How could he own Crossroads and not know?"

Portnoy shrugged.

"You've never had big money. That said, he probably would know, but he's just come into his inheritance in the last six months or so. It was tied up in court. And Tanner Linden just so happened to run a big chunk of Wendell Evans' estate since he died."

"OK. So pestering Tanner Linden makes sense. How we gonna do that? I liked the pushy reporter thing."

"We could do that again, I think."

When Tanner Linden left his office in the Evans Building for the trip home that evening, he was accosted on the sidewalk by a reporter with a cameraman along.

"Gladys Mint, Capital Newsfeed. Mr. Linden, do you plan

any changes for your management of Crossroads space station and its manufacture of RDT?"

Linden stopped and held a finger up in Dent's face.

"Listen you," he said with heat. "That's libel. You publish anything along those lines and I will sue you into penury."

Linden turned and stalked to his limousine where the driver held the door for him.

"Well, that got a reaction," Portnoy said.

"Yeah. I thought he was going to herniate his spleen or something."

"Which means he's guilty."

"You think?"

"Oh, sure. Evans acted like 'what the hell is going on?' He was truly surprised. Linden acted like he knew what was going on and was counter-attacking. Wrong response for an innocent man."

"I see."

"For all that, Linden wouldn't sue anyway."

"He wouldn't?"

"Of course not. Truth is an absolute defense in libel cases. Which means we would get court-mandated discovery on what the truth is."

"Ah. Got it. So maybe we get an illegal reaction from Linden. Which would give us an opening."

"Yeah. You identified yourself as Gladys Mint, though. They may have a hard time finding us."

Dent smiled.

"Claude, dear. I'm booked into the hotel as Gladys Mint."

"Excellent. We should probably be on our guard, then."

"Oh, I would think so. Mr. Linden looked very angry."

Reaction On Crossroads

There was a buzz on Stavros' office door. She was seated at her desk, and enabled the door from her display.

Two large patrolmen stood in the doorway. Two large patrolmen she knew. Had worked with before.

"Sorry, Elina, but we have orders to arrest you. You need to come with us."

"On what charge?"

"They didn't tell us the charge."

"Yeah. Right. Not happening, guys."

"C'mon, Elina. We don't want to have to get rough with you."

"Have you guys seen the latest in high technology purses?"

They blinked at the non-sequitur.

"You gonna come quietly, Elina?"

"Not a chance."

The leader – Ted Gorski – sighed.

"All right. We do it the hard way."

"Don't try it, fellas. You're gonna get hurt. And for what? Some bullshit arrest, with no stated charges? Just run along now."

"We can't do that, Elina."

Gorski started to advance on her, while the other – Andy Conner – moved to one side and started to draw his sidearm.

Two quick shots rang out from Stavros' purse. One hit Conner in the right upper arm, the other hit Gorski in the right thigh. Both shots were aimed for the bone, and both hit home.

"Shit!"

"Owww!"

Conner no longer had the use of his gun hand. He held his left hand over the bullet wound in his broken right arm.

Gorski's leg buckled and he went down, hard, to his right, clearing Stavros' path to the door.

"Sorry, but I warned you guys. I'm not going to be disappeared just because I spoke up on what is really going on around here. And you two should know better than to try to arrest me without stated charges."

Stavros picked up and slung her purse, then walked to the door.

"I'll see you boys later. Good luck with your recovery."

Stavros' unsuppressed weapon made enough noise to attract attention, and people were rushing to the scene. None of them knew, though, that Stavros was supposed to be taken into custody.

"Two men down. Get a doctor," she called to those police responding.

"Yes, Detective."

Stavros turned and walked toward the main P.D. entrance, turning her back on the scene. She knew Jules would have eyes behind.

Arriving in the entrance lobby, she found Mangum and Sam, in his Jack Sturm persona, waiting for her. They stood when she entered.

"Come along with me."

Mangum, then Sam, followed her back into the police headquarters area of the station. There seemed to be a lot of activity, with people hurrying about.

"So what's happened?" Mangum asked Stavros in a low voice as they walked.

"Two patrolmen were sent to arrest me without charges.

Jules took them down, but nobody else knows it's me they're after yet."

"Where we going now?"

"Head of the RDT control unit. Dart him immediately when we walk in. Then Sam holds him until it takes."

"Got it."

They walked across the pool area of the RDT control unit toward the office of the head of the unit. There were some raised eyebrows, but nobody made a move against them.

Stavros had worked on the door code last night, and she flashed her ID, overriding the lock on the door, and strode in, Mangum and Sam on her heels.

"You!" Warren Heston said, then dove for his side desk drawer.

But Stavros stepped to one side just inside the door, opening Mangum's field of fire. He shot Heston in the neck with a Com-Ply dart, then stepped to the other side.

Sam came through between them, and he was moving fast. He dove across the desk, grabbing Heston's wrists, and took him and his desk chair to the floor.

Stavros closed and locked the office door with her ID. Her jimmying of the codes on the door meant only she could open it. Short of an oxyacetylene cutting torch, nobody was getting in without her permission.

It took mere seconds for Heston to stop fighting. Sam got off of him and then lifted Heston and his chair back to a sitting position behind his desk.

"Sorry to have taken you down so hard," Sam said.

"Oh, that's OK," Heston said.

Heston was feeling very good at the moment. And it was so nice of that fellow to apologize.

"Hello, Captain Heston," Stavros said, sitting in one of Heston's guest chairs before his desk.

"Hello, Detective Stavros."

Stavros was nice, too. She was good people.

"So why don't you talk to me about the RDT manufacturing facility here on Crossroads?"

"We're supposed to keep that a secret."

"Tell me about it anyway. How long has it been there?"

Heston shrugged. He couldn't see any reason not to tell her.

"Since the station was built, I think. As long as I've been here, anyway. Twelve years."

"And the RDT control unit exists to keep it a secret?"

"Yes, of course."

"Have you ordered people killed to keep it a secret?"

"No. Not on my own authority."

"Has anyone been killed by the RDT control unit to keep it a secret?"

"Yes. Half a dozen times, at least. Maybe a dozen."

"People who didn't do anything else wrong?"

"Yes, that's right."

"People like Clark Jones?"

"Yes."

"Those orders come from the chief of police?"

"Sometimes. Sometimes I bring him the situation and he gives the order."

"But it was always on his authority?"

"Yes. Of course."

"I think we should get the chief down here to tell us about that, don't you?"

"I could do that, I think. If I just call him."

"Do that for me, Captain Heston."

"All right."

Heston turned to the display on his desk and called the chief's office.

"Chief Harker's office."

"Let me talk to him, Margaret."

"Of course, Captain Heston."

Crossroads Police Chief Adam Harker's face appeared in Heston's display.

"Warren," Harker said. "Have you got that Stavros woman in custody?"

"Yes. I have her here, sir."

"Good. Excellent work."

"Thank you. I was actually calling to have you come down here, sir. There's some aspects of this we should talk about."

"Why not here?"

"Do you want to talk about these things in your office, sir?"

"No. No, you're right. I'll be right down."

Harker cut the connection.

"Very nicely done, Captain Heston."

"Thank you, Detective Stavros."

It was only five minutes before Chief Harker buzzed the door. Stavros let him in, and Mangum, standing to one side of the door, shot him in the neck as he walked in. Sam stepped up and grabbed his wrists until he settled down.

"Have a seat, Chief Harker."

"Thank you, Detective Stavros."

"Captain Heston and I were just talking about the RDT manufacturing facility here on Crossroads."

"You know, we're supposed to keep that a secret."

"We are, Chief Harker. It's just us, here."

"Oh. All right."

"You sometimes order people on Crossroads killed to keep that secret, don't you, Chief Harker?"

"Well, yes. Of course. We have to keep the secret."

"Who told you that you have to keep the secret?"

"The Station Manager."

"Carl Ikenberry?"

"Yes. That's right."

"Even if it means killing someone who did nothing else wrong?"

"Yes."

"Does Mr. Ikenberry tell you to kill them, Chief Harker?"

"Not in so many words. Sometimes he lets me know we have a problem. You know. Sometimes we find the problem ourselves."

"But Mr. Ikenberry knows about the RDT manufacturing facility?"

"Oh, yes. We don't actually have anything to do with the manufacturing and shipping part of it. You know. The police. That's not our job."

"You just keep it a secret."

"Yes. That's right."

Stavros looked over at Mangum and nodded.

Mangum and Stavros had talked about it the night before. Keeping the organization in place to continue manufacturing and shipping RDT under Mangum's plan did not need to include the police.

And Stavros had been adamant. Someone who so flagrantly violated their oath to enforce the law – to the point of multiple murders! – was not to be allowed to skate.

At the same time, Mangum was the one who had the experience with Com-Ply, and how to give lingering orders.

Mangum nodded back to Stavros, then stepped forward so Heston and Harker could see him.

"You fellows know that you did some very bad things,

right?"

"Oh, yes," Harker said, and Heston nodded.

"I'm afraid you can't be allowed to get away with that. But I have a fun way to solve the problem. Do you want to hear it?"

"Yes, I'd like to hear it," Harker said.

"Me, too," Heston said.

"All right. Here's how it goes. We all leave, leaving just the two of you here. Once we leave, Captain Heston, you reach into your desk drawer for your pistol and shoot Chief Harker in the chest two times. Right here."

Mangum put two fingers on his sternum, just over his heart.

"Then you put the gun to your head and shoot yourself in the temple, right here."

Mangum put his finger to his temple.

"That way, you both get punished for being very bad, no one else gets hurt, and it's all over very quickly. No arrest or trial or any of that nonsense. Doesn't that sound like fun?"

"Yes, actually," Heston said.

"Sounds good to me," Harker said.

"And can you do it, Captain Heston?"

"Oh, yes. That's easy."

"All right, then. We're leaving now. Give us one minute, then do just as I said."

"OK," Heston said.

Sam, Stavros, and Mangum walked out the door, Mangum turning as he left.

"Start counting now."

"OK," Heston said.

Stavros closed the door behind them, but did not lock it. Instead, she removed her control from the door using her ID and the 'Clear' button on the panel.

The trio walked across the RDT control unit pool area. Some

people turned to watch them go.

Just as they reached the far end of the room, two shots rang out in Heston's office, then a third. People in the pool area jumped up and ran to Heston's door.

Stavros, Mangum, and Sam walked down the hallway to the entrance of the police headquarters where she had picked them up earlier.

"Just that easy?" Stavros asked.

"Just that easy," Mangum answered.

"Good. Couldn't happen to a nicer pair of assholes."

Reaction On Wilbourne

The newsfeeds on Wilbourne that Tuesday morning were full of news and speculation about the murder-suicide on the Crossroads space station the day before.

The head of the Crossroads' police department's RDT control unit had asked the chief of police to stop by his office. He then shot the chief of police twice in the chest, killing him almost instantly, lifted the gun to his own head, and shot himself in the temple.

William Taylor Evans read the reports over breakfast with growing interest. That reporter had said something yesterday morning about RDT and Crossroads, and that Evans' companies were involved. He hadn't even started looking into it yet.

And here was a major news story about Crossroads and RDT. That was a strange coincidence.

Tanner Linden read those same reports over breakfast with growing alarm. It was just yesterday that he had been accosted leaving the office by a reporter asking about Crossroads and RDT.

Unlike Evans, Linden did not believe in coincidences.

The implications were clear. He had to do something.

And when Tanner Linden needed something done, he knew just who to call.

Every organization that operates on the edge of the law has a fixer. Not an attorney, though they have those, too, but someone who can fix things by stepping outside the law, making an end-run around the rules.

Not themselves, of course. They would never break the law in their own person. But they maintain the right contacts and know how to find the right people to get illegal things done.

In Tanner Linden's side of the Evans organization, that man was Brad Clark.

"Something's going on, Brad," Linden said. "I don't know what it is, but I don't like it. The head of the RDT control unit in Crossroads police – which is supposed to keep everything under wraps for us – pops the police chief and then himself. Right there in police headquarters. And now we have this pushy reporter asking about Crossroads and RDT."

"What's the shape of your preferred solution, sir?"

"We need to find out what's going on at Crossroads. I don't for one minute believe that this Captain Heston killed the police chief and then himself. He's been in that job twelve years. Maybe it was staged or something. I don't know. But we need to find out what really happened."

"And then fix it, I assume."

"Something. Keep it from blowing up in our faces."

Clark nodded.

"And the reporter?"

"That problem needs to be dealt with, too."

"Are you worried that, if something happened to her, it would indicate she was on to something?"

"No. Pushy reporters like that always have a lot of enemies. Powerful ones. Besides, deterrence works, too."

"I understand, sir."

One reason Clark had been successful for Linden was that he did his research. He started by looking at the security recordings for the Evans building. These had both video and sound.

Gladys Mint, Capital Newsfeed. Hmm.

Start with Capital Newsfeed. No such thing. That was not a good sign. If not Capital Newsfeed, then who did she work for? What organization was he up against?

Finding her could be an issue as well. If the organization was an alias, the reporter's name probably was, too.

Clark did a search over the residents of Somerset, then Wilbourne, and found no Gladys Mint that was within decades of her apparent age.

He switched to transient listings – passenger manifests, hotel guests, and the like – and had better luck. While he did not have access to every such database, he did have access to Crossroads' database, and that of the Wilbourne passenger liners that called there.

So Gladys Mint had most recently come from Crossroads. That was surely suggestive. And the passenger line had delivered her baggage to the Somerset Plaza Hotel downtown.

The Somerset Plaza Hotel was an Evans Group hotel, and Clark did have access to that database. Yes, here she was. Staying on the penthouse floor, and she'd been there six weeks so far.

Shit. That meant, whoever she was working for, they had money to spend on this operation.

He adjusted his estimation of the kind of operator he was looking for. It would be more expensive, but Linden didn't nickel-and-dime him on expenses as long as the job got done.

Gloria Dent and Claude Portnoy had not been idle. Much like Dent and Mangum had on Abelon, Dent and Portnoy had placed surveillance cameras in the elevators and the penthouse floor lobby plants so they could monitor their approaches.

Dent also set alarms on the surveillance feeds to pick up movement, especially movement in the penthouse floor lobby and the 'Penthouse' buttons in both elevators. All of this was done Monday evening before they retired for the night.

They eschewed eating out – leaving the room at all, in fact – and ordered several days food ahead from room service so their food couldn't be tampered with, and kept the curtains on the French doors out onto the patio closed.

Portnoy had a dart gun with Com-Ply darts, and he kept that handy. For Dent's part, she got a cricket bat out of her baggage.

Portnoy raised an eyebrow at that.

"You just nail him with the dart when he comes through the door, Claude. I'll take care of him from there."

The result of their preparations was that they had plenty of advance notice when Hugh Parker came to visit.

Tuesday late afternoon, the alarm went off on Dent's roll-up display, and she went over to check it.

"We've got a penthouse floor call on one of the elevators, Claude."

Portnoy picked up the dart gun and moved over to the hinge side of the door.

"Yeah, he's coming here. Pistol. Knock or pass-key, do you think?"

"Pass-key. This is an Evans Group hotel."

"OK. Good."

Dent grabbed the cricket bat and took up station on the other side of the door, the handle side.

There was a soft click from the door, then Parker edged into the room, looking for the inhabitants. As he passed the doorframe, Portnoy shot him in the neck with the dart gun through the crack between the door and the doorframe.

THE FAVOR

As soon as she heard the dart gun go off, Dent brought the edge of the cricket bat down hard on the wrist of Parker's gun hand, and his pistol clattered to the floor. Parker turned to her in surprise just as Dent brought the cricket bat back up and clocked him upside the head with the flat of the bat.

Parker went down like a sack of potatoes.

"Nice," Portnoy said.

"And people told me sports wasn't good for anything."

"Well, they were wrong. Clearly."

Portnoy pulled Parker into the room and retrieved his pistol from the floor before closing the door.

"You think he's OK?" Dent asked.

"Yeah. Just out. I'm gonna wait, though. No sense lugging him anywhere when he'll be able to walk in a minute."

They sat at the table and waited. A few minutes later Parker started groaning on the floor.

"Oh, man," he said. "What happened?"

Portnoy got up and walked over.

"You fell and hit your head. Are you OK?"

"Yeah. I guess so."

"Here. Let me help you up."

"Thanks."

Portnoy extended his hand and helped Parker get to his feet.

"Why don't you sit down there on the sofa until you feel a bit better."

"OK. Thanks."

"Oh, and here's your pistol. You dropped it when you fell down. You should reholster that so nobody gets hurt with it."

"Good idea. Thanks."

Parker took the pistol from Portnoy and reholstered it under his jacket. Dent gave him a glass of water, and he nodded his thanks and drank half of it.

"Are you feeling a bit better now?" Portnoy asked.

"Yeah. Much better, actually."

"Do you mind if I ask you some questions, then?"

"No, not at all."

"What's your name?"

"Hugh Parker."

"And you came here to kill us, is that right, Hugh?"

"Yeah. Her mostly. You, too, if you were around."

Parker looked over to Dent.

"Sorry."

Dent nodded once, in acknowledgement of the apology.

"Who hired you to kill us?"

"Guy name o' Brad Clark."

"Who's he?"

Parker shrugged.

"Some guy. Works in the Evans Building downtown. At least, that's where I picked him up."

"So does he work for the big boss there, at Evans Group?"

"I dunno. I haven't worked with him much."

"When did he give you the job?"

"This morning. He said he was in a hurry to have it done."

Portnoy looked over to Dent, and she piped up.

"Did you get paid half in advance for this job, Hugh? That's the normal setup."

"Yeah. Ten thousand now, ten thousand later."

"Directly into your bank account?"

"Yeah."

"Can you give us that account ID and login?"

"Sure."

Parker rattled off the access information.

"Thanks, Hugh."

Dent nodded to Portnoy, and he cleared his throat. Parker

turned to him.

"Have you killed other people for hire, Hugh?"

"Yeah. Not real often. Mostly I do other odd jobs. But once in a while I get called for that."

"You know that's bad, don't you, Hugh?"

"Yeah. But if it isn't me, someone else will do it."

"I suppose. Still, it strikes me that we can't just let you go after doing such bad things. But I think I have an alternative to getting arrested by the police and jail and having a trial and all that stuff. Would you like to hear it?"

"Sure. That sounds good."

"OK. There's a park across the street from the front of the hotel. Right across from the entrance. Did you see that when you came in?"

"Yeah. It's pretty."

"It sure is, Hugh. I think what you ought to do is go down to the park, and sit on a bench there. All pretty and everything. And then put your gun to your temple and shoot yourself in the head. Could you do that?"

"Sure. That's easy."

"I agree, Hugh. Much easier than getting arrested and going to jail and all that. I think that's what you should do. And it'll frustrate the cops."

Parker laughed.

"Yeah. The cops'll never get me."

Portnoy laughed along.

"So go ahead and do that now, Hugh."

"All right. Thanks."

"No problem."

Parker got up and let himself out. Dent and Portnoy went over to the French doors, drew back the curtains, and went out onto the patio. The park was across the street, twenty-five stories below them.

After a few minutes, Parker exited the front of the hotel and walked across the street into the park. He selected a bench and sat down there. He looked around at the park and laughed, then pulled his pistol out of the holster, released the safety, and shot himself in the head.

Dent and Portnoy went back inside as the first sirens started up.

"OK, so now what?" Dent asked.

"I think we need to talk to Mr. Brad Clark next."

Dent nodded.

"I might suggest something first."

Portnoy looked at her and raised an eyebrow.

"Well, we have Mr. Parker's banking information. We could pull all of his funds for ourselves."

"Sounds good."

"And we could return the advance for assassinating me."

"What?" Portnoy asked.

"Mangum did that in the Evelyn Barnes case. Sent the money back on each assassin, with a note that the refund was for non-performance. And he included a note to Barnes in the transfer."

"So we could send a little note to Mr. Clark, you think?"

"Sure. Why not?"

"I like it."

Portnoy nodded.

"I like it a lot."

Dent went over to her roll-up display and accessed Parker's bank account. She set up the reverse transfer and showed it to Portnoy. He chuckled.

"Gloria Dent, you are an evil person."

THE FAVOR

"Claude Portnoy, you say the sweetest things. So I send?"

"Sure."

Dent looked at the note once more before hitting 'Send'. Looked good to her.

Brad Clark: I am returning your advance payment, due to non-performance, to Hugh Parker (deceased). If you have any questions, you can ask me when I see you. Gladys Mint.

"OK. Sent," Dent said.

Portnoy looked up from his own display.

"We'll see what he does next, Gloria. Maybe we'll even go visit him."

"We need to research him first, Claude."

"Already under way," Portnoy said, returning his attention to his roll-up display.

Dent nodded, then pulled the remaining funds – several hundred thousand credits – out of Parker's account. It was in royals, which were not worth quite as much as Crossroads credits or Abelon dinars, but it was still a tidy sum.

Brad Clark was scanning the newsfeeds, looking to see if he found anything on the sudden and messy demise of one Gladys Mint.

Instead he found an article on the suicide of Hugh Parker in the city park across from the Somerset Plaza Hotel where Gladys Mint was staying.

He read it with growing alarm, when he got a beep from his display. He looked at it, and found it was a notification from one of his blind bank accounts. The one he used to make payments for certain off-the-books expenses.

It was a return of funds from his earlier transfer to the account of Hugh Parker.

Clark read the note on the transfer, and all the blood drained from his face.

Fuck! Who the hell did Gladys Mint work for? The Devil?

THE FAVOR

Gone To Ground

Mangum, Stavros, and Sam – still in his Jack Sturm persona – did not go back to Mangum's first-class suite.

"I rented another place. In the transient crew area."

"They have no surveillance there," Stavros said. "They won't be able to find us."

"Or so they claim, anyway. And we do have surveillance there. Plus the residents of that section of the station will be loath to cooperate with the police in any case."

"Oh, yeah. The police hate going in there. But wait. Can't they find you just from the rental?"

"Under the name of Frank Cox. Different account and all."

"Nice. That'll slow them down."

As the head of Investigations of the Crossroads P.D., Captain Brendan Daley was brought in to investigate the apparent murder-suicide of Chief Adam Harker and Captain Warren Heston. The forensic team returned nothing unexpected.

Daley turned his attention to surveillance recordings. There were no cameras in Heston's office, or in the RDT control unit area, but there were in the outer police headquarters lobby.

Witnesses said that three people walked out of Heston's office just a minute or two before the shootings. One of them was Detective Elina Stavros. The other two, both men, were not recognized by anybody in the unit.

But Daley picked up the trio walking out through the lobby after the shootings. The woman was definitely Stavros, with a look of grim satisfaction on her face.

A look Daley was familiar with, since she told him to go fuck himself this morning.

Daley didn't immediately recognize either of the two men, though the younger one seemed familiar. He set a facial search algorithm going on them both and sat back to await results. For databases he used both the Crossroads immigration control records and the cluster newsfeeds.

With that running, he sat back to await results, if any.

It didn't take long. The match on the younger one came in first. Daley looked down it quickly.

"Oh, shit."

When the match on the older one came in, Daley's heart skipped a beat.

"Fuck me."

Daley put in a call to the assistant police chief – he supposed the chief now – Glen Holbrook.

Glen Holbrook had his hands full. He had just, unexpectedly and suddenly, become the chief of police of the Crossroads P.D. He had already spoken to Carl Ikenberry once today, and the station manager was most interested in finding out what had happened.

Holbrook wasn't surprised by the intense scrutiny. He had been brought into the circle of people who knew the big secret of Crossroads when he was made assistant police chief. This apparent murder-suicide touched awfully close to that, being that the head of the RDT control unit was involved.

But he wasn't so busy as not to respond to the call request from Captain Daley. The head of Investigations may have learned something about what had really happened.

"Yes, Captain Daley. How can I help you?" Holbrook asked.

"I hate to bother you, sir, with so much going on, but I think it's important."

"You've learned something about what happened then, Captain? And why?"

"Not what and why, sir, so much as who."

"I don't understand, Captain."

"Just before the shootings, three people walked out of Captain Heston's office. One was recognized by all the witnesses as being Detective Stavros, of my department."

"Yes, Captain. I heard that earlier."

"Yes, sir. But she was accompanied by two men. I've run facial-match searches on those two men and can now identify them. There's no mistake, I checked them myself."

Holbrook wondered if he was going to have to beat it out of Daley.

"Yes, Captain. I understand. And?"

"Well, sir, one of them comes back as a match for a fellow known as Bert Mangum."

"That name's familiar."

"Yes, sir. He shot and killed Morton Van Dyke in his cabin six months or so ago now. The guy was armed and in Mangum's cabin, so it was pure self-defense. Detective Stavros handled that investigation. Mangum then left the station.

"Apparently he's back, sir. But during the Van Dyke investigation, Detective Stavros told me that Bert Mangum was likely a foreign intelligence operative. In her opinion, he was from the Association's intelligence branch. The Agency."

"There's no such thing as the Agency, Captain Daley."

"So everyone says, chief. Loudly and repeatedly. Nevertheless, he got the drop on an armed man lying in wait, coming home with his arms full of groceries, and killed him without so much as being injured."

"I see. And the other man, Captain?"

"That's even worse, if possible, sir. The other man is a facial match for Jack Sturm, who recently became the head of the Abelon Intelligence Service."

"That's not possible, Captain. Sturm must be on Abelon."

"That's what I said, sir, but if it's not him, it's his twin brother."

"A ringer do you suppose? A look-alike?"

"I guess it could be, Chief. But then you have to ask, Which one is the real Jack Sturm, the one on Abelon or the one here?"

"Ouch."

"Yes, sir."

"Where are they now, Captain?"

"We don't know, sir. Bert Mangum has a first-class suite on the station. He's been there over two months."

"In first-class?"

"Yes, sir."

"He's on some kind of budget, then. What about Stavros?"

"Detective Stavros took seven weeks' vacation, returning this morning. Looking back at surveillance, though, she hasn't been living in her own apartment. We checked the limited surveillance in the first-class section, and she appears to have been staying with Bert Mangum that entire time."

"In first-class."

"Yes, sir. But they did not return to the first-class section today after the shooting. A check of surveillance shows that conclusively. We can't find them."

"They must be in the transient crew section."

"Yes, sir. That's my conclusion as well."

"What a mess."

"Yes, sir. And if anything happens to Mangum or Sturm, either the Agency or AIS is going to swarm this place. That's their history, anyway. Especially if it really is Jack Sturm."

THE FAVOR

"I'm not sure which would be worse, Captain."

"I am, sir. At least with AIS, you hear tales about what happened when they showed up with vengeance in their eye. But when the Agency shows up angry, there's nobody left to tell you about it."

Holbrook broke off the call with Daley and considered his options. The next liner out from Crossroads was looking better and better, no matter where it was going.

Holbrook had looked forward to becoming police chief when Harker retired. The money was better. The perks were better, including a bigger apartment. Five or ten years as chief and he would be set. Retire with his twenty-five and settle down some place. Get some fishing in. Maybe find a partner.

Now it looked like he would be lucky to survive a month.

Holbrook sighed and considered whether to tell Ikenberry. Or, rather, what to tell Ikenberry.

People like Bert Mangum and Jack Sturm didn't get involved in things unless their government was behind them. And if the governments of Abelon and the Association were involved, things were about to get very dicey on the Crossroads station.

Carl Ikenberry was fretting over the murder-suicide of Harker and Heston. He had worked with both men for years. To have them both gone at once like that, with no warning, was disorienting.

The manner of their deaths was even worse. Shocking. That someone as stable and rock-steady as Warren Heston would go off like that didn't make any sense.

Ikenberry had been station manager on Crossroads for over ten years, taking over from the legendary Miles Borsten. Borsten had been the station manager that had come out here with the original construction crew, had lived in their habitat with them as they built the first iteration of Crossroads, the original cylinder. With the gardens.

With the RDT facility.

It was Borsten who had told Ikenberry of the RDT manufacturing and distribution operation, during the several years he had been assistant station manager. Ikenberry had been shocked.

Borsten had told him it was the only way to build Crossroads. The only way to make it financially workable. But Ikenberry hadn't liked it, and he still didn't. His hands were dirty, he knew. It was a dirty business. But he didn't have to like it.

For a dozen years, Ikenberry had expected the whole thing to be found out. To blow up in their faces.

Was that finally going to happen?

And, if so, what did he do about it?

What *could* he do about it?

"Ikenberry."

"Holbrook here, sir."

"Yes, Chief. Do you have any news for me?"

"Yes, sir. Not good news, though, I'm afraid."

Ikenberry braced himself for the worst.

"Go ahead."

"Minutes before the shooting, sir, Detective Elina Stavros of Crossroads P.D. left the meeting in Captain Heston's office with two men. We've identified the two men. We think we have anyway."

"You think you have, Chief?"

"Yes, sir. It's just hard to believe. One of them is a match to Bert Mangum, the fellow who shot Morton Van Dyke in self-defense during a robbery of his apartment six months ago. He has a beard now, but the facial match is at high percentage. We had identified him at that time as likely a foreign intelligence asset, probably from the Association of Planets."

"From the Association?"

"Yes, sir. We think he's an operative for the Agency."

"Oh, shit."

Ikenberry was under no illusions that the Agency didn't exist. There was a very big something in that space nobody talked about, at least. That the Association of Planets would have *no* intelligence service was not credible. The rumors of the Agency filled the bill nicely.

"And the other?"

"That's even worse, sir. The facial match came back as Jack Sturm, the new head of the Abelon Intelligence Service."

Ikenberry opened a sidebar in his display and did a search of newsfeeds on Jack Sturm, setting it for the last two weeks.

"Sturm's still on Abelon, Chief. Within the last two weeks. He can't have gotten here by now."

"Yes, sir. We came to the same conclusion. But if there's a look-alike to Jack Sturm running around, which one is the real one? Could it be the one here on Crossroads?"

"And even if it isn't, what kind of stones do you have to have to impersonate the head of the Abelon Intelligence Service? Who would even dare to do that, if not one of his friends or operatives?"

"I see your point, Chief."

"The bigger issue is that we have two extremely dangerous people running around with Detective Stavros, who is not only dangerous herself but a squeaky-clean straight arrow.

"And they're clearly not above arranging some, uh, premature mortality among some high-ranking people."

"You think they arranged the shooting somehow, Chief? Staged it or something?"

"That's my assumption, sir. Warren Heston just isn't the sort of guy to go off like that. Not without help."

"I understand, Chief. I've been wrestling with that myself."

Ikenberry paused and considered before continuing.

"So where are Detective Stavros and her friends now, Chief?"

"We don't know, sir. They did not return to Mangum's suite in the first-class section. We think they've gone to ground in the transient crew section."

"He was in the first-class section, Chief? In a suite?"

"Yes, sir. For the last two months or more. For an individual, that's a lot of money, so I don't think he's here on vacation. But for the Association? The Agency? That's nothing."

Ikenberry nodded.

"All right. Thanks, Chief. Keep me informed."

"Of course, sir."

Mangum went out to the transient crew section cafeteria to get a couple of pizzas and some sodas.

When he got back to the studio apartment in the transient crew section, Sam and Jules were sitting on the sofabed and Stavros was sitting on one of the two chairs at the small table. She had her roll-up display open on the table.

"Well, this is cozy," Stavros said. "How do we all eat? Do we take turns?"

"No, Sam prefers to eat pizza in the bathtub."

"What about Jules?"

"The bathtub is fine, Elina," Jules said.

Sam and Jules walked into the small bathroom and returned to their natural state, a couple of irregular brown masses lying in the bottom of the tub. Mangum dumped a whole pizza in on top of them and poured a couple of sodas in after it.

Coming back out into the main room, Mangum saw Stavros had stowed her display. Mangum set the remaining pizza box and two sodas on the table.

"Not exactly first-class room service," he said.

"That's OK. That gets old, too," Stavros said.

She looked around the apartment as they dug into the pizza.

"I'm surprised the sofabed is so big."

"Prostitution is legal on Crossroads, but not in the staff section of the station. The prostitutes don't take you back to their place, they come to yours."

"Oh, right. Of course."

"One nice thing, it means you're safe walking around the transient crew section, at least as long as you're dressed like a prostitute."

"How so?"

"Transient crew won't allow violence against prostitutes. They don't want prostitutes to feel unsafe here. If anybody gave you any trouble, half a dozen guys would jump him."

"What about Carmen? She was murdered."

"But not in the transient crew section. She was followed back to her apartment in the staff section. Her friend found her in her own apartment."

"That's right. So I'm safe here in the transient crew section as a prostitute, but not as a police officer?"

"Yes. Of course."

"You learn something every day."

"One thing, though. You can't be as, er, expressive here as in first-class. The sound insulation is nowhere near as good, and you'll piss off the neighbors."

"I'll try to remember that."

"If you don't, I'll have to stuff a towel in your mouth or something."

Stavros looked up at him with a twinkle in her eye.

"That sounds like fun anyway."

After dinner, they sat on the sofabed to talk. They each half-turned toward the other.

"So you've been checking the newsfeeds. What's going on?" Mangum asked.

"Well, there was a shocking murder-suicide today, right in the police department."

"You don't say. What are they saying about it?"

"Murder-suicide. Open-and-shut case. Some people are quoted as saying they were surprised Warren Heston would do that. He was always so grounded a guy, it's weird that he would go off like that. The internal police communications tell a different story, though."

"Internal police communications, Elina?"

"Yes. In all the excitement, they apparently forgot to close down my access. My extra logins, anyway."

"Extra logins?"

"Well, yeah. I don't need some asshole system administrator deciding when I can log in and when I can't, Bert."

Mangum chuckled.

"Well, that's handy. So what's the inside skinny, Elina?"

"Oh, you'll love this. The gossip going around is that I apparently left the meeting with Harker and Heston minutes before the shootings, in the company of two men."

"There were witnesses to that, Elina."

"Yes, but they've now identified the two men."

Mangum glanced toward the bathroom, then turned back.

"They have?"

"Yes, Bert. One of them was the notorious Bert Mangum, an operative of the Association of Planets' intelligence agency. And the other is no less than Jack Sturm, the new head of the Abelon Intelligence Service."

Mangum laughed aloud.

"Sam just picked Jack because he knew him well enough to mimic him."

"Well, it fooled Crossroads P.D."

"But that's easy to debunk, Elina. There should be newsfeeds showing Jack still on Abelon. Within the last two weeks anyway. It's two weeks' transit from Abelon to Crossroads."

"Right, and they've done that, Bert. So they know there's a real Jack Sturm and a look-alike. They just don't know which is which. Maybe the one here is the real one."

"Oh, that's just too good."

Stavros nodded.

"The other thing, of course, is that, even if this Jack Sturm is the impersonator, what kind of person would have the sheer balls to impersonate the head of the Abelon Intelligence Service?"

"That's priceless, Elina. I wonder how we can use this."

"The other interesting thing is that Mr. Ikenberry has apparently been on the phone with new police chief Glen Holbrook several times today. And the police guard on the station manager's residence and office here on the station has been doubled."

"So Ikenberry's nervous, huh? Good. I'll have to figure out how to work that in as well."

That night, Mangum was awakened by Stavros tossing. She was having a nightmare, and he woke her gently. As the disorientation of the nightmare passed, and she realized where she was, she started to cry.

Mangum held her close and cooed to her with soft reassurances while she clung to him and sobbed.

"That's OK, Elina. I understand. It'll be all right. We'll make it better. I promise."

And Mangum did understand. The nightmare had passed, but so had the dream.

The dream of being an honest cop, on an honest police force.

On Mardouk

Henry Grant was reviewing the reports coming in from the Agency's operatives on Crossroads and Wilbourne, Bert Mangum and Claude Portnoy. As the situation moved toward its crisis, he was reviewing the raw reports, not a précis prepared by the operations unit.

Mangum had verified the existence of the RDT manufacturing facility by simply going to it and asking for a tour. After dosing the guard with Com-Ply, of course.

Detective Elina Stavros had confronted her boss over the facility. She had avoided arrest and, together with Mangum, arranged the murder-suicide of the Chief of Police and the head of the so-called RDT control unit.

That bothered Grant a bit at first. One thing they did not want to do is destroy the manufacturing and distribution of RDT. Instead they wanted to control it, so they could avoid catastrophic social and economic damage from addicts dying or suffering severe mental and cognitive issues.

But, on reflection, the police weren't part of that operation, they were simply there to protect its secrecy, a function no longer needed. And Grant could understand Stavros' determination that those who had so significantly violated their sworn oaths as law enforcement officers not escape justice, which Mangum had mentioned in his report.

They had now gone to ground, and were likely hidden enough from Crossroads police to be able to operate without hindrance.

Next up for them was probably to confront Ikenberry, the station manager. Hopefully they left him in place, though the assistant station manager would likely do as well.

Meanwhile, Portnoy, together with Gloria Dent of Gaston's Bureau of Espionage and Intelligence, had inspired and then defeated an assassination attempt against Dent on Wilbourne. The questioning of the assassin had turned up the name of his boss, one Brad Clark, who had links to the Evans Group and Tanner Linden.

That seemed to confirm that conclusion as well, the deduction that it was the Evans Group that controlled Crossroads and the RDT trade.

Good work all around. He was happy it had been Mangum and Portnoy who had been in place to address this issue when it came up. They were so competent, their results often seemed much like magic.

Now, with the RDT manufacture on Crossroads verified and the links to the Evans Group confirmed, it was probably time to update Chairman Febo.

Grant put in a meeting request with Febo, then moved on to his next action item for today.

"Good day, Mr. Grant."

"Good day, Madam Chairman. Thank you for taking this meeting."

"You have news for me, Mr. Grant?"

"Yes, ma'am."

"Proceed, Mr. Grant."

"Thank you, ma'am. Our operatives have confirmed a number of conclusions we had previously reached. First, our operative on Crossroads has confirmed the presence of an RDT manufacturing facility there and that it has the capacity to supply all the RDT we are seeing in the whole cluster."

"Excuse me, Mr. Grant, but this is an essential point. How

confirmed is that?"

"We have recordings of the actual operation in process, Madam Chairman, and our people here have confirmed the quantities observed and the quantity possible with this equipment."

"Very good. Carry on, Mr. Grant."

"Yes, ma'am. Second, our operative on Wilbourne has confirmed the connection between the Crossroads RDT operation and the Evans Group, a major business interest on Wilbourne."

"And how was that confirmed, Mr. Grant?"

"Our operative and the cooperating Gaston operative posed as a reporter and cameraman and asked pointed questions of the chairman of the Evans Group and one of his top assistants. They were subsequently targeted for assassination."

"Oh, my. Are they all right, Mr. Grant?"

"Yes, ma'am. The assassin, however, is deceased."

"Oh, good."

"Also, the chief of police and one of his chief deputies on Crossroads are deceased. They admitted to our operative to a number of murders, over the years, of people who had stumbled onto the existence of the RDT operation."

"Yes, I saw something about that in the newsfeeds, Mr. Grant. I thought it was a murder-suicide."

"Yes, ma'am, it was. Arranged by our operative on the scene and the police detective who brought us the problem in the first place. She was incensed that sworn law enforcement officers would be so corrupt."

"Will that hamper our efforts to preserve the manufacturing and distribution operation to maintain those currently addicted, Mr. Grant?"

"No, ma'am. The police were involved in keeping the

operation secret. If the operation is public, however, we do not need their involvement."

"I see, Mr. Grant. Is there anything else for me today?"

"No, ma'am. I just wanted to let you know we had confirmed those earlier conclusions."

"Very well. Thank you, Mr. Grant. Keep me informed."

"Of course, Madam Chairman."

When she got off the phone with Henry Grant, Association of Planets Chairman Isabela Febo put in a call request to Gaston Alliance Speaker Michael Corliss.

"Hello, Isabela. How are you today?"

"Good, Michael. And you?"

"Very good. How can I help you?"

"I wanted to make sure you were being kept informed of developments on this Crossroads business."

"I believe so, Isabela. I was just briefed on the assassination attempt on Wilbourne and the murder-suicide of the police officials on Crossroads."

"Oh, good. Michael, I think it's important you and I stay together on this whole thing to bring it to a successful conclusion."

"I agree. If we stay together, we can keep the rest of the cluster on the plan."

"My thoughts exactly. You're not concerned, Michael?"

"No, Isabela. We're together."

"Are you at all worried about the loss of those police officials, in terms of carrying out the plan?"

"No, I don't think there's any cause for alarm there, Isabela. As a matter of fact, I'm not sure some of the administrators and such are indispensible either. It's the chemists and technicians I worry about."

"All right. Good. Because it seems we're going to get a certain amount of breakage in this effort."

"Understood. But I think we're good."

"Excellent. And while I have you on the call, I do want to thank you for the assistance in this matter, Michael. This is the second operation in a row we've collaborated on."

"And to good effect. I think the whole Abelon affair worked out tremendously well."

"Agreed. Very well, Michael. Thank you for your time today."

"Of course, Isabela. Stay in touch."

Meeting With Ikenberry

Mangum and Stavros were up early the next morning, Tuesday. Mangum knew what he wanted to do about Carl Ikenberry.

"All right, Sam. You understand? Put this on his desk, then watch what he does. I'm particularly interested if he says 'Yes' or not."

Sam, in his utility persona, read the note.

"I understand, Bert. This should be interesting."

Sam went over to the ventilator, then oozed through it and was gone.

Carl Ikenberry arrived at his office the next morning after a fitful night's sleep. The murder-suicide had just been yesterday, and he couldn't believe it was an isolated incident or that it would stop here. He was waiting for the other shoe to drop.

When he got into his office and sat at his desk, he found a three-by-five card in the middle of his desk. He picked it up and read the handwritten note.

Mr. Ikenberry:

We need to talk. There is a way out of this RDT business that does not require your immediate demise. If you wish to meet, just say "Yes." You are being watched.

Bert Mangum

THE FAVOR

Ikenberry looked around. He was alone in his office. He knew his office had no surveillance cameras. No approved ones, anyway. He tucked the note into his pocket and tried to ignore it as he went about his day.

Sam, watching from behind the ventilator grille in his office, gave it fifteen minutes, then returned to Mangum's room in the transient crew section.

"So now what?" Stavros asked after Sam returned back without a 'Yes' from Ikenberry.

"We'll play a similar game tonight. It's going to drive him nuts all day, and he should be primed."

That night, after a very nervous day, Carl Ikenberry went to bed in the station manager's residence on Crossroads. Even with the increased police presence in his office and residence, he did not feel safe.

When he pulled the bedspread back to get into bed, he found another three-by-five card on his pillow.

Mr. Ikenberry:

Are you sure you don't want to talk? I suppose I can just kill you and meet with Mr. Thorne instead, but that's not my preference. If you wish to meet, just say "Yes." You are being watched.

Bert Mangum

Vernon Thorne was the assistant station manager, and Ikenberry's replacement if something should happen to him. Like Bert Mangum killed him, for instance.

That would have sounded ridiculous two days ago, but that

was before Warren Heston had shot and killed Chief Adam Harker and then himself yesterday. Death now seemed just around the corner.

And it was clear to Ikenberry that Mangum would have no trouble breaching his security and killing him.

Ikenberry looked around the room. He couldn't see anybody or anything, but the note said he was being watched.

"Yes," Ikenberry said. "I'll meet with you."

Sam pulled back from the ventilator grille and headed back to Mangum's room in the transient crew section.

"OK, so he's going to meet with us. How do we handle that?" Stavros asked.

"This is what I want to do."

Mangum explained the plan to Stavros, with Sam and Jules looking on.

"Does that work for you, Elina?"

"Yeah. Sounds good. I think especially to meet him in this section. No surveillance."

"What about you, Jules? Any problem?"

"No. I get it, Bert."

"Sam?"

"Just one thing, Bert. Who do I impersonate? I can do a better job if I have a model."

"Can you do Jimmy Forney, Sam? A big guy like that?"

"Sure, Bert."

Sam changed into the spitting image of Jimmy Forney, the big RDT control unit guard they had met at the RDT manufacturing facility.

"Someone will recognize him, though, Bert," Stavros said.

Mangum nodded.

"All right, Sam. Keeping that body, can you change the head

and face to Rodney Stephan, the assassin on Mystik?"

Stephan had tried to kill Mangum and Dent on Mystik during the Evelyn Barnes affair, and Sam had deflected his gun arm.

"Sure, Bert."

The head and face changed, but it was the agreeable Stephan, after Dent had injected him with Com-Ply.

"No, Sam. Rodney Stephan before Gloria injected him. When he was holding me at gunpoint."

"Oh. OK."

The face changed, and now it was the face of a stone-cold killer.

"Perfect," Stavros said. "Nobody will mess with him, even in the transient crew section."

The next morning, Wednesday, when Ikenberry got to work, there was another three-by-five card on his desk.

Mr. Ikenberry:

How nice that you'll meet with me. You are to go to the entrance to the transient crew section on Aisle B-7 at ten o'clock this morning. My assistant will meet you there. Do not bring any friends from the police department. There's no need for anyone to die. You are being watched.

Bert Mangum

At quarter to ten, Ikenberry got up from his desk and left his office. In the lobby, he spoke to the police guard.

"Everyone stay here. I don't need any guards where I'm

going."

"But, sir, we have our orders."

"Yes. And you get those orders from me. Stay here."

"Yes, sir."

Stavros was watching all this on her roll-up display in the transient crew bar on B deck. The bar didn't open until noon, but that did not stop her and Mangum from getting in.

She was tapped into both the station surveillance system and police communications, as well as Mangum's surveillance cameras in the transient crew section.

"They're reporting in to headquarters. The RDT control unit has a tail on him."

"That's fine," Mangum said.

He turned to Stavros' purse on the table.

"You ready, Jules?"

"I'm good, Bert," her purse answered.

Ikenberry walked into the small lobby by the transition from the resident section to the transient crew section on B deck at aisle 7. A very large fellow who looked like somebody one did not want to mess with walked up.

"Mr. Ikenberry. This way, please."

Ikenberry would not normally have wanted to follow someone like that without backup, but Mangum had already shown him that he could kill him any time he wanted.

So Ikenberry followed Sam in his big Rodney Stephan persona into the transient crew section.

The big, intimidating guide was actually a pretty good choice, Ikenberry had to admit as he followed Sam through the transient crew section. There were some people out and about, and he got curious looks in his business suit, but nobody was willing to interfere with whatever business Sam was on.

It looked like it would be distinctly unhealthy.

After a few minutes they came to the door of the transient crew bar on this deck. It should be closed at this hour, but the big fellow grabbed the handle. Ikenberry heard the lock click, then Sam opened the door and held it while waving Ikenberry ahead.

Sam followed him to the table where Bert Mangum sat. Ikenberry saw a woman he recognized as Detective Elina Stavros also sitting at the table, though she was engrossed in a roll-up display.

"Mr. Ikenberry, Mr. Mangum."

"All right. Thank you, George. Could you tell Jack we're ready to start."

"Yes, Mr. Mangum."

The big fellow left, and Ikenberry looked at Bert Mangum curiously. He was fairly young. Early thirties. But he had an air, an attitude. It occurred to Ikenberry that, though only medium height and slender, Mangum was much more dangerous than the fellow who had led him here. He seemed to radiate competence, assurance, and more than a little menace.

Sam went out into the vestibule of the bar out of sight of Ikenberry, waited a minute or so, then came back in. He was now in his persona of Jack Sturm, the head of the Abelon Intelligence Service.

"Hi, Jack," Mangum said.

"Hi, Bert. Mr. Ikenberry."

Mangum nodded to Sam, then turned to Carl Ikenberry.

"Thanks for coming to see me, Mr. Ikenberry. You see, we have a problem. We know all about the RDT manufacturing facility under the hill in the gardens. We know all about the distribution of RDT to planetary drug dealers by Griffin Interstellar. We know all about the involvement of Evans Group on Wilbourne.

"All of this has been communicated to our superiors, and they are not amused. The chief executives of the six local star nations have therefore decided to do something about it."

"The six chief executives? They all know?"

"And have agreed on a solution. Yes, Mr. Ikenberry. Since the Evelyn Barnes affair on Abelon a few months back, they have a consortium of the six for handling big problems. And they have a navy. Were anything to happen to us–" Mangum waved a hand indicating himself, Sam, and Stavros "– you would likely get to see that navy and its boarding personnel up close and personal.

"As I say, though, they have agreed on a solution. A workable solution to the problem you have created here is a thorny issue. There are millions of addicts who would die or be cognitively impaired if the flow of RDT stopped.

"Almost worse, from their point of view, Crossroads would likely close. As you know, the station is not profitable on its own without the RDT business. But if Crossroads closed, the interstellar hub-and-spoke trading system would collapse, plunging all of their economies into a long-lasting depression."

Ikenberry nodded. This was exactly the situation Miles Borsten had presented him with when he became assistant station manager more than a decade ago.

"What is their solution, Mr. Mangum?"

"You will remain in place and continue to run the Crossroads station, including the RDT facility. But the RDT facility will now be run above board. The RDT shipments will be made to government franchises in the six star nations, who will each make it available to their addicts on the terms they think best.

"There will be no more RDT control unit in the Crossroads Police Department, no more murders to ensure its continued secrecy, and no more black-market payments to Evans Group by the planetary drug dealers. Those people are out of business. I think in most cases, they will be very permanently out of business."

Ikenberry sighed.

"Good."

Mangum raised an eyebrow.

"You have to understand, Mr. Mangum, this situation you describe was all in place when I became assistant station manager. There was damn-all I could do about it. It was already a threat to the cluster's economy when I took over as station manager. That and the so-called RDT control unit is a very dangerous bunch, even for me.

"I've been waiting for this thing to blow up in my face for ten years."

"You're hardly an innocent, Mr. Ikenberry," Stavros said over her roll-up display.

"I didn't say that, Detective Stavros. But I also didn't know what, if anything, I could do about it."

"OK. That's probably fair," Stavros said.

Ikenberry turned to Mangum.

"I can tell you, though, Mr. Mangum. The people in Evans Group who were behind this from the beginning will be much harder to deal with than the Crossroads end."

"We understand that, Mr. Ikenberry. Mr. Linden and Mr. Evans are more than evenly matched. My own employers and the Gaston Bureau of Intelligence and Espionage are involved in that effort right now."

Ikenberry raised an eyebrow. He looked aside to Jack Sturm,

head of the AIS, then turned back to Mangum, reputedly of the Association's 'non-existent' Agency, and added Gaston's BIE into his thinking.

"Yes, Mr. Ikenberry. As I said, all six chief executives are agreed this is the solution that causes least harm while getting the worst offenders proper justice. And that includes King Ferdinand on Wilbourne."

Ikenberry nodded. Yes, they would be able to deal with Tanner Linden.

"One thing I think I must tell you, Mr. Mangum. I don't think Bill Evans knows anything about any of this. My report was always to Tanner Linden, and he warned me that Bill Evans was not in the know. Your trail at that end probably stops with Tanner Linden."

"Thank you for that, Mr. Ikenberry."

Mangum looked over at Stavros, and she nodded back. She had already sent that intelligence on to Dent and Portnoy on Wilbourne. Mangum looked back to Ikenberry.

"As far as Tanner Linden and the Evans Group is concerned, Mr. Ikenberry, you are no longer to take any orders from that organization."

"Then who do I report to, Mr. Mangum?"

Mangum looked to Sturm, who stirred and turned to Ikenberry.

"For the time being, Mr. Ikenberry, you will report to Mr. Mangum. When the consortium of chief executives establishes your permanent reporting structure, Mr. Mangum will inform you."

"Very well."

"And with that, Mr. Ikenberry, I believe our meeting is coming to a close. You are to support the conversion of the RDT business to a legal government franchise. You are to instruct the police to leave the three of us alone.

"And you should be aware that we are monitoring everything that goes on. Any attempt to double-cross us will be answered by our superiors with force exceeding anything you or Tanner Linden can bring to bear."

"I understand, Mr. Mangum, but I have no desire to do that anyway. I've wanted a way out of this situation for a long time, and you've given me one."

Mangum stood up and so did Ikenberry, and they shook hands. But Stavros spoke up from behind her display.

"Contrary to orders, Crossroads P.D. followed Mr. Ikenberry here."

"Holbrook?" Mangum asked.

"No. Cooper. Heston's replacement in the RDT control unit. He's down the hall now, with a couple squads of their enforcers. Gonna arrest us, I guess."

"Time to clean 'em out?"

"Yeah. I'll be right back."

Stavros got up from the table, picking up her purse and slinging it over her shoulder. She walked over into the vestibule inside the entrance.

"All right, Jules. First cross-corridor. Four on the left and five on the right. Kill shots. Head or heart."

"I understand, Elina."

Stavros held her purse out in front of her and Jules changed into a bowling ball. She opened the door into the hallway and rolled the bowling ball down the hallway, closing the door behind it.

"All right. So I don't know what the hell Ikenberry is up to, but we know Stavros and those other two assholes are hanging out here in the transient crew section. So when Ikenberry comes out, we arrest anybody in there. Anybody who comes out with him. Anybody involved. Everybody got that?" Curt Cooper asked.

"Yes, sir. We got it."

"And don't take no for an answer. Whatever it takes. Kill them if you have to."

One fellow was keeping an eye out around the corner. He saw Stavros open the door at the end of the hallway, the door into the bar, and roll something down the hallway. A bowling ball.

"Hey, boss. Stavros just rolled a bowling ball down the hallway."

"What?"

"What if it's a bomb?"

"On a space station? Nobody's that stupid. Let it roll by us."

The bowling ball rolled until it got to the midpoint of the cross-corridor, then unrolled into a flat circle on the floor. In the middle of the circle was a semiautomatic pistol, held in something like a hand, with something like an eye behind it.

The bowling ball or whatever it was on the floor opened fire. Nine shots in under five seconds, every shot a kill shot.

The flat circle gathered itself up around the gun, then changed into a cute golden doodle puppy and went running back down the hallway to the door of the bar.

Stavros opened the door of the bar once the gunfire was over, and the puppy jumped up into her arms, then turned back into a purse, her gun inside.

"Thanks, Jules. Nice job."

"No problem, Elina. Easy," her purse said.

When he heard rapid multiple gunshots out in the hallway, Ikenberry looked at Mangum, then Sturm. Both men sat composed, apparently not at all concerned.

Stavros walked back into the bar.

"All taken care of?" Mangum asked.

"Yeah. No problem."

Ikenberry raised an eyebrow, but said nothing.

"See you later, Jack. Thanks."

"Sure, Bert."

Sam, as Jack Sturm, got up and left the bar. A minute or two later, Sam, as the big fellow, George, came back.

"Can you escort Mr. Ikenberry back to the resident section, George?"

"Yes, Mr. Mangum. This way, please, Mr. Ikenberry."

Ikenberry nodded to Mangum and Mangum nodded back.

Ikenberry followed 'George' out of the bar and down the hallway. He was shocked when they passed the cross hallway and there were nine men down, dead, in the cross corridor.

Ikenberry had only heard nine shots.

Detective Stavros hadn't been gone two minutes.

"Shame some people can't follow orders, ain't it, Mr. Ikenberry," the big fellow said as they passed the carnage.

One thing was certain to Ikenberry. He wasn't going to double-cross the Mangum-Sturm-Stavros trio. Even the police wouldn't be able to protect him.

The entire Crossroads P.D. was outmatched by that bunch.

Outgunned, anyway.

Wilbourne Gets Involved

Gaston Alliance Speaker Michael Corliss put in a call request to King Ferdinand IV of Wilbourne on Wednesday after lunch. It was Wednesday morning Somerset time.

"Good afternoon, Michael."

"And good morning to you, Ferdinand."

"To what do I owe the pleasure of your call today?"

"I need to let you know what we've confirmed about this whole Crossroads business we talked about, Ferdinand. Wilbourne plays a major part in it, I'm afraid."

"All right, Michael. Tell me what's going on."

"Crossroads is a clandestine project of the Evans Group, a major Wilbourne business interest. Most or all of the RDT in the cluster is being manufactured on Crossroads and distributed by Griffin Interstellar. We believe both are wholly owned subsidiaries of the Evans Group."

"That's shocking, Michael. Wendell Taylor Evans was one of our most prominent citizens."

"Yes, I know. His son and heir, William Taylor Evans, appears not to be involved, but the father's chief assistant, Tanner Linden, is up to his neck in this whole business."

"This is very disturbing news, Michael. What are we to do about it?"

"We need your help to clean this all up, Ferdinand. Some police or intelligence organization in your government you trust absolutely. We don't know who might have been co-opted in all this, but we suspect some must have or it couldn't have stayed hidden this long."

King Ferdinand nodded. Criminal organizations like this

almost always had the help of someone in the government. Who could he trust absolutely?

There was only one organization that met the bill.

"Very well, Michael. I will give this assignment to the King's Own, the Royal Guard. Them I trust absolutely."

"Excellent, Ferdinand. Isabela and I have operatives in Somerset tracking this all down. They were involved in shutting down that sex-trafficking ring, and in that earlier Abelon affair. They're some of our best people, but they need backup on this."

"I will have our people coordinate with your Mr. Petrov. Does that work for you, Michael?"

"Absolutely, Ferdinand. Thank you."

"Not at all, Michael. We need to get this cleaned up.

When he got off the phone with Speaker Corliss, King Ferdinand summoned General Hugo Sinclair, the eighth Earl of Dunharrow. The Earls of Dunharrow had been the head of the Royal Guard for generations, and were beyond suspicion, the eighth Earl no less than his predecessors.

Sinclair was located inside the palace itself, and came to the king's summons. Ferdinand's liveried man showed him in.

"Your Highness," Sinclair said, bowing to the man behind the desk.

"Be seated, Earl Dunharrow."

"Thank you, Sire."

Sinclair sat in one of the two guest chairs facing the desk.

"I have a matter requiring the uttermost sensitivity and discretion to be attended to, Dunharrow, and your organization is the only one I trust enough for this assignment."

"Thank you, Your Highness."

"We'll see if you still thank me when you know the facts,

Dunharrow. It is shocking," Ferdinand said.

Ferdinand then filled in Sinclair on what the Association had found on far Crossroads, and how it had led back to the very center of the Kingdom of Wilbourne, to one of its most prominent citizens.

"Wendell Taylor Evans, a major illegal drug supplier? That is incredible, Sire."

"Yes, well, old Wendell wasn't above being a rules mechanic, and he set up the rules so it wasn't actually illegal, on Crossroads, to be doing just that."

"Even so, Sire."

Ferdinand nodded.

"Yes, even so. And I have it on the best authority, from Gaston's Speaker Corliss himself. Not through channels, not through the foreign service, but directly from the Speaker."

Sinclair nodded. Corliss was a remarkably straight shooter for a head of state, and he had a good relationship with the king. This would be the facts, at least in Corliss' own mind.

"I see, Sire."

"Now Speaker Corliss and Chairman Febo both have operatives active in Somerset right now tracking this down. They were instrumental in shutting down that sex trafficking ring as well as in the Abelon affair. They pulled us away from war with Villacqua, and we owe them one."

"I understand, Sire."

"More to the point, Dunharrow, they're here doing our laundry, to some extent. There's no way this Crossroads thing should have gotten so out of hand right here on Wilbourne. I suspect someone in the police or the courts has been shielding them."

"If someone violated their oaths to the Throne, Sire, that's treason. Will you be invoking high justice, then?"

"If I have to. But they are not getting away. So I need you to contact Ivan Petrov of the BIE. Get your best espionage people in touch with these operatives. Back them up. And then take it all down, Dunharrow. Root and branch."

"Do you trust their information, Sire?"

"Right now I trust them more than my own police and courts. Find out who's behind the RDT trade, Earl Dunharrow. Find out who's been getting payments to keep it quiet. And then lock them all up."

"I understand, Sire."

"At that point, *I* will deal with them."

"Yes, Sire."

"And, Dunharrow?"

"Yes, Sire?"

"This is a very short term need. Things are moving quickly."

"We're on it, Sire."

Sinclair called Ivan Petrov on Gaston.

"General Hugo Sinclair on Wilbourne here, Mr. Petrov. I am the head of His Majesty's Royal Guard."

"Good to meet you, General. I was told someone would be in touch."

"Yes. At the orders of King Ferdinand, our espionage section is prepared to move to the assistance of your operative in Somerset. I just need to know who that is."

"Our operative on the scene is Gloria Dent, currently checked in to the Somerset Plaza Hotel as Gladys Mint. The Association also has someone on Wilbourne, but I will leave that to Ms. Dent."

Sinclair nodded. One might identify one of one's own agents, but someone else's? No. Never. Not, at least, if they were on your side.

"Excellent. We're on it, Mr. Petrov."

"I won't keep you, General. Good hunting."

Lieutenant Colonel Lance Peabody did not often get assignments directly from General Sinclair, but it had happened before. When the need for speed and discretion were paramount.

They certainly appeared to be so here. He had been numb with shock when Sinclair briefed him. How could this have gone on in secret for so long? To Peabody's mind, someone was clearly getting help in keeping it so.

It was certainly a high priority. Instructed to drop everything else for the moment, it was just early afternoon Wednesday that Peabody, in a civilian suit, approached the lobby desk of the Somerset Plaza Hotel.

"Yes, I'm calling on Gladys Mint, a guest of the hotel."

"Just one moment, sir," the desk clerk said.

Peabody looked around. The Somerset Plaza was the best hotel on Wilbourne. Little touches here and there made that clear.

"Yes, sir. Let me connect you to her room."

The clerk put a house phone, audio only, on the desk. Peabody picked it up and listened.

"Mint."

"Lance Peabody, here. I understand you're expecting me."

"Or someone like you. Yes, Mr. Peabody. Someone will be down to pick you up shortly."

Peabody hung up the phone and nodded to the desk clerk.

"Thank you."

"No problem, sir."

Peabody stood there in the lobby, looking out through the glass front to the park opposite. One of the elevators dinged its arrival, and he turned toward them. A young man walked out, caught his eye, and headed toward him across the lobby.

Neither Peabody nor Portnoy had any trouble recognizing each other. They recognized each other as someone not to be messed with, someone not to be underestimated. The younger man – perhaps thirty to Peabody's thirty-eight – walked up to him.

"Mr. Peabody?"

"Yes."

"Chuck Pendergast. This way, Mr. Peabody."

Portnoy led him to the elevators, and had no trouble directing one to the penthouse floor, presumably with a room tab. Peabody raised an eyebrow. The penthouse floor at the Somerset Plaza Hotel was known for its service – and expense.

Once they came into the room, a voluptuous brunette came forward.

"Mr. Peabody, I am Gladys Mint. Please do come in."

Dent waved them both forward to the sitting arrangement, with a lovely view out over the large city park in the middle of Somerset. The palace glittered in the sunlight in the commensurate position at the other end of the park.

"Perhaps some introductions are in order, Mr. Peabody. My name is Gloria Dent, and I am a computer adept, hacker, and database analyst for the Bureau of Intelligence and Espionage on Gaston."

Peabody nodded. What he expected, but to be considered computer adept in the BIE was an extraordinarily high bar.

Peabody turned to the young fellow who had brought him up to the suite.

"My name is Claude Portnoy. I am a direct-action operative for my employer on Mardouk."

"The Agency, Mr. Portnoy?"

"There is no such thing as the Agency, Mr. Peabody."

Of course, Peabody knew better, and Portnoy said it as something of a formula, something said many times before.

Peabody was impressed. As with Dent, being a direct-action operative – a wet-work man – for the Agency was a very high bar. Claude Portnoy was indeed someone not to be messed with.

For Peabody, it was nice to know he was working with the best. Literally so. He doubted his own service could match Dent's or Portnoy's abilities in their specialties. But it was clear he need not worry about the abilities of this pair.

"As for me, I am Lieutenant Colonel Lance Peabody, of His Majesty's Own, the Royal Guard. I am the commanding officer of the clandestine operations group."

"Indeed?" Dent asked. "Excellent. We have need of your assistance, Colonel."

"So I was advised. Why don't you brief me in?"

It took two hours to brief Peabody in on everything that had happened, from Stavros' and Mangum's hypothesis that RDT was being manufactured on Crossroads through Mangum's takeover of Crossroads and William Taylor Evans' non-involvement, which they had just heard about.

"This drug of yours–" Peabody began.

"Com-Ply," Portnoy said.

"Yes. Com-Ply. Can it be used on someone to find the truth, without having them kill themselves after?"

"Yes," Portnoy said. "On Abelon, we asked people directly about their involvement with Evelyn Barnes' complex treason, under the influence of the drug. If they were involved, they simply told us, and were subsequently executed. If they were not involved, we gave them the antagonist and let them go."

"So if we wanted to, we could simply take Tanner Linden into custody and question him under the drug, and he would tell us the truth. About everything and everybody."

"Bill Evans, too, for that matter. All the motivations for lying disappear under the drug. Now, if someone believes something that is in fact false, he will tell you that as well, so we always wanted more than one person's say-so to determine guilt, unless we heard it from them directly."

"I understand."

Peabody pondered Com-Ply for a moment. The hardest thing to know in questioning is whether someone was telling you the truth or not. With this drug, though, at least you heard what they *thought* was true.

"What are you thinking, Colonel?"

"Lance. Please. I'm thinking the best way to proceed is to lock up the Evans Building, question Tanner Linden, and then take everyone he names as involved into custody."

"Can you even do that?" Portnoy asked.

"Of course. I put a company of His Majesty's Marines on hot standby before I came over here, and I have the entire battalion as immediate backup."

"Yeah. A hundred and fifty guys or so? That would do it," Portnoy said.

Dent turned from Portnoy to Peabody.

"But when?" she asked

"It's just after three. Let's do it right now."

Dent raised both eyebrows, and Peabody shrugged.

"I'm told His Majesty wants this done on the short term. In my opinion, that does not excuse waiting around."

"All right, Lance. If you're ready to go, I guess we're ready to go."

"And do you have sufficient supplies of your interrogation

drug available, Claude?" Peabody asked.

"I'll have to bring extra down from the ship, but yes, including that I have plenty. I do have to do the administration, however."

"I understand. Well, let me get this party started."

"Great," Dent said. "Then we can grab a bite. You caught us before lunch."

Peabody took a roll-up display out of his pocket and unrolled it. Portnoy went over to the suite's refrigerator behind the bar and started to put lunch together for three from their supplies, laid in after they had confronted Tanner Linden coming out of the Evans Building Monday evening.

It was cold from the refrigerator but it was still first-class room service of the Somerset Plaza Hotel, bought specifically with the idea of eating it cold or heating it up later.

Peabody took several minutes on his display, then looked up at Portnoy.

"Do you have enough there for me as well, Claude? I skipped lunch as well trying to be responsive to His Majesty's command."

"Sure, Lance. We laid in food for several days when we expected assassins. Didn't want to trust room service. As it turned out, the first assassin was just a shooter."

Peabody nodded. Easy to forget that these two operatives had been targets of Tanner Linden after they purposefully antagonized him. They did that to force Linden to react, inviting assassination so they could interview the assassin.

Right here in Somerset, the capital city of Wilbourne.

Getting Tanner Linden would be satisfying.

They ate lunch out on the patio, which had a splendid view

of the park and the palace. It also had a splendid view of the Evans Building, to their right along the edge of the park.

It was fifteen minutes later, just after three-thirty, when six Royal Marines assault shuttles flew across the park, hovered over the Evans Building, then slowly came down onto the city streets below.

"How do they land on the streets without accidents?" Dent asked.

"They can control the street lights. All the lights into the block in front of the building go red, all the lights out of the block in front of the building go green. Same with the street past the rear entrance."

"Then they land on the empty street."

"Right. And seal the entrances to the building."

"Wow. That's pretty slick."

"Probably about time we headed over there. Are you ready?"

"Let me get my kit," Portnoy said.

Portnoy headed off to the second bedroom of the suite, then came back to the others, waiting in the living room of the suite.

Portnoy nodded to Peabody, and Peabody motioned Dent toward the door.

"There should be a car waiting for us," Peabody said.

His Majesty's Royal Marines

The men of the Capital Regiment of His Majesty's Royal Marines were used to weird jobs in and around the capital. They had cooperated with His Majesty's Own, the Royal Guard, on numerous occasions. So it was not a big surprise when they got a short-notice warning to prepare a ready company for action, potentially today.

The company got a short briefing from their company commander, Major Peter Swanson, just before noon.

"OK, so we're doing something a little different today. We got a building downtown got some bad guys in it. Really bad guys. His Majesty wants their asses in a really big way.

"So we can't let any of those guys get away, right? At the same time, the building is in the middle of downtown, and everybody outside the building is, for today's purposes, a model, upstanding citizen deserving of every courtesy.

"So are most of the people in the building. The bad guys are mixed in with them. So we can't just go in and clear the building. We will be sending arrest squads in later, once the Royal Guard asks real nice and polite who the bad guys are.

"But the first job for us is to seal the building, and do it quick. So we're gonna drop down right on the street. We'll jimmy the stoplights and such, but be careful.

"Then we seal up the doors to the building, and don't let anybody in or out. We also keep people from getting in the way by asking them, all pretty-please and polite, to stay away from the building.

"Anybody in the building tries to make a break for it, that's different. We keep them in the building no matter what. If somebody gets past us somehow, we shoot them. His Majesty is probably going to shoot them anyway, so we're just arguing about the timing.

"You get that? Nobody gets out of that building alive until the Royal Guard shows up and starts vetting people.

"Any questions?"

One captain held his hand up.

"Yes, Captain Moore."

"Who is the Royal Guard commander on the scene, Sir?"

"Lieutenant Colonel Peabody."

"Oh, good."

"Yeah. We've worked with him before and he knows what he's doing. I'm also told he's gonna have a couple of intelligence people with him. Don't mess with them, or you could get hurt."

Some people laughed and Swanson held up his hand.

"Anybody want to mess with a wet-work guy direct from the Agency on Mardouk? Let me know, so I can start writing the sympathy letter to your parents now, OK?"

The company got serious all of a sudden, and Swanson nodded.

"That's more like it. I'm told it's a man and a woman. Do not fuck around with these people. They're dangerous as hell. They uncovered this whole thing in the first place, so the bad guys sent an assassin after them, and they put him in the morgue. They're actually running this operation for His Majesty, so act like they're a general or something. Polite, you know. You guys still got some polite in you, right?

"Personally, I think it's a good thing we have them. The people we're up against – the bad guys in the building – aren't any slouches, either. So I'm glad we got some serious hard-types on our side.

"All right. That's it, everybody. Hit the mess and then dress for the party. We could be leaving any time after thirteen hundred hours.

"And remember. We're First Company, First Battalion of the Capital Regiment of His Majesty's Royal Marines. We don't fuck up. We leave that to other people."

"Gee, Sergeant. Did you hear what the Major said about those intelligence guys?" PFC Paolo Motta asked.

"Guy and gal. Yeah, I heard Major Swanson," Staff Sergeant Lars Iverson said.

"You think that's real?"

"You ever known Major Swanson to overestimate someone's competence, Motta?"

"No, Sergeant. It just seemed over the top."

"Then I guess we gotta think Major Swanson knows shit we don't know, and he's impressed."

"The Major? Impressed? Wow."

"Yeah. That's my reaction, too. I'm sorta looking forward to meeting these two. Since they're on our side."

"You are, Sergeant?"

"Yeah, Motta. But if they weren't on our side, I wouldn't be interested in meeting them at all. In fact, I'd go to some serious lengths to avoid them."

On the Marine Annex to the Somerset Capital Shuttleport, First Company waited just inside the ready building, their armored assault shuttles idling outside.

It cost an extra minute or two not to have them preloaded on their shuttles, but experience showed it increased combat effectiveness for them to load on the alarm. Something about adrenalin peaking and the like, the psych boys said. The calm before the storm, where the guys could sit and joke around before getting serious set in.

But it was observable, so the Royal Marines didn't care what the underlying reason was.

First Company sat and waited inside the building.

A single loud buzzer sounded for one second, and Iverson and his peers were on their feet.

"GO, GO, GO!"

Marines exploded up out of their chairs and out the doors of the building. The far-side thrusters of the shuttles were already spooling up as they started loading, and the near-side thrusters started spooling up as the last men were getting aboard.

Loadmasters stood by at the doors of each of the six shuttles. When all were aboard their shuttle, each loadmaster hit the close-door button, then hurriedly sat down in their seat by the door.

When the 'Load Door Secure' light lit on their instrument panels, each pilot hit the oxygen and focused thrust, and his shuttle leapt into the air and headed for downtown Somerset.

The sudden vertical and then horizontal acceleration was a big signal to the Marines aboard. A ferry run was a much more sedate affair. Even drills and exercises, nominally at the same accelerations, didn't seem to have the urgency of today's lift.

First Company, First Battalion, Capital Regiment, His Majesty's Royal Marines, was in the air.

Iverson stood up in front of his platoon – everybody in this shuttle – hanging on to an overhead grab bar with both hands.

"All right, you guys. Listen up," Iverson bellowed over the roar of the thrusters. "Remember. Anybody outside the building, that's fine. Anybody inside the building, that's fine.

For them, we're all polite and shit. Anybody inside the building who gets outside the building, we shoot 'em. Got it?"

A roar went up from the platoon.

Iverson sat down and turned to Lieutenant Pierson in the next seat and nodded. Pierson nodded back, though he looked nervous.

First-timer, Iverson thought. *Well, that's why I'm here.*

"We're good, Sir. Just another day at the office," Iverson said with a smile, and Pierson seemed to relax a bit.

Unlike the platoon shuttles, the cabin of the company command shuttle was divided into a forward and an aft cabin.

Major Swanson sat in the forward cabin of the command shuttle with his exec, Captain Henri Dornier, and his top sergeant, First Sergeant Helmut Nieman, and the rest of his headquarters staff. The pilots were in the cockpit in front of them and his headquarters rifle squad in the after cabin behind them.

They were just three minutes out when Swanson gave the order to the pilots.

"Begin traffic diversion now, Lieutenant."

"Yes, Sir," the pilot answered.

In the streets of the city below them, the traffic lights away from the Evans Building went green, the traffic lights toward it went red.

The company's shuttles hovered over the four corners of the block the Evans Building was on, plus one on the front door and one on the back door. They were waiting for the final traffic to clear before descending to the empty street below.

"Sir, what do you make of this?"

The pilot's voice came over the speaker, and the forward

display showed the roof of the Evans Building. The pilot had drawn a circle around a structure in the middle of the roof.

"Equipment building for the HVAC equipment?" Swanson asked.

"Then why does it have a twenty-foot roll-up door to a hard point, Sir?"

"A hangar, do you think?" Swanson asked.

"Could be, Sir."

"Let's occupy that hard point, Lieutenant."

"Yes, Sir. Traffic is clear. Shuttles descending now."

Tanner Linden heard the commotion outside. Thruster engines. Very loud. Whoever it was would be in a lot of trouble for violating capital airspace.

When he looked out the windows, though, he saw Marine assault shuttles descending to the street below, one at each end of this block.

Brad Clark came into Linden's office without a knock.

Without preamble, he said, "Have you looked out the windows, sir?"

"Yes. What's going on, do you think?"

"I don't know, but I think it's time to be somewhere else."

"Good idea."

Wendell Taylor Evans and his chief henchman, Tanner Linden, had anticipated the need at some point to get out of town on an expedited schedule. A small private shuttle in a rooftop hangar had been the means, and the fleet little craft had been maintained to a fare-the-well over the years despite never being needed.

Brad Clark had initially come into the organization as their getaway pilot.

Linden walked over to a bookcase on the wall and pushed a

button under one shelf. The bookcase slide aside, revealing a doorway. There was a short hall, with a door on the other end, and a stairwell in the middle leading to the rooftop hangar.

The other door terminated at a similar bookcase in Wendell Taylor Evans' office, now the office of his son, though William Taylor Evans knew nothing about it.

Clark and Linden headed up the stairs, emerging in a small hangar, the shuttle sitting in the middle of the floor.

Clark went on into the shuttle to begin flight preparations, while Linden went over to the hangar door controls.

When the door went up, however, Tanner Linden found himself staring into the starboard rocket launchers of a Royal Marine assault shuttle.

"FREEZE!" a sergeant bawled.

Tanner Linden was the target of the unwavering aim of the rifles of a squad of Royal Marines.

Linden raised his hands in surrender.

They took him into custody, then the sergeant looked over to the shuttle. Someone had started pre-flight. The sergeant walked over to the shuttle's open hatch and banged on the side of the shuttle with his open palm.

"Come on out, in there. Shut the shuttle down and come on out. You do not want us to come in after you."

The shuttle's fuel pumps shut down and Brad Clark appeared in the doorway, hands in the air.

The loadmaster of Lieutenant Pierson's shuttle hit the 'Door Open' button before the shuttle hit the ground. When it shut down, Marines boiled out of the door, setting up a perimeter on the main entrance of the Evans Building.

Anyone trying to get out, they waved back, anyone trying to get in, they waved away. They were getting no argument.

THE FAVOR

Staff Sergeant Lars Iverson looked down the block in each direction. Platoons from shuttles there had blocked the streets, and the traffic lights had returned to normal. While traffic was now moving, no one was being let into the block.

Lieutenant Pierson walked up.

"Looks like it went really well, Sir," Iverson said. "All boxed up, no shots fired."

"Excellent, Staff Sergeant. Let's keep it that way if we can."

"Yes, Sir."

When Lieutenant Colonel Peabody led Gloria Dent and Claude Portnoy out of the Somerset Plaza Hotel, a Royal Guard staff car and a troop carrier were just pulling up at the curb.

The command car was a big vehicle, with dual-facing rear seats and the look of being armored. Flags flew at the front fenders with the insignia of the royal guard: a crown, surrounded by a chain, with the silhouette of a combat rifle, vertical, on each side.

The front passenger door opened and the shotgun got out and opened the rear passenger door. He saluted Peabody as Peabody got in.

With all three of them seated, the shotgun closed the door, re-entered the front cabin, and the big car moved away from the curb.

The Marines manning the road block had no trouble recognizing a Royal Guard command car, and the car and troop carrier were waved through the road block. They pulled up at the front of the Evans Building and the trio got out.

Staff Sergeant Iverson could hardly believe his eyes. All three of the passengers were in civilian clothes. Peabody, in his business suit, Iverson recognized, of course. The two people with him, though, were maybe thirty or thirty-two years old, and were dressed for a day in the park. Slacks and casual shirts.

He was good-looking, in a hard kind of way, and she was beautiful. A real knock-out. And these people were dangerous?

Then the young man turned to look down the block, and Iverson caught sight of a top-of-the-line Siegfried Arms semiautomatic 8mm pistol with integral suppression in a pricey Woods Leather shoulder holster. That was top-shelf equipment right there, and he wore it like it had been part of him for years, not something he occasionally put on.

Iverson gave the young woman the once over, and realized she was carrying at least one and likely two small pistols, one in her left armpit, the other in the small of her back under her over-blouse. The guy who thought he had disarmed her could get a nasty surprise.

Iverson inconspicuously nudged Pierson, and the lieutenant moved forward and saluted Peabody.

"Good afternoon, Sir."

"What's our status, Lieutenant?"

"We're all boxed up, Sir. No shots fired. Everyone's been playing nice so far. Major Swanson advises they captured two people trying to make a break from a roof hangar. With a small personal shuttle. They've identified them as Tanner Linden and Brad Clark."

"Excellent," the woman said.

Peabody nodded.

"Where are they holding them, Lieutenant?"

"In the executive offices on the top floor, Sir. Major Swanson is sending someone down to guide you there."

"Excellent. Thank you, Lieutenant."

Peabody, Dent, and Portnoy waited at the front doors until a Staff Sergeant came out to the front door and opened it.

244

THE FAVOR

"Colonel Peabody? This way, Sir."

When all three had disappeared into the building, Iverson came up behind Pierson.

"Nicely done, Lieutenant."

"You think so, Staff Sergeant?"

"Yes, Sir. Minimal words, full information. Nice."

"Thank you, Staff Sergeant."

Iverson noticed Pierson seemed more at ease in his skin after that. Like this was where he belonged, rather than being out of place somehow. Being an impostor.

Iverson nodded. Pierson was coming along. He'd be OK. Probably be a good one when it all shook out.

The Interrogation Of William Taylor Evans

Major Swanson was waiting for Lieutenant Colonel Peabody in the outer office of the executive offices on the top floor of the Evans Building. The staff sergeant who had shown them up waved them ahead and then went off to look after his rifle squad, who had secured the top floor.

"Colonel Peabody. Good to see you, Sir."

"Hello, Major. It's been a long time."

"Yes, Sir."

The two men shook hands. Then Peabody waved a hand at his two companions.

"These are Gladys Mint and Chuck Pendergast. They've been operating this investigation from the beginning."

"Good to meet you, ma'am. Sir."

"So what have we got, Major?"

"William Taylor Evans is in his office, there," Swanson said, pointing. "He seems confused as to what's going on and why. Tanner Linden is in his office, there. He seems to understand exactly what is going on and why. As does Brad Clark, whose office is on one of the floors below, but we're holding him in that room there."

"And where did you apprehend them, Major?"

"Evans was in his office. Linden and Clark, though, were up on the roof trying to escape in a personal shuttle that's located in a small hangar there. My pilot noted the hangar door and the hard point on the roof from the air, however, and, well, he sort of parked in the way, Sir."

Peabody chuckled.

"Nice," Dent said.

THE FAVOR

Peabody turned to Portnoy.

"Where would you like to start?"

"Evans. Let's see if he knew anything at all. We know Tanner Linden did, and that's going to take longer."

Peabody nodded and waved Portnoy forward.

Bill Evans was waiting in his office, trying to be patient. He had no idea what was going on, but clearly someone had irritated the king in a major way. King Ferdinand IV was not noted for being a tyrant per se, but some things would set him off. Evans wondered what it was.

Did it relate somehow to that reporter's question Monday morning? Was someone making RDT on the Crossroads station? Did he have any interest in Crossroads station? He might have, through Tanner Linden's organization.

Into which he had no visibility whatsoever.

His thoughts had gone around this circle a dozen times or so when his office door opened and three people walked in. He recognized the reporter and her cameraman from Monday morning.

The other fellow also seemed familiar as well. Evans couldn't place him, but from his military posture he imagined him in uniform, and he had it. An officer in the Royal Guard. Major or lieutenant colonel. Something like that. Evans would have seen him at a palace reception, most likely.

"Good afternoon, Mr. Evans," the older fellow said. "I am Lieutenant Colonel Peabody of His Majesty's Royal Guard. These are Gladys Mint and Chuck Pendergast. They are intelligence agents, assisting His Majesty in an investigation into the RDT trafficking in the kingdom."

Evans nodded. So it was part of what she had asked him about on Monday.

"Good afternoon, Colonel. Ms. Mint, Mr. Pendergast. I hadn't thought I would see you again so soon."

"Mr. Evans, we are going to get to the bottom of this business one way or the other. Ms. Mint and Mr. Pendergast have told me, based on their investigation, you are most likely innocent of any wrongdoing. I am charged by His Majesty to make sure, however. No guilty party will be allowed to escape."

"But how are you to be sure, Colonel?"

Peabody looked to Portnoy, and Evans followed his gaze.

"We have an interrogation drug, Mr. Evans. Under its influence it is simply not possible to lie. We would like to administer this drug to you, then ask you a few questions."

"What's the drug do?"

"The drug makes it impossible to lie. I have been trained in the use of this drug, and, in fact, have had it used on myself as part of that training. The effect is rather pleasant. You will feel very good, and happy, and think we are wonderful people, to whom you would not consider telling a lie. We also have an antagonist, that will neutralize the drug within minutes, rather than waiting for it to wear off. There are no long-term effects."

Evans turned to Peabody.

"And this will clear me in His Majesty's eyes?"

"Yes, Mr. Evans."

Evans turned back to Portnoy.

"Very well, Mr. Pendergast. You may proceed."

Portnoy pulled his kit out of his shoulder bag and opened it on Evans' desk. Evans shuddered a bit as he saw the hypodermic needles and ampoules, but he would not live his life under a cloud of suspicion.

Portnoy came around the desk and raised an eyebrow at Evans, and Evans nodded. Portnoy injected Evans in the side of the neck just above his collar.

Almost immediately, Evans felt a relaxing of the tension that had been building since being accosted Monday morning by that reporter, now revealed to be this intelligence agent before him.

She seemed a very nice lady. After all, she had concluded he was innocent. She was beautiful, too. One of those people who had everything going for them. Evans liked her. Pendergast, too. Very nice people. Trying to prove him innocent.

Even Peabody had Evans' respect. Serving His Majesty. Keeping the kingdom safe. What a noble cause.

Deep contentment settled on Evans. Life was good, and he was surrounded by friends.

The three settled in chairs around Evans's desk, Portnoy and Dent in his guest chairs, while Peabody sat in one of the chairs of the conversation group off to one side, content to watch from a distance.

"Can I ask you some questions now, Mr. Evans?"

"Of course, Mr. Pendergast."

"Were you aware that the illegal drug RDT was being manufactured on Crossroads?"

"No. Not at all. That's terrible, if true."

"Did you know that Crossroads Corporation owns the Crossroads station?"

"Yes. Of course. Everyone knows that."

"Did you know that the Evans Group is the sole owner of Crossroads Corporation?"

"We are? No, I didn't know that. Of course, I have no visibility into Mr. Linden's part of the organization."

Portnoy took his cue off Evans' answer.

"Did Tanner Linden run part of the Evans Group?"

"Yes. For a long time now."

"How long has Tanner Linden run a big portion of the Evans Group?"

"Twenty-five years now, I think."

"When your father died, did you inherit all of Evans Group?"

"No. There were other claims against the estate."

"Have you by now inherited all of Evans Group?"

"Yes. In the last six months or so."

"But you did not have visibility into Mr. Linden's part of the organization?"

"No. I began to suspect he was hiding something from me."

"Why did you suspect he was hiding something from you?"

"I would ask him for simple things, like an organization chart or a balance sheet, and I wouldn't get them."

"Why wouldn't you get them?"

"Mr. Linden always had some excuse or some delaying tactic. 'I'll see if I can find that.' Things like that."

"So you could own Crossroads Corporation, and you wouldn't know."

"Yes, that's right."

"Do you know if the Evans Group owns Griffin Interstellar?"

Evans thought about it, then shook his head.

"Never heard of it."

Portnoy looked to Dent, who shrugged. He looked over to Peabody, who nodded.

Portnoy turned back to Evans.

"That's all the questions we have, so I'm going to give you the antagonist now, Mr. Evans."

"All right. Whatever you think is best."

Portnoy filled another hypodermic needle from another ampoule, then injected Evans in the neck just above the collar, as before.

The contentment almost immediately receded, to be replaced by a strange mix of anger and sorrow.

"Mr. Pendergast, I must ask you. Was my father a part of all this?"

Portnoy looked to Peabody, who rose and came over to the desk.

"We think so, Mr. Evans. I'm sorry."

Evans nodded dumbly. Many things fell into place now. How he was asked to leave the room when Tanner Linden reported to his father. How his father never shared with him the reports from Linden's part of the organization.

Evans looked back up at Peabody.

"And am I now proved innocent in this matter, Colonel Peabody?"

"Yes, Mr. Evans. You're free to go."

"What about the rest of my people?"

"As soon as we can clear them, Mr. Evans, they'll be released."

"How long will that take?"

Peabody looked to Portnoy.

"We should know a lot more once we talk to Linden and Clark. A couple of hours, perhaps."

Evans nodded and got up. He came around the desk.

"Well, if I'm free to go, Colonel Peabody, then I think I'm going to go home and have a drink or three."

Peabody grabbed his forearm.

"Mr. Evans, will you be OK?"

"Oh, yes, Colonel. I'm not going to go home and swallow a bullet. Not my style. Besides, I want to see Tanner Linden hang."

Peabody summoned Major Swanson over to Evans' office door.

"Yes, Sir."

"Major, Mr. Evans is permitted to leave. You should give him an escort downstairs. And his car is permitted to enter the enclosure and depart with him in it. Is that understood?"

"Yes, Sir. This way, Mr. Evans."

"All right. Let me call for my car."

On the way down to the entrance, Evans asked his escort to wait a moment, then went over to the ground-floor restaurant that had just been gearing up for dinner when the lockdown came. All the staff was trapped inside the building, and no customers could get in.

"Charles," Evans said, pronouncing it in the French fashion, "dinner this evening for everyone held in the building is free. It's on me. You can let people on every floor know that."

"Yes, sir. Thank you. We were going to have to just throw everything out."

"While everyone in the building is missing their supper. Yes, I know. So it's on me tonight. And twenty-percent tips for the wait staff. Just let me know what I owe you when this all blows over."

"Thank you, sir."

Evans waved his guide on, and they came out the front entrance to find his car was already there.

The driver held the door for him as Evans walked up.

"That was fast."

"I was just down the block, sir. It is your normal pickup time, after all."

Evans was surprised. It felt like a week had passed.

"Why, so it is."

THE FAVOR

Evans got in, the driver closed his door, walked around the car and got in, and the big car pulled out from the curb and moved slowly down the empty block.

Marines at the road block waved it through.

"Well, that was simple," Dent said. "He didn't know anything about anything. Linden kept him in the dark."

"And so did his father," Portnoy said.

"Poor bastard," Peabody said.

Dent looked at him in surprise.

"The richest man on Wilbourne, Colonel? Poor bastard?"

"His old man was in this filthy business up to his neck, and he just now found out. Imagine having your father's memory gutted like that."

"Ah," Dent said, then turned to Portnoy. "So now what? Linden or Clark?"

"Clark," Portnoy answered. "Let's come at Linden from above and below."

Portnoy looked at his kit.

"And I should probably get additional supplies from the ship."

"Yes, Mr. Portnoy," said Timothy Langdon, captain of *Silverheel*.

"Captain, I need one of my equipment cases from the ship. I need someone trustworthy to run it down here for me."

"Of course, Mr. Portnoy. Is this one of the drug cases?"

"Yes, Captain. It's marked C-P-times-one-thousand, I think. There are several. I just need one of them."

"Yes, Mr. Portnoy. I recall. Land at the shuttleport and bring it to you at the hotel?"

"No, Captain. Land at these coordinates."

Portnoy shoved the coordinates over the link. Langdon looked at them curiously, then his brows shot up.

"That's right in the middle of downtown Somerset, Mr. Portnoy."

"That's correct, Captain. His Majesty's Royal Marines will mark the landing spot with flares."

"Yes, sir. If you're sure it's OK...."

"Yes, Captain. It's good. Remember. Someone trustworthy."

The Interrogation Of Brad Clark

Brad Clark was sitting in one of the offices in executive row, on the top floor of the Evans Building. It was the office of one of Bill Evans' people, who was traveling on business. His own office was two floors down, but this one was handy for the moment. Handy for them to hold him pending questioning.

Clark guessed that was their purpose, because they had not simply arrested him and dragged him away. That was fine. He wasn't going to tell them anything.

Clark had been careful, had covered his tracks well. He'd used blind accounts for anything shady, limited his contacts with the people he used for anything nefarious, encrypted his files.

They had nothing on him. He just had to not give anything away. Not fall for any tricks. The Kingdom of Wilbourne had pretty strong defendant protections in the criminal law. Only the system of high justice could set those aside, and then only if the king were personally involved.

He should be good.

In the meantime he sat here, in the side seating arrangement of this office. Two armed Royal Guard men stood at the door, while two big unarmed Royal Guard men stood behind him. No chance to start something, steal a gun, and shoot his way out.

Anything like that was not going to work anyway. So Clark sat and waited for the questioning.

The things Clark had failed to take into account were two-fold. One is that the king was already involved, and was not amused.

The second was that there were certain things even the courts could not undo.

The guard on the outside of the office containing Brad Clark opened the door for Dent, Portnoy, and Peabody. Dent walked in first. Clark immediately recognized her as the nosy reporter, the one who had taken out Hugh Parker somehow.

"Hello, Mr. Clark," Dent said cheerily. "Do you have any questions for me?"

"Fuck you."

"Keep dreaming, boy," Dent said with scorn. "I don't do scumbags."

The dismissive 'boy' from someone fifteen years his junior, and her tone, angered Clark further, and, his focus on Dent, he didn't pay attention to Portnoy.

Portnoy raised the hand he had held behind his back and shot Clark in the right shoulder with the dart gun.

Clark jumped out of the chair, but the two guards behind him pulled him back and parked him back in the chair.

"Hang onto him, please," Portnoy said. "Should be just a couple of seconds."

"Yes, sir," one of the guards said.

"How long?" Peabody asked.

"Not long. I dosed him pretty hard. Much more than Evans, who was cooperating. He'll try to fight the drug, but it's a fight he can't win."

In fact, Clark was already subsiding, and the guards let him go and took up their positions again.

Dent and Portnoy crossed to the side seating area and sat opposite Clark.

"You're going to answer some questions for me."

"All right."

"Who do you work for?"

"Tanner Linden."

"How long have you worked for Tanner Linden?"

"Twenty-two years."

"What do you do for him?"

"I am his shuttle pilot and his fixer."

"What sort of things do you fix?"

"People he needs taken care of. Stuff like that."

"Did you hire Hugh Parker to kill Gladys Mint?"

"Yes."

"Have you hired assassins to kill other people before?"

"Yes."

"How many times?"

"Usually only once or maybe twice a year."

"So in twenty-two years you've had perhaps thirty people murdered?"

"Something like that, yeah. I don't remember the exact number."

"Would your blind bank accounts show those payments?"

"Yes."

"We need the account numbers and login credentials for all your bank accounts, including the blind accounts. Can you give me those?"

"Sure."

Clark began rattling off account numbers and login credentials, one after the other, a total of six in all.

"Are your computer files encrypted?"

"Yes."

"We need the crypto keys for your files then. Can you give me those?"

"OK."

Clark rattled off three crypto key seeds.

"Did you know about the RDT manufacturing business on the Crossroads station?"

"Yes."

"Who ran that whole operation?"

"Tanner Linden."

"I need the names of everyone else who you definitely know is in on the RDT operation. Can you tell me the names?"

"Yes. There's actually a file in my machine of who knows."

"Just tell me the names now, please."

Clark rattled off names, beginning with Tanner Linden and himself, and including Carl Ikenberry and Vernon Thorne among others on Crossroads.

"Did you ever hear of a company called Griffin Interstellar?"

"Yes."

"Where is Griffin Interstellar?"

"Downstairs."

"Downstairs? Where downstairs?"

"On fifteen, I think."

Dent looked up from her roll-up display.

"There's no listing in the building for Griffin Interstellar."

"Explain, please, Mr. Clark."

"Griffin Interstellar here is called Hippocamp Logistics."

"So the company has two names?"

"Yes."

Dent looked up from her display again.

"Hippocamp Logistics is on the fifteenth floor of this building. A side note: the griffin and the hippocamp are both mythological creatures that are half one thing and half another."

Clark chuckled.

"Tanner Linden's joke."

"Half a legitimate company and half a drug-running operation?" Portnoy asked.

"Exactly," Clark said. "Tanner thought it was funny."

"So who at Hippocamp Logistics knows about the RDT operation? All of them?"

"No. Just the top guy and his assistant."

"That would be Ralph Carson and Brenda Bansberg?" Dent asked from behind her display.

"Yes, that's right."

"The rest of the people don't know?" Portnoy asked.

"No."

"What do they think they're doing?"

"Shipping supplies and such around."

"So they just ship containers and receive the money?"

"That's right."

"They don't know what's in the containers?"

"Right. Oh, there's some bill of lading of some kind, but it's bullshit."

"Who are the consignees for these shipments?"

"The drug dealers on each planet."

"And the Hippocamp Logistics people don't know the consignees are drug dealers?"

"No, they all have legitimate front companies."

"Do you have the names of the consignees and who they front for?"

"No. Ralph has those."

"Ralph Carson?"

"Yes."

Portnoy turned his head to look at Peabody and raised an eyebrow. Peabody thought about it, sighed, and nodded.

Portnoy turned back to Clark.

"You know these are very bad things you did, don't you?"

"Yes."

"And you know that you will be arrested, and jailed, and put on trial, right?"

"I suppose so."

"You will probably be executed, and your name and reputation will be ruined forever."

"Yes."

"I have a way out of that for you. Would you like that?"

"Oh, yes."

Portnoy put a hypodermic needle on the coffee table between them.

"All you have to do is inject yourself with this hypodermic needle. Can you do that?"

"Sure. Sounds simple enough."

"The compound in that hypodermic will kill you, without pain, and then you don't have to go through all that other nonsense. Does that sound good?"

"Yes. It does."

"Inject yourself in the arm now, then, and you'll be rid of all that."

"All right."

Brad Clark picked up the hypodermic needle from the table and, using his right hand, injected himself in the left arm. He set the hypodermic back down on the coffee table.

"That's it?" he asked.

"That's it. You should feel sleepy soon. Do you feel sleepy yet?"

"A little bit. Oh, suddenly I feel really sleepy."

Brad Clark was still leaned forward in the chair. His eyes closed and he pitched forward onto the floor.

Peabody looked to the Royal Guard men standing behind Clark's chair.

"Bag him," he said.

"Yes, Sir."

Dent, Portnoy, and Peabody stayed in the office while other Royal Guard men, called by radio, brought in a body bag and bagged and tagged Brad Clark.

"OK, I'm getting into all of his accounts," Dent said from behind her roll-up display. "There's a lot of stuff here. I can see the payments to the assassins for the various murders he hired out. I'm still looking for the file of people in the know."

"That's how they made it all work," Portnoy said to Peabody. "The largest drug-running operation in the cluster, being run out of a major downtown building within sight of the palace."

Peabody nodded.

"I'm told His Majesty is not amused."

"I can imagine."

"Here it is. The list of people in the know. Not as many as you might think. Most of them are on Crossroads. The station manager, the assistant station manager, the chief and assistant chief of police, the entire RDT control unit, the chemists and technicians and packers."

"We can leave all those to our people on Crossroads. Many of those we need for the sanctioned trade in RDT. But it seems like all the top dogs here are dispensable. The logistics people could be run by any good administrator."

"And we already control Crossroads," Dent said, "and have an administrator in place there."

"I would think Bill Evans could hire or promote someone to run the Hippocamp Logistics operation, and both Crossroads and Hippocamp would report to him," Peabody said.

"Sounds like a plan," Portnoy said. "And His Majesty's

desires with the rest of them?"

"I think Mr. Clark's fate is too good for them, but I have my orders. They can check themselves out as he did, but they don't leave this building alive."

Portnoy nodded.

"Let's go deal with Mr. Linden, then."

THE FAVOR

The Interrogation Of Tanner Linden

Tanner Linden smugly waited in his office for the interrogation he expected. They couldn't do anything to him. He had already sent the orders, effective tomorrow.

If Linden didn't rescind those orders, the entire edifice would collapse. Millions would die, millions more would need assisted living for the rest of their lives, and, with Crossroads off-line, the entire cluster would be plunged into an economic depression that would last years.

Linden knew he would have to act fast, get his threat out there, before they executed him.

He could do that.

One of the Royal Guard men opened the office door, and Dent, Portnoy, and Peabody walked into Tanner Linden's office.

"Good afternoon, Mr. Linden."

"I've already transmitted the orders," Linden said. "Unless I rescind them, millions will die and the entire cluster will be plunged into economic depression. You need to let me go, or I'll pull the whole thing down around your ears."

"But there's something you don't know, Mr. Linden," Dent said sweetly. "We already control the Crossroads station. Your minions are either dead or co-opted."

Linden gaped at her, and so he missed Portnoy pulling out the dart gun. Portnoy shot Tanner Linden in the right shoulder, but Linden did not respond as Clark had. Instead, he sagged in his chair as the implications of Dent's statement sank in.

They had taken Crossroads first. The Evans Building was a

263

follow-up, not the initial push.

His orders would have no effect whatsoever.

He had no way out.

"I see," he said simply.

Portnoy and Dent sat in the guest chairs in front of Tanner Linden's desk, while Peabody stood, leaning against the back of one of the armchairs of the side seating arrangement.

As the Com-Ply kicked in, Tanner Linden went from despairing and subdued to more animated and happier. Dent hadn't seen that before, but Portnoy nodded.

"I'm going to ask you some questions if I could."

"Of course."

"Did Wendell Taylor Evans know about the RDT manufacturing on the Crossroads station?"

"Yes. It was his idea."

"How did he come by that idea?"

"He had gone to the Earth sector looking for things he could bring back to the cluster."

"He went to the Earth sector? That's a long way off."

"Oh, yes. He was gone a year."

"He was looking for things to bring back?"

"Yes. Products. Ideas. Technologies. You know."

"And he brought back RDT?"

"Yes."

"Who ran the company while he was gone?"

"I did."

"So you and he put together the idea for Crossroads?"

"No. That was an idea he got on that trip. Hub and spoke."

"But the funding was a problem, right?"

"Right. We couldn't make it work."

"So RDT then became part of the plan?"

"Yes."

"Did you not know of the harm from the drug?"

"We did, but there was a cure in the works."

"There was a cure in the works?"

"Yes. In Earth sector."

"So the idea at some point was to go back to get the cure?"

"Yes. After the station was built and paid off."

"But he never went back, did he?"

"No. He became too ill to travel like that."

"He was too ill for such a long trip?"

"Yes."

"And Crossroads wasn't paid off yet anyway, right?"

"Right."

"Who owns Crossroads Corporation?"

"The shareholder."

"And who is the shareholder?"

"Evans Group."

"That's on your side of the house?"

"Yes."

"So Bill Evans actually owns Crossroads Corporation right now?"

"Oh, yes."

"Were you hiding the operations in your side of the house from Bill Evans?"

"Yes."

"Why?"

"Because he didn't know about the RDT."

"His father never told him?"

"No. I told Wendell to tell him, but he didn't."

"And you didn't tell him after his father died?"

"No."

"Why not?"

"He'd grown up to be a straight arrow."

"You thought he would have disapproved?"

"Oh, yes."

"Do your computer files contain all the information on your side of the house?"

"Yes."

"Are they encrypted?"

"Yes."

"I need you to give me the encryption keys."

"All right."

Linden then rattled off half a dozen crypto seeds for the keys.

"Were you skimming money off the Evans Group?"

"No."

"You were not?"

"That's correct."

"Why not?"

"That would be dishonest. And I was well compensated."

"Wendell Evans took care of you?"

"Yes."

"Does Bill Evans know about all your compensation?"

"No, I don't think so."

"We need your bank account information, too."

"All right."

Linden then rattled off the bank account numbers and login credentials for three bank accounts.

"Are all three of these accounts in your name?"

"Yes."

"Why three?"

"I didn't want everything in just one bank."

Portnoy looked to Dent and raised an eyebrow.

"You said you transmitted orders?" she asked Linden.

"Yes."

THE FAVOR

"What were those orders?"

"To abandon Crossroads and blow it up."

"There's a demolition charge on Crossroads?"

"Yes."

"Crossroads is huge. What is the demolition charge?"

"A ten-megaton warhead."

"There's a thermonuclear demolition on Crossroads?"

"Yes."

"Where is it?"

"In the distribution facility. It's a container that never moves."

"Where in the distribution facility is it?"

"By the RDT factory."

"What is the container identifier?"

"GIX 748931162."

"GIX? So it's a Griffin Interstellar container?"

"Yes."

"You know, it doesn't really make any difference, but I want you to send the message rescinding those orders anyway."

"OK. Should I do that now?"

"Yes. Send the transmission rescinding your orders now."

"All right."

Linden turned to his display. It took just a minute, then he turned back to Dent.

"You transmitted a message rescinding your orders?"

"Yes."

Dent nodded to Portnoy, then bent over her own display.

Portnoy looked to Peabody and raised an eyebrow. Peabody nodded, and Portnoy turned back to Linden.

"You know a lot of the things you did were very bad things, don't you?"

"Yes."

"And you're going to be arrested, and put in jail, and put on trial, right?"

"Oh, yes."

"And then you'll likely be executed, and your reputation will be destroyed."

"Yes, I know."

"Would you like a way to avoid all that?"

"Oh, yes. That would be wonderful."

Portnoy put a hypodermic needle on the desk.

"If you inject yourself with this hypodermic needle, you won't have to go through all that. Can you do that?"

"Sure."

"What will happen if you inject yourself with that needle is that you will die here, now, and escape all that unpleasantness. Wouldn't that be nice?"

"Yes. Very much so."

"All right. Inject yourself with the hypodermic needle now. In the arm is fine."

"OK."

Linden picked up the hypo and injected himself in the left arm, then set the needle back on the desk.

"That's it. You've escaped."

"Wonderful."

Linden grew sleepy, then his eyes closed and his head thumped to the surface of his desk.

Peabody turned to the Royal Guard men standing inside the door.

"Bag him."

"Yes, Sir."

Two more Royal Guard men entered and bagged and tagged the body of Tanner Linden.

"Still too good for him, from my way of thinking," Peabody

said.

Portnoy nodded, but he was looking at Dent.

"Did you send that information to, um, our people on Crossroads?"

"Yes. It's after hours there now. They'll have it first thing in their morning."

"OK, good."

"So now what?" Dent asked.

"We have other interviews to do," Portnoy said. "And we have the list of those who knew what was going on. I guess we can let everyone else go home now."

"Let's round up the ones in the know first," Peabody said. "That makes it easier on the Marines. Target differentiation isn't their strong suit."

Portnoy chuckled.

"OK. Let's get the list to the Royal Guard and round 'em all up."

Timothy Langdon sought the exact coordinates he was given, creeping along over the tall buildings of downtown Somerset in *Silverheel*'s landing shuttle. He couldn't see down to the street between buildings except for the one right below him.

He crept just a bit further north, and the street in the gap before him became visible. There were the marker flares.

He eased off on the engines and started coming down between the buildings for a landing on the street below.

The Royal Marines had a landing spot marked out with flares on the street. This was ho-hum to them, as they often had to light the approach for their ride home.

The small personnel shuttle came slowly over the buildings

of downtown Somerset to the spot above the Marines' flares, then started slowly down between the buildings.

"All right," Iverson bellowed. "Eyes on top. Don't get in his way."

"Is he all right, Staff Sergeant?" Lieutenant Pierson asked.

"Yes, sir. Looks like he knows what he's doing. He's just taking it easy, which is all right with me."

"Ah," Portnoy said as *Silverheel*'s shuttle passed the top floor windows on its way down. "Looks like my supplies are here."

Portnoy headed back down to the entrance to the building. Nobody should handle that case except him and whoever Captain Langdon sent down with it.

Portnoy exited onto the street level just as Langdon was exiting the shuttle with the case of interrogation drugs. He walked up to Langdon.

"I didn't expect you to bring them down yourself, Captain."

"You said pick someone I could trust, sir, and I had an easy answer."

Langdon handed the case over to Portnoy.

"Very good, Captain. Thank you."

"Yes, sir."

Langdon saluted Portnoy, then got back into the shuttle. Portnoy was already on his way back up to the top floor as Pierson and Iverson watched Langdon take the shuttle back up between the buildings – faster this time – and off to orbit.

"He's got a navy captain delivering his luggage, Staff Sergeant?"

"As the Major said, sir. Treat them like they was generals or somethin'."

Major Hazard On Crossroads

When Carl Ikenberry got back to his office after meeting with Bert Mangum, Jack Sturm, and Elina Stavros, he called Crossroads police chief Glen Holbrook.

"Hello, sir," Holbrook said.

"Hello, Chief. We need to talk about some things."

"Can it wait for when I get a chance, sir? We just had nine men killed in the transient crew section."

"That's one of the things we need to talk about, Chief."

"Yes, sir. Would later this afternoon work? We're trying to track down Stavros and those other guys now. I have nine men down, and we need to get on top of this."

"Chief, will you just shut up and listen to me for a few minutes?"

That pulled Holbrook up short.

"Yes, sir. Sorry. Go ahead."

"Those nine men were shot for breaking my direct orders. Heston and Cooper and that whole RDT unit was out of control. I told them not to follow me, and they did. Now they have a serious case of dead, and I couldn't be happier. Understand me? I will not permit insubordination in your police force."

"Yes, sir."

Holbrook said 'Yes, sir' but Ikenberry didn't care for his tone.

"So you are to call off the search for Stavros and the rest. I have cleared them of any wrongdoing in any of these matters. They are free to come and go as they please. And if anybody on your police force doesn't get that message, they're going to be recycling material as well."

"Stavros, Mangum, and Sturm just walk, sir?"

More pushback, in tone alone. Time to bring the hammer down.

"They're completely clean, Chief Holbrook. On my say-so. And if that's not good enough for you, you can look for another fucking job. Understood?"

"Yes, sir."

That was better. A 'Yes, sir' that didn't have a 'Fuck you' built into it.

"There will be no more RDT control unit. We will have an RDT security unit, which will be solely responsible for guarding the production facility in the distribution center. They will have no jurisdiction in the rest of the station. If I see one of those guys in uniform in the rest of the station, I'll fire him *and* you."

"Understood, Sir. But then how do we keep the RDT operation secret?"

"We don't, Chief. We're out of that business. I now work directly for the chief executives of the six local star nations. Isabela Febo and her friends. I no longer work for Tanner Linden and the Evans Group. I'm not even sure Tanner Linden is still alive."

"Really, sir?"

"Really. The Association of Planets got wind of what was going on, and Isabela Febo and the other chief executives decided they didn't like it much. That's why Mangum and Sturm are here. They've taken over the station, and have probably taken down Evans Group on Wilbourne by now as well."

"Wow."

"Yes. Wow. That's what all this is about. The last two days.

Heston went after Stavros and Mangum, and the two of them and their team took down Harker, Heston, Cooper, and pretty much the whole RDT control unit. And they're just getting started. I bought a free pass for you and me, but only if we play ball. I for one don't want to go into the recycling loop."

"Yes, sir. Now I understand. And thank you for that, sir."

"You're welcome, Chief. And now see to it that you call off the search for Stavros and Mangum and the rest, because quite honestly the last thing you want to do is find them. You don't stand a chance in hell against them and whoever else they have along. And the Association and Abelon Navies are their backup."

"Yes, sir. I'm on it."

"Let me know when your department is up-to-speed, Chief."

"Yes, sir."

"Today."

"Yes, sir."

By late that afternoon, Holcomb had called back with a status report. Ikenberry called Mangum to tell him that all the police on the station had been informed that he, Stavros, and their companions had been cleared of any wrongdoing in the events since Monday. It should be safe for them to return to their first-class suite.

"So, dinner in first-class tonight?" Mangum asked Stavros when he got off the call.

"Even better would be sleep in a first-class bed."

"It's only been two nights here, Elina."

"Oh, I know. But I need to work off some stress. We need more room."

"Ah. But of course, my lady. I live to serve."

Stavros laughed and Mangum grinned.

The hair-raising part of the op was over.

Or so they thought.

The message from Dent came in overnight.

Mangum sighed and sat back in his chair after a wonderful breakfast.

"That was nice, Elina. I missed the first-class food."

"Last night was nice, too. I missed the first-class bed."

Mangum nodded.

"That little bit of extra room does make a big difference, doesn't it?"

"Oh, yes, and so does being clean-shaven again. I wasn't a big fan of the beard."

Mangum had shaved when they got back to the suite last night.

"Well, that was just for the transient crew section. Blending in. You know."

Mangum pulled out his roll-up display and put it on the table, shoving plates out of the way.

"Time to check the mail."

Mangum saw the priority mail from Dent right away.

"Oh, this is lovely," Mangum said, with sarcasm.

"What's that?"

"Message from Wilbourne overnight. There's a ten-megaton demolition on Crossroads."

"Oh, no."

"They think it's OK from their end – you know, that the firing sequence is secure – but they also think we should probably get it off the station."

"Well, yeah."

"Let's go take a look at it."

THE FAVOR

Mangum, Sam as Jack Sturm, and Stavros, with Jules as her purse, went up to the distribution center office. The counter man waved them through on Stavros' police ID.

They walked down to the RDT facility, about two city blocks away. When they got there, Jimmy Forney was sitting out front.

"Hi, Jimmy. They have you sitting out front now?"

"Hi, Elina. Yeah. It's all new rules now. Ain't that somethin'?"

"Jimmy, I got a question for you. Any of these Griffin containers never move? One that's just always there, in the same place?"

"Yeah. That one on the end. It's spare parts or something. For the lab. You know."

"OK. Thanks, Jimmy."

They walked down to the container. It looked like it had been there quite a while. Years.

"GIX 748931162," Mangum read off the end doors. "Yup. That's the one."

"All this time, they were prepared to blow up the station. Whatta buncha bastards."

"That's all right, Elina. The bastards are mostly dead now."

"Are they?"

"Yeah. They've been drugging them, interrogating them, and executing them on Wilbourne, one after the other."

"Good to hear, Bert. So what do we do about this thing?"

"Have them put it in with the trash containers and shoot it into the sun, I guess."

Stavros bent down and looked at the frame rails along the bottom of the container.

"Bert, this thing is welded to the deck."

"Then I guess we have them cut it loose, then put it in with the trash containers, and shoot it into the sun."

"OK. Fair enough. Ikenberry?"

Mangum nodded.

"Ikenberry."

"Ikenberry."

"Good morning, Mr. Ikenberry. Bert Mangum here."

"Yes, sir. What can I do for you this morning?"

"Well, it turns out your former management had an ace in the hole, Mr. Ikenberry. They secreted a ten-megaton demolition onto the Crossroads station. It's been here for years. Probably since the beginning."

"You're kidding."

"Not at all, Mr. Ikenberry. I'm looking at it as we speak."

"What do we do about it, Mr. Mangum?"

"We need to have some people down here with some big weld grinders and the like to cut it loose from the floor. But it is in a container, so I think we put it in with the trash and dispose of it. Soon."

"I agree. Tell me where to have the workmen show up."

It was only about fifteen minutes before a maintenance team showed up. A supervisor and half a dozen guys, all with big gas-powered angle grinders.

"Mr. Mangum?" the supervisor asked.

"I'm Mangum. We need to cut this container free of the floor. It's welded down."

The supervisor went over and looked at the frame rails of the container closely.

"Half a dozen foot-long welds on each side. This won't take long, sir."

"Have at it then."

"Yes, sir."

THE FAVOR

The supervisor turned to his crew.

"All right. We need to cut this thing loose from the deck. Three guys on each side so we're not in each other's way. Let's go."

The crew started up the grinders and soon sparks were flying from the welds.

While they were at it, a container lift came down the aisle toward their location. Mangum walked over to talk to the operator.

"Boss says we got a container here needs to go in the trash?"

"Yeah. Fucker's welded down. They're cutting it loose, then straight into the trash with it."

"Sounds good."

"When does the trash go out?" Mangum asked.

"Right away. Mr. Ikenberry put a hold on today's load waiting for this one. What the hell's in it, anyway?"

"Some chemical or something that's way out of date. Somebody finally got around to checking on it. Surprised the damn thing hasn't popped already. So real nice and easy, OK? Last thing we want to do is have the fucker let go on us."

"Got it. Kid gloves all the way, then off it goes with today's trash."

"Perfect."

Mangum made an OK sign to the driver and walked back to where Stavros, Sam, and Jules watched the maintenance crew grinding away.

"They're each on their second weld now, Bert," Stavros said. "They should be done soon."

"Good. I get itchy looking at it."

"You and me both."

The grinders finished and the supervisor came over to Mangum.

"It should be free now, Sir."

"Hang around until he gets it lifted in case there's a problem, would you?"

"Of course, sir."

Mangum waved the lift operator forward, and he inched the lift up to the container, then lowered the carriage down onto the container. The latches caught the container at the lift points, and the operator tested his connection by slowly lifting the container just a couple inches off the deck. It came free without any problem.

The operator gave Mangum a thumbs-up, and Mangum returned it. The operator lifted the container a foot clear of the deck, turned, and headed off down the aisle.

Mangum turned to the maintenance supervisor.

"All right, we're good. Thanks a lot."

"No problem, sir."

The supervisor turned to his crew.

"OK. That's it here. Let's get these stowed and then it's time for an early lunch."

"All right!"

Once back in the suite, the four of them settled down in the living room.

"It's lucky they had those grinders handy," Stavros said.

"Pretty common tool when you have a metal space station to maintain. They probably have a hundred of them," Mangum said.

"It was interesting to watch," Sam said. "Humans have the strangest tools. All with some specific purpose."

"That's one definition of human in anthropology, Sam. Tool user."

"Well, they clearly knew what they were doing with them,

Bert, and it was fascinating to watch."

"So now that container goes out with the trash?" Jules asked.

"Yes. They lash a bunch of containers full of garbage together, use a cargo shuttle to get them up to speed, and then let them go on a vector toward the sun."

"Will the nuclear demolition go off when it gets to the sun, Bert?" Stavros asked.

"I don't think so. The detonator will die first, from the heat. Of course, the sun will burn up the nuclear fuel, but it's less than a drop in the ocean."

Stavros nodded.

"And when does it leave the station?"

Mangum checked his roll-up display for the Crossroads shuttle log.

"This says it's already gone. Five minutes ago."

"Oh, good."

"So how about some lunch?"

They took a siesta after lunch, nude in the big bed, cuddled up together under the blankets.

When they got up and redressed, Mangum spent some time reading Portnoy's reports out of Wilbourne.

Portnoy had gone through the entire Wilbourne-based roster of people in the know on the RDT operation. Most people in Tanner Linden's portion of Evans Group hadn't known. The mechanics of arranging the shipping of containers and billing for them was independent of what they contained, and they simply hadn't known. Fake bills of lading kept them in the dark, and routine scheduled deliveries over time to consignees was routine shipping business.

Those in the know had each been interrogated, then executed on the king's orders. It had gone on into the night before they were completed.

The innocent had been released earlier, once all those in the know had been rounded up. Bill Evans had popped for dinner for everyone at the pricey restaurant on the ground floor, and most people had been released after a nice dinner with their coworkers.

The best part, from Mangum's point of view, was that those not in the know were the ones they actually wanted to keep. The people responsible for keeping the operation running. The management types who knew what was really going on, and who were now all bagged and tagged, weren't essential to Mangum's plan.

Similarly on Crossroads, with the exception of Ikenberry and Holbrook, the people remaining were the ones who were essential to the operation. Harker, Heston, Cooper, and the enforcers of the RDT control group were gone, though perhaps a bit more mechanically than Portnoy had managed.

Ikenberry and Holbrook were the exception, an exception Mangum was OK with. Ikenberry was adept at running all the other operations on Crossroads – as the timeliness of his response to the nuclear demolition showed – and that was no small thing.

As for Holbrook, Crossroads did need a police presence for normal police functions, and police were clanny. Not good to bring in an outsider to replace him. Retaining Holbrook, who was in the know but not in the command chain of the nasty side of the business, worked for Mangum.

Mangum wrote his own report for transmission to Mardouk.

That evening after supper, Mangum got a call from Ikenberry.

"Mangum here."

"Carl Ikenberry, sir. Sorry to bother you after hours."

"No, that's fine, Mr. Ikenberry. What's going on?"

"That container we threw out this morning? It detonated."

"No shit. Was the shuttle clear?"

"Oh, yes. Well clear. Everybody's OK, but somehow that demolition got the signal."

"Or it got the signal earlier, and it was a time-delayed detonation."

"Whatever, Mr. Mangum. But it detonated. Very impressive, actually. It's on the station's surveillance recordings."

"What's the official story?"

"The official story is yours from earlier. That it was an extremely out-of-date chemical shipment that we threw out."

"Ten megatons?"

"The size of an explosion in space as seen from a distance is hard to estimate, sir. Particularly if one doesn't know the distance."

"Ah. Of course. Excellent, Mr. Ikenberry. Thanks for letting me know."

"Of course, sir."

Mangum cut the connection and brought up the station surveillance recordings on his roll-up display. He found the explosion and checked the timestamp.

Eight hours. That's how close it was.

"Elina, take a look at this a moment."

Stavros came over and looked into the display.

"I don't see anything."

"It's surveillance video of the trash shipment. It's a ways away already, so you can't see much. Until you play it forward."

Mangum allowed the recording to run, and several seconds later a pinprick of bright white light expanded into an orange cloud and dissipated over several seconds.

"My God. It went off."

"Yup. About eight hours clear."

"So there's still someone out there high enough in the organization to have the detonation sequence and send it."

"Or Tanner Linden's delayed detonation just went off. The timing is about right for a twenty-four hour delay, depending on the exact time he sent the initial transmission."

"I thought Portnoy reported Linden sent the transmission rescinding his orders."

"Yes. Under the influence of Com-Ply. Maybe he screwed it up. Or maybe the second transmission was garbled, or the device – which was twenty years old, remember – didn't receive it or inaccurately decoded it."

Stavros watched the recording, replaying through the explosion. Thought of such a thing going off on Crossroads. The station, reduced to fragments, chunks of it flying through space. People dying of the blast or suffocating in the vacuum.

Stavros shuddered.

"Damn. That was close."

Their lovemaking that night seemed even more special, for both of them having survived at all.

On Mardouk

Henry Grant reviewed Mangum's and Portnoy's reports with interest. Clearly it had been a near thing.

But everyone did what they needed to do to head off disaster. Portnoy had gotten Evans Group locked down quickly. BIE's Gloria Dent had followed the necessary line of questioning to surface the existence of the device. And Mangum had found the device on Crossroads and gotten it off the station before it detonated.

Just another reason Henry Grant was happy he had his most competent people in position to carry this operation through.

In an unusual move, Grant copied Chairman Febo on the raw reports rather than give her an operations department précis.

Only the operatives' names were redacted.

"Grant here."

"Good afternoon, Mr. Grant."

"Good afternoon, Madam Chairman."

"Thank you for the raw reports on the crisis point of the Crossroads affair. It's clear we got lucky, Mr. Grant."

"It was definitely a near thing, ma'am. I think lucky is what one gets when one has the right people in place."

"And this is the same crew from the Abelon affair?"

"Yes, ma'am. Including Gaston's operative on the scene. Only Detective Stavros of Crossroads police is new here."

"I know one does not give awards or honors to clandestine operatives, Mr. Grant, but I hope you compensate these people adequately."

"Yes, ma'am, we do, even though they are both adrenaline junkies and would probably do the job whether we paid them or not, just for the thrill of it."

Febo chuckled and nodded.

"So what is to happen now, Mr. Grant? It looks like our man on Wilbourne has cleaned out the management ranks that were party to this knavery."

"Two things, ma'am. One is that William Taylor Evans was not involved and remains in place. He will likely move some of the executives on the legitimate side of the house in Evans Group to the RDT operation, while moving subordinates up on the legal side. He wins twice there. The old hands get a new challenge, while talented subordinates get a bump.

"The other is that we have the complete listing of the planetary drug dealers who are the retail side of the RDT business. The six nations of the star cluster can move against them individually as they each see fit."

"And what of Crossroads, Mr. Grant? Our operative there has left Mr. Ikenberry and Mr. Holbrook in place."

"Yes, ma'am. With regard to Mr. Ikenberry, he has prime responsibility for all the operations that form the basis for keeping Crossroads in place. The hub-and-spoke freight and passenger operations and the refueling operation. He was in the know on the RDT operation, but not a prime mover there.

"Mr. Holbrook was the assistant chief of police. While the RDT control unit was a significant player on the criminal side of this organization, Holbrook was not the major player there, either. Harker was, and Heston and Cooper. Holbrook was primarily involved in running the day-to-day police operations."

"In the opinion of your operative, Mr. Grant?"

"Yes, ma'am. I will point out this is the operative who came up with the solution we are pursuing in this matter. It is also the operative who tracked down the instigator in the developing hostilities between Wilbourne and Villacqua, Evelyn Barnes, and came up with the solution there as well.

"In cases like this, ma'am, I tend to trust the judgment of the operative on the scene. Not in all cases. But if one has an operative of this caliber on the scene, it is difficult to second-guess them from afar with any success."

Febo nodded.

"Very well, Mr. Grant. For what it's worth, I agree with you. So what is on my plate at the moment is to get the dealer data to my cohorts across the six star nations and coordinate, to the extent we can, going after the planetary dealers. At the same time, we need to get our own retail operation in place to take up the maintenance of our current addicts."

"Yes, ma'am. That's correct."

"And we trust our people on the scene to leave Wilbourne and Crossroads under competent management."

"Yes, ma'am. Although you do need to set up a management structure within the consortium to manage Mr. Evans and Mr. Ikenberry."

"Yes, that's right. OK, so that's on my plate as well. Anything else today, Mr. Grant?"

"No, Madam Chairman."

"Very well. Have a nice day, Mr. Grant."

Febo cut the connection and Grant thanked his lucky stars once again that the other asshole hadn't won the last election for chairman.

Isabela Febo placed a call to Speaker Michael Corliss on Gaston. Their close cooperation was a big part of this all working out so well. They would need to keep it up to bring this situation to a successful closure.

"Good morning, Michael."

"And good afternoon to you, Isabela."

"Have you seen the latest reports from our agents on Wilbourne and Crossroads?"

"Yes. That was a very near thing on Crossroads, wasn't it?"

"Yes, Michael. But our people pulled it off. We are now in control of Crossroads and Griffin Interstellar. The question now is, What do we do with them? I mean, we have a broad plan, but we're getting down to specifics now."

"Yes. I understand, Isabela. It's a matter of who and when and how. Who is in charge of all this, and when do we make the transition to a government franchise, and how do we pull that off?"

"The coordination issues as well, Michael. We can't each go on our own schedule, or the planetary drug dealers will get away. They have been the dirty end of the stick all along."

Corliss nodded.

"I think we need to get everyone else involved now, Isabela. Then get a council meeting together once we are all more or less of one mind. Do you have a proposal for who controls this whole thing? Who manages it for us?"

"I think so, Michael. My understanding is that the Crossroads station manager, this Ikenberry fellow, used to report to Tanner Linden of the Evans Group on Wilbourne. The central coordination was all there.

"Rather than invent a new structure, would it be best to sort of keep that structure in place, but pull it all together under William Taylor Evans?"

"The son of the fellow who set all this up?"

"And, according to our reports, is mortally ashamed of that fact. Yes, Michael. Let him clean up his father's mess. He is by all accounts a capable manager, and already has a management structure in place in the rest of his organization. He has tried and tested people under him now.

"With some shuffling around, he can staff the now-empty positions in the prior structure with people who are already in place and with whom he already has a relationship. It seems to me the lowest-risk strategy. Much better than setting something up from scratch, with all the teething issues that's likely to have."

"I can see that, Isabela. I think I'm with you there. Let's start working this with the others and see where we get. You going to take Catherine and Jacques again, and leave Randall and Ferdinand to me?"

"Yes, Michael, I can do that. What do we do in the interim?"

"I think have Evans take temporary control now, then we can confirm him in that once we have everyone else aboard. Or if the council decides something else, we can transition it then. As you've noted, he has most of it right now, in some sense."

"All right. We can do that. Put him in charge while we work up a consensus, which will probably coalesce around that as a permanent solution anyway."

"Very well, Isabela. Then once that plan is in place, we need to each decide our distribution mechanism before moving against the existing dealers, or we're going to have serious problems with the existing addicts."

"Yes, we should all be thinking about that as well. Another topic for our conversations with our peers. Get them working on their distribution systems. Figuring out how they'll handle it. Because we want to move on those drug dealers."

"What were you thinking of for the Association, Isabela?"

"We have local health clinics now. For the poor. For disaster response. Things like that. We think we can fold this into that organization's activities pretty easily. And you?"

"We have similar organizations here, though the best ones are private charities. We may do it through them. It's a current topic of conversation with my Internal Affairs chairman."

"Then I think we're in pretty good shape, Michael. Let's tag up again early next week and see where we've gotten."

"All right, Isabela. We'll see you then."

Henry Grant was surprised to get a call from Isabela Febo less than two hours after their previous call.

"Hello, Mr. Grant."

"Good afternoon, Madam Chairman. Did I forget something in our previous call?"

"No, Mr. Grant. Most thorough. But I have been in touch with Speaker Corliss of Gaston and we are agreed. Mr. Evans should take control of Crossroads and Griffin Interstellar. This may in fact be permanent, but we need to get the six nations council to agree first."

"But in the meantime, we should turn over control to Mr. Evans?"

"Yes. And have him carry on as they have been until we're prepared to move against the dealers."

"Very well, Madam Chairman."

"Good day, Mr. Grant."

On Wilbourne

It was after midnight Wednesday night before Claude Portnoy and Gloria Dent got back to their penthouse suite at the Somerset Plaza Hotel on Wilbourne.

All those on Wilbourne who were on Brad Clark's in-the-know list had been detained by eight o'clock, despite some of them hiding out in bathrooms and janitor closets. The Royal Guard had been most thorough in searching the building for them, and all were found.

Everyone else was then released from the building, usually after having a splendid dinner on Bill Evans' tab in the four-star restaurant on the ground floor. The Royal Marines withdrew, and traffic was restored.

There was still plenty of work for Portnoy and Dent, however. They had conducted interviews of all of the in-the-know people, working right through from the interview with Tanner Linden, even as the Royal Guard was rounding up the holdouts.

These interviews were typically short. Portnoy asked for and got the encryption keys for their files. Their bank account numbers and login credentials. Their part in the operation, and any information that was unique to them. All of this was recorded by Dent.

Portnoy also got their admission of their wrongdoing. Admission of their certain knowledge that they were part of the massive – and, on Wilbourne, illegal – drug-running operation. He walked them through an admission of their guilt, and the offer of an easy way out. Suicide by drug with the hypodermic needle he supplied them.

All, under the influence of Com-Ply, took the easy way out.

They had finally finished. The Royal Guard withdrew. Peabody gave them a lift back to the hotel in the Royal Guard command car and wished them a good evening, and they had trudged up to their room.

"Damn, but I'm beat," Portnoy said as they entered the suite.

He had not said anything since leaving the Evans Building save for a 'Good evening' to Peabody.

"How many was that, all told?" Dent asked.

"A couple of dozen or so. It's amazing how closely held it was. I guess that's how they kept it a secret for twenty years."

"Still a long day."

"Oh, yeah."

Portnoy headed off to the second bedroom, but Dent stopped him with a word.

"Claude."

Portnoy turned around and Dent pointed to the master bedroom.

"Active phase of the assignment is over, and I could use some cuddles."

Portnoy nodded, and redirected his trudging walk to the master bedroom.

They were so tired, they undressed, crawled under the blankets, and clung to each other.

They were asleep in seconds.

Claude Portnoy woke eight hours later to find himself in a tangle of limbs with a ravishingly beautiful nude woman.

"I love the end of an assignment," Dent said.

Portnoy agreed.

THE FAVOR

Their morning lovemaking having pushed yesterday's grim business to the back of their minds, breakfast was a convivial affair.

"Getting time to head back, I guess," Portnoy said.

"Back to where?" Dent asked.

"Mardouk for me."

"Can you drop me at Crossroads?"

"Sure, Gloria. That'll give us a couple of weeks to unwind on the way."

"I'd rather spend the couple of weeks getting wound," Dent said with a wink.

"I'm sure that can be arranged."

"Oh, good."

"So what do we need to do before we leave, Gloria?"

"We should probably stop over and talk to Bill Evans at some point."

"I wonder what they're going to decide to do. The big shots."

"No telling, Claude. But we need to file reports."

Portnoy nodded. No matter what happened, there were always reports.

"We better get on that. I sent some quick interim stuff last night, but I should round everything up in a final."

"Yeah. Me, too."

When he opened his roll-up display, though, Portnoy had a report from Mangum on Crossroads.

"Hey, Gloria. You know that nuclear demolition on Crossroads?"

"Yeah?"

"They moved it off the station and put it in the trash shipment. Eight hours out on its way to the sun, it detonated."

"No shit."

"Yeah. Look at this."

Dent walked over and looked into Portnoy's display and watched the sequence play out.

"Wow. Good thing we caught that."

"Good thing *you* caught it, you mean."

"Yeah. That's what I said."

Dent peered at the timestamp.

"That's about right for a twenty-four-hour delay, if I have my time conversions right."

"Yeah. Looks like."

"So Linden's rescind order didn't get there."

"Or he botched the transmission somehow. He was under Com-Ply, Gloria, and I dosed him pretty hard."

"Well, I'm glad they got that damned thing off the station. Can you imagine?"

Portnoy nodded.

"It would have been a disaster, and caused all the things we've been trying to avoid."

"Tanner Linden was such a bastard."

"Do you think it was Linden put that thing on Crossroads, Gloria? I think it was Wendell Evans."

"Yeah. Yeah, you're probably right."

Dent looked at the sequence again, still spooling in Portnoy's display.

"But it was Linden's order that armed it, Claude."

"Yeah. Can't get around that."

"Mangum got lucky."

"Again," Portnoy said. "Luckiest bastard I ever met."

Portnoy and Dent prepared and filed their reports. They sent the appendices on after, including the list of the guilty and

THE FAVOR

Dent's recordings of all the interviews. By the time they were finished it was time for lunch. They took lunch out on the patio. It was a beautiful day.

After lunch, they were more or less at loose ends.

"Well, nothing to do until we get some sort of instructions," Portnoy said.

"Well, I don't know about you, Claude, but I am not going to waste this sunshine."

With that, Dent stripped down, right there on the patio. She threw a towel across a chaise lounge and lay out nude in the sun.

"You look absolutely fabulous, my dear," Portnoy said.

"Strip down and enjoy the sun, Claude. Sun first, then a great fuck, then dinner. How's that for afternoon plans?"

"You had me at fuck, Gloria."

"Sun first."

Dent patted the chaise next to hers.

William Taylor Evans got up Thursday morning a bit the worse for wear. He wasn't a big drinker, and he had exceeded his usual consumption the night before. The revelations about the RDT-running operation had hit him hard.

Dammit, Dad. What the hell were you thinking?

There had been no answer.

Evans didn't want to go into the office today. Didn't want to face the wreckage of his dreams. But people relied on him. Good people he had recruited and mentored over the years. It wasn't fair to them for him to abandon them to the results of his father's– What? Misconduct? Lawlessness?

Criminality?

So Evans forced himself to dress for the office and head downtown.

It was the hardest thing he had done in his thirty years in business.

Once at his desk, Evans found his mail choked with requests from people wanting to know, What do we do now? Most of these people were missing managers above them, and had resorted to asking Evans himself for direction.

There were no easy answers. Did he continue the drug operation? Did that put himself at risk? But if he cut it off, existing addicts would die or be horribly impaired.

What was the proper course?

Evans thought about it, then put in a call to Lieutenant Colonel Peabody. If he did not know the answer, he was in a position to get it. From the king if nobody else.

"Peabody here."

"Yes, Colonel Peabody. Bill Evans here."

"Good morning, Mr. Evans. What can I do for you?"

"Answer me a simple question, Colonel. What do I do now? Do I shut down this drug business, abandoning addicts across the cluster to their fates? Do I continue it? And at what risk to myself, because to continue it is an illegal act under the laws of this kingdom."

"I understand, Mr. Evans. These issues are being discussed at the very highest levels, and I cannot give you a final answer. I can, however, give you near-term guidance. Continue as you were – continue the drug business as it was – until a final decision has been made."

"I'm happy to do that, Colonel, but I don't want to hang for it. Can you send me a mail telling me to do just that? If I have the Royal Guard's OK for those actions, I'm happy to do them."

"Yes, Mr. Evans. I can arrange that. It will probably come

from General Sinclair, the head of the Royal Guard."

"The Earl of Dunharrow?" Evans asked.

"Yes, Mr. Evans. As I said, the ultimate resolution of this matter is being discussed at the very highest levels."

"That would be excellent, Colonel. I appreciate it."

"Not a problem, Mr. Evans. Thank you for asking the question."

That settled it for Evans. The Earls of Dunharrow were known to be the most loyal subjects to the occupant of the throne in the whole kingdom.

Which is why they always commanded the Royal Guard.

To all of his mails, Evans gave the same answer. 'Carry on as you were. We are working to resolve the management issues as fast as we can. Thank you for your understanding.'

Friday morning, Portnoy and Dent had both received new instructions overnight. They talked about them over breakfast.

"New instructions for me," Portnoy said. "Close the loop with Peabody and Evans, then proceed to Mardouk by the best route."

"I got more or less the same. Best route? Does that mean you can't drop me at Crossroads?"

"No. It doesn't say the fastest route, or the most direct route, or anything like that. It says the best route, which is to say, it's my judgment call. I think we should continue the extraordinary cooperation between our agencies while we can."

"Oh, good. Because I would like to get extraordinarily cooperated a bunch more times before we split up."

"Gloria, I think you're mixing up cooperated and copulated."

"Whatever," Dent said, waving a hand. "Either works."

Portnoy chuckled.

"It looks like they're closing in on putting Bill Evans in charge of the whole RDT operation going forward."

"Yeah. He's definitely the interim solution anyway, while they figure it out. But I think the council is just going to stick with that. Wilbourne would likely have little objection, and it looks like my Speaker Corliss and your Chairman Febo are agreed."

Portnoy nodded.

"That's the interim plan, anyway. Should I put a call into Colonel Peabody, Gloria?"

"Yeah, Claude. I'll check if we can meet with Mr. Evans this afternoon."

"And I'd better let Captain Langdon know to prep *Silverheel* for departure. You want to leave before dinner or after dinner?"

"How's the food on the courier ship?"

"Pretty good, actually."

"Before dinner."

Lieutenant Colonel Lance Peabody's command car pulled up in front of the Somerset Plaza Hotel at one o'clock. Dent and Portnoy were waiting at the curb. The shotgun got out and opened the rear door for them. They entered, and he closed the door, got back in the front cabin, and the big car pulled away from the curb.

Peabody was in the rear-facing seat.

"Good afternoon, Gloria. Claude," Peabody said.

"Hello, Lance," Dent said.

"I thought we would just make sure we were all on the same page before speaking to Mr. Evans."

"My understanding is that he will run the RDT operation, including Crossroads and Griffin/Hippocamp, while the council decides what to do, but that will also likely be the council's decision. To keep him in place on the long term."

"That's my understanding as well, Gloria. I'm told His Majesty has already signed up for Speaker Corliss' and Chairman Febo's plan."

"Excellent. So we're all good, I think."

"What are your plans after the meeting? My understanding is that your assignment here on Wilbourne is then completed."

"We'll be going up to my courier ship and leaving for Crossroads immediately after the meeting. Our baggage has already been picked up from the hotel," Portnoy said.

"Allow me to give you a lift to the shuttleport, then, Claude."

"That's very considerate, Lance."

Peabody waved it away, and Dent stifled a chuckle.

The head of clandestine operations for His Majesty's Royal Guard would probably like nothing better than to see these two foreign clandestine operators got off-planet expeditiously.

William Taylor Evans wasn't quite sure what to expect at his one-thirty meeting with Lieutenant Colonel Peabody and the two agents who had interviewed him – under drugs – Wednesday afternoon. When she called for the appointment, the woman of the two – Gladys Mint – had said it was just to have a talk before they left Wilbourne.

Evans' secretary showed them in at one-thirty.

"Colonel Peabody. Come in, come in. It's good to see you again."

They shook hands.

"Ms. Mint. Mr. Pendergast. It's good to see you as well. Please. All of you. Have a seat."

Evans waved them to the side seating arrangement, and they

all sat in the big armchairs, arranged around a central coffee table.

"Would you care for refreshments? Coffee, perhaps? Or tea?"

"No, thank you, Mr. Evans," Portnoy said. "We have a shuttle to catch. My courier ship is preparing for departure right now."

Evans re-evaluated the young man's standing yet again. Courier ships were insanely expensive to operate. Which is why even important people took liners.

Not Pendergast, however.

"Very well, then. How can I help you all today?"

"We think we can help you, Mr. Evans," Peabody said. "After your call yesterday, I sought further guidance. And I am now prepared to pass that on."

"Indeed? Proceed, Colonel."

"Thank you, sir. Your instructions are to continue to operate the RDT manufacturing and distribution business as Tanner Linden had been doing. That includes having the station manager of Crossroads reporting to you. They expect that the council of six star nations will confirm that as the permanent situation sometime in the next week."

"They expect, Colonel?"

Peabody nodded.

"His Majesty King Ferdinand, Speaker Corliss of Gaston, and Chairman Febo of the Association of Planets."

Evans raised an eyebrow, and Dent nodded.

"Per my most recent instructions, my government on Gaston supports this plan, Mr. Evans."

That was a surprise. Peabody had introduced them as agents helping His Majesty's government, but had not said they were foreign agents. In Mint's case, that probably meant the BIE.

THE FAVOR

"Per my most recent instructions, so does my government on Mardouk," Portnoy said.

That was an even bigger surprise. The two were clearly working together, which meant Gaston and the Association were working together at very high levels. And the Association had no intelligence outfit, unless of course Pendergast was from the officially non-existent Agency. Evans bumped his standing yet again.

"And General Sinclair told me this morning that His Majesty is behind this plan as well, Mr. Evans."

This whole thing went all the way to the king. Which meant Evans was being trusted at the highest levels, across multiple star nations, to carry out their plan. That was humbling. And more than a little daunting.

"I see. That's three of the six governments right there."

"Yes, sir," Peabody said.

"So I run this drug operation into the future?"

"Yes, sir. On the near term, the expectation is that the distribution of the drug will be transferred to government healthcare facilities within each of the six star nations. Your current customers will then be removed from the business."

"I see."

And Evans did see. The planetary drug dealers were likely in for some rough times.

"That last is confidential, sir."

"Of course, Colonel. Their removal from the business will not be voluntary. I understand."

"We thought you would likely have seasoned managers in your organization, people already tried and tested, who could be moved into the open positions you now have, while others might be up for promotion within your organization."

"I see, Ms. Mint. That is likely true. There are always some people ready for promotion, operating at that level, awaiting only the opportunity."

Dent nodded.

"But it is up to you to manage this organization, Mr. Evans. You know your people. You make the calls."

Evans nodded. He could do this. The product, such as it was, was different, but the management of the business was the same.

"Very well. I suppose this is the least disruptive solution, after all. Since I already own the RDT business, much to my chagrin."

"That's what makes you such a good candidate for the job, Mr. Evans," Portnoy said.

Evans nodded again. He wondered how much of this solution had been crafted by the two enigmatic agents here in his office.

"That's all we had for today, Mr. Evans," Peabody said. "If you have any other questions, I would direct you to General Sinclair. He has the ear of His Majesty, and would be happy to give you whatever guidance you need."

"I have met the Earl of Dunharrow, Colonel. At social events. I think we can make that work."

"Excellent, sir. Then I think our business is done for today."

The personnel shuttle was waiting on the pad when the big command car pulled up. Captain Timothy Langdon was waiting with it.

Figure Portnoy to show up for lift in a military command car, flying the fender flags of His Majesty's Royal Guard.

Langdon liked assignments with Claude Portnoy. You never knew what was going to happen, but it was always interesting.

Portnoy and a stunningly attractive young woman got out of

the car, followed by a man with military bearing but wearing a civilian business suit. They all shook hands, the military man got back in the car, and it was away.

"Hello, Captain. I don't think you've met Gloria Dent."

"Actually, sir, I have. On a mission with Mr. Mangum, I think."

"Yes, Captain. You have a good memory. It's good to see you again."

"And our destination, Mr. Portnoy. Is it still Crossroads?"

"Yes, Captain. We will be dropping Ms. Dent at Crossroads and picking up Mr. Mangum there. Then it will be off to Mardouk."

"Very good, sir."

Langdon waved them to the shuttle door, and they entered.

One day out of Wilbourne, *Silverheel* opened a rift in space-time in front of itself. It passed through that rift and disappeared from reality.

On Crossroads

Friday morning at breakfast was a slow, lazy time. Finally.

"So what craziness is in store for today, Bert?"

"What do you mean, Elina?"

"Well, Monday, I confronted my boss at Crossroads P.D., and then we took out Harker and Heston. That put us on the run. Tuesday, we started on Ikenberry, pushing him for a meeting. Wednesday, we had a meeting with Ikenberry, took over the station, and took out Cooper and his goon squad. Thursday, we found and removed a nuclear demolition, which went off mere hours later.

"So I was just wondering who we were going to kill or what we were going to blow up today."

"Getting to you, huh?"

"A little bit, I admit."

Mangum nodded.

"Yeah, the end of an op is always like that. All the pieces come crashing together. Usually right in front of you."

"So what's for today?"

"Nothing, I think. I'm waiting to see what higher-ups are going to do next to transition to a government-run RDT maintenance program. That may involve me to some extent. But I think mostly anything I can do is over."

"So then what?"

"I wait for another assignment. Maybe here, maybe back home on Mardouk. Don't know. But I've been in space a lot. I have some planet time coming."

Why did that last bother Stavros so much? Mangum, Sam, Jules all going back to Mardouk? How empty would that leave the station?

How empty would that leave her?

She'd always had her job, her career, but did she even have that anymore?

Did she even *want* it anymore?

They took a walk in the gardens after breakfast. In the dog run area, there was a little boy playing with his dog, the parents looking on. There were never many children on Crossroads, but there were some, and this child was squealing with delight as he played catch with the dog. They stopped to watch for a few minutes, then walked on.

Stavros wondered if this would be their last time in the gardens before Mangum left Crossroads?

Would Stavros be asking herself that question about everything they did? Their last this, their last that?

What did she really want?

How would she know?

Mangum picked up on Stavros' mood. They would have to talk about it, he supposed. There were few other people she could talk to about– whatever it was.

Mangum suspected he knew. It was about her job. Her career. Did she really want to be back on Crossroads P.D., which had turned out to be such a violation of her standards? Her morals?

Sure, the police department was mostly cleaned up now, but how soured was she on it at this point? Could she even trust it going forward?

One thing was sure. Elina Stavros would never be so naive again.

When they got back from the gardens just before lunch, Mangum had new mail waiting.

"I have my new orders."

Stavros got up from the table and came over to sit in the other armchair, across from Sam and Jules on the sofa.

"What are they?"

"It looks like Bill Evans is going to be put in charge of the whole RDT operation."

"Tanner Linden's old boss."

"Yes. But uninvolved, based on the investigation, and by all accounts a good businessman. So they'll put him in charge."

"And Ikenberry?"

"Will report to Evans."

"Just as he reported to Tanner Linden before."

"Right. Gloria and Claude are going to talk to Evans today. Make sure he's willing to take the job."

"Then what?"

"Then I tell Ikenberry he now reports to Bill Evans."

"And you're out of the loop."

"Right."

"Then what?"

"I'm to return to Mardouk. Best route, which would likely be a liner."

"So you're leaving Crossroads? When?"

"There's a liner every Tuesday."

"I see."

Stavros was quiet after that, staring at the far wall of the room, and Mangum didn't disturb her.

Sam and Jules looked on with concern.

That evening, after a supper during which Stavros was very subdued, Mangum got a mail from Portnoy. He mentioned it to

Stavros.

"I got a note from Claude. Evans took the job, so they're done on Wilbourne. He and Gloria are on their way here in the courier ship he's been bouncing around in. He'll drop her here to catch a liner home to Gaston, then give me a lift to Mardouk."

"So you're here another two weeks?"

"Until Claude shows up. Yes."

"With Dent?"

"Yes."

Stavros wondered why that should fill her with such foreboding.

"Ikenberry."

"Hello, Mr. Ikenberry. Bert Mangum. Sorry to interrupt your evening, but I thought this shouldn't wait until Monday."

"Yes, Mr. Mangum. That's fine. What's going on?"

"Things have been resolved, on the medium term at least. William Taylor Evans is taking over the RDT operation."

"The head of the Evans Group?"

"Yes. Apparently his father and Tanner Linden left him in the dark about what was going on. He's untainted. He's agreed to take over the RDT operation."

"That's probably a smart move. He's got it now, with Tanner Linden gone, and has the people and organization to continue operations already in place."

"Correct. That was our recommendation, and the council of the six star nations has agreed. The news tonight is that Evans has agreed."

Ikenberry wondered who Mangum meant with that 'our'. How high was he, anyway?

"What does this mean for Crossroads, Mr. Mangum?"

"From this point forward, you will report to Bill Evans on Wilbourne, Mr. Ikenberry. I'm out of it."

"And what does the future hold for you, Mr. Mangum?"

"A courier ship is on the way here from Wilbourne. I will be taking it home to Mardouk."

"Well, I won't say I'll be sorry to see you go, Mr. Mangum. It would be nice to have things around here settle down for a bit."

Mangum chuckled and Ikenberry smiled. He could certainly understand Ikenberry's point. It echoed Stavros' question of this morning.

"And what are Elina Stavros' plans, Mr. Mangum? Do you know?"

"She hasn't shared them with me, Mr. Ikenberry. I suppose she's not sure about her status with Crossroads P.D."

"That question I can answer. I've talked to Holbrook about it. He needs a new assistant police chief. So he was thinking about moving Daley up into that spot and making Stavros head of investigations."

Mangum thought that would be nice. It was a big career bump, and it also implicitly endorsed the actions she'd taken since Monday.

"I'll let her know, Mr. Ikenberry. I don't know what she'll do, however."

"I understand, Mr. Mangum. Give her my best, and thank you for the information about Bill Evans."

"You're welcome, Mr. Ikenberry, and good luck to you and Crossroads going forward."

"Well, that was interesting," Mangum said when he got off the phone with Ikenberry.

"What did Ikenberry have to say?"

"He likes putting Bill Evans in charge of the RDT operation. He thinks that will work out well."

"So you transferred his report to Evans?"

"Yeah. He also said he wouldn't be sorry to see me go. Let things settle down a bit."

"Yes, I can see that. From his point of view."

"He asked me your plans and I said I didn't know. He told me Holbrook was going to make Daley assistant chief, and move you up to head of Investigations. If you wanted it."

That floored Stavros. This was Friday. They had been trying to kill her Wednesday.

But did she want it?

It was an endorsement of all she had done since Monday. And before. As a detective.

Two months ago, it would have been a dream offer, but there had been a lot of reaction mass through the thruster since then, as the spacer saying went.

She had to admit that Captain Elina Stavros, head of Investigations, had a nice ring to it. And she could go anywhere with that hit on her résumé.

But did she want it?

Mangum thought Stavros would likely take the head of Investigations position. She was young for such a position, and it was a huge vote of confidence in her. Her character. Her skills. She could go anywhere from Crossroads after a stint like that.

It was a great opportunity, and Mangum was happy for her.

Then why did she cry herself to sleep in his arms that night?

After his first ninety-minute sleep cycle, Mangum got up and went into the living room for a nightcap. He closed the bedroom door softly, so as not to wake Stavros.

Sam and Jules were sitting at the table, Mangum's roll-up display open. Both were staring into the display. Mangum noted they maintained contact with their feet, one against the other, under the table. Communicating, though not talking.

When Mangum came out, mixed a drink, and sat in one of the armchairs, Sam and Jules came over and sat on the sofa.

"Hi, Bert."

"Hi, Sam. How you guys doing?"

"We're good. How are you doing?"

"OK, I guess. I just don't know what's going on with Elina."

"Yes, we had noted her growing unease."

"Unease, Sam?"

"Concern. Worry. Pensiveness. Pick one, Bert. English has several hundred words to describe when one is unhappy. Honestly. A casual observer might wonder if that's all you think about is being unhappy. Or miserable, or depressed, or sad, or melancholy, or...."

Mangum chuckled.

"Yes, Sam. We do seem to talk about it a lot. And I don't understand what's going on with Elina. They are promoting her to the head of investigations, so that's a huge positive for her. And she seems sad about it."

"We may be able to offer some insight there, Bert."

"You? What do you know about human emotions?"

"Not much, but we've been reading up."

Mangum glanced over to his roll-up display. He had always left it out, convenient for Sam to use when Mangum was in bed.

"We think it comes down to one of three things. Or some combination. Or all three."

"OK, Sam. And those are?"

"First, there is often expressed within human literature a nostalgia for what was, especially if it involved participation in a group. 'The good old days.' 'Putting the band back together.' 'Wedding bells are breaking up that old gang of mine.' The anticipation of breaking up a close group can result in melancholy."

"So she's sad to break up our little group."

"Yes, Bert. That is one option. Second is that when anything comes to a stop, one has options about how to proceed. Much like a stop sign on a road. That stop sign is typically at an intersection, and one has choices about which way to turn that had not presented themselves along the prior stretch of road.

"Elina has options about how to proceed now, and she may be having difficulty with that decision. This is an anticipation of the 'road not traveled' problem, in which one has doubt or regret about one's past decisions. Elina may be anticipating such regret no matter what she chooses."

"All right. I get that one, too, Sam."

"The third one is generally more obvious than the other two, but, curiously, may be least obvious to you."

"And that is?"

"She may have pair-bonded to you, Bert."

"Elina's in love with me?"

"Yes, that's one of the several hundred ways to say that in English. Looking at English vocabulary, one would think all humans did was fall in love and then be sad about it."

Mangum laughed. Sam had a serious point, though. Could Stavros have fallen in love with him? He knew her initial stimulus in seeking him out had been sexual release after several years of frustration on Crossroads. But they had been through a lot since then, and always together.

"It could also be a combination," Jules said. "You know, she regrets in advance taking either path, especially because she's torn between the advancement here and being in love with you. Either way, she loses. Something like that."

Mangum nodded. Yes, he'd had to make decisions like that. Never easy. He had learned to set them aside, finally, and stop regretting the path not chosen. Down the other path could have been disaster, just around that first corner. How could one know? So he didn't spend a lot of time on regret.

And his job didn't lend itself to a lot of introspection.

"As for breaking up the group, Bert, I admit to some hesitation there myself. For one thing, how does the group break up? Does Jules stay here with Elina? Or do we three go to Mardouk and leave Elina here alone?"

Mangum considered. Another good question.

"Well, she would hardly be alone. There are a hundred thousand people on Crossroads."

"Yes, Bert. But none of her friends have stopped by to see her in eight weeks, though her whereabouts are known. I conclude she has few close friends here. The authority of her position has limited her social opportunities."

Mangum nodded. That was certainly true. It was her isolation that had brought her to him in the first place.

"That seems likely," he said.

"So what will you do, Bert?"

"I don't know, Sam."

"Please let us know what you decide, for it affects us as well."

"Of course, Sam. You'll be the first to know."

"Thanks, Bert."

Mangum went back into the bedroom and climbed into bed with Stavros. She turned toward him, pulling herself close, and murmured something in her sleep.

For his part, Mangum took a while to fall asleep. While his job didn't lend itself to introspection, he pulled his feelings out now, with this assignment complete, and considered them.

What would life be like with Stavros? If he took her back to Mardouk with him? What would she do for a career? Would she like his condo, or would she want to choose another place? What would daily life be like?

The questions, and the opportunities, were endless.

Then he considered what life would be like without Stavros.

He came up empty.

No questions.

No opportunities.

The next day they walked in the gardens again. This time Jules went as Stavros' purse.

"Why a purse today?" Mangum asked.

"I got Jules a ball this morning."

"You did? Where?"

The various ball games didn't work on Crossroads. The spinning space station made things not – apparently – go straight when thrown or hit. Of course, they were going straight, but the station wasn't.

In any case, when one hit or threw a ball on Crossroads, it curved in the station's rotation direction.

Which was also counter-intuitive.

"At my apartment. Something I brought from Mardouk and never used here. Jules wanted to try it."

Stavros had ducked out while Mangum was writing up his final impressions of the operation after breakfast, but he hadn't given it any thought.

"So what's Jules going to do?"

"You'll see."

When they got to the dog run, Stavros set her purse down on the ground. She looked around. Nobody else here.

"All right, Jules."

The purse turned into a ten-year-old boy, the age of the child they had observed yesterday, holding a ball.

Mangum chuckled and unclipped the leash from Sam.

"Fetch, Sam. Fetch!"

Jules threw the ball and Sam tore off after it. Damn, he was fast. Jules laughed. Sam caught the ball after the first bounce, then came trotting back with it, and Jules threw it again.

Mangum and Stavros watched the two aliens playing with the ball. Such a normal scene, apparently, but it was actually the weirdest thing in human space.

After lunch, Stavros and Mangum were sitting in the armchairs in the living room. Sam and Jules had left after lunch and gone into the kids' bedroom, sensitive to the moods of the two humans.

"Elina?"

"Yes?"

"Are you going to take the head of Investigations position?"

"I don't know, Bert."

"I think you should."

"You do?"

"Yes. It will make finding a job on Mardouk much easier."

"On Mardouk?"

"Yes."

Mangum turned to her and caught her eye.

"Elina, will you go back to Mardouk with us? With me?"

"As your passenger, Bert, or as your partner? Your woman?"

"As my wife."

THE FAVOR

"But can you settle down with one woman, Bert Mangum? Is that even a possibility?"

"Yes. Oh, I've catted around, Elina, but not when I'm with someone. When I'm with them, I'm with them. In between, well, that's different."

"What about Gloria Dent?"

"Gloria Dent is– not tempting. Gloria is just Gloria. She's all about Gloria. About what Gloria wants. She's fun, as long as she wants to be. But for her, it's all about her. Always was, for that matter. And I've known her a long time."

Stavros considered him a long time. Until Mangum started to squirm under her regard.

Then she smiled that beautiful smile.

"Yes, Bert Mangum. I will be your wife."

Mangum thought he must be truly in love.

Otherwise why would he feel such relief at her answer?

RICHARD F. WEYAND

Heading Home

Silverheel exited hyperspace close in to the Crossroads station. There was no planetary gravity well here to be avoided, and no day's travel in normal space to reach the station.

The passenger shuttle cut loose from *Silverheel* as the courier ship passed by the station, decelerating all the way.

Dent and Portnoy checked into a first-class room down the hall from Mangum and Stavros' first-class suite. It was in Dent's name, as it was Thursday and the liner *Gaston Galactic* would not be leaving until Tuesday.

Silverheel would depart Crossroads on Saturday.

"We have an invitation to join Bert Mangum and Elina Stavros for drinks and dinner," Portnoy said once they had settled in and he checked his mail.

"How sweet," Dent said. "I've never met her, but it will be nice to see him again."

"We're invited over to celebrate their engagement."

"Engagement of what?"

"To be married."

Dent almost choked on her drink.

"Bert Mangum? Married? Is she a witch?"

"Could be, I guess. Never thought I'd see it, myself."

"How interesting."

"Claude. Gloria. Come in, come in."

"Hi, Bert," Dent and Portnoy said together.

They came in and Mangum waved Stavros forward.

"I want you to meet my fiancée. Elina Stavros, Claude Portnoy and Gloria Dent."

There were handshakes and 'pleased to meet you's all around.

Stavros, like most women, was painfully aware of every little shortcoming, every blemish, every imperfection she had. Dent, though, was a ravishing beauty, a near-perfect rendition of God's plan. Mangum's dismissal of her seemed surprising.

Dent's self-esteem did not have that little quirk, however, and she was surprised to find Stavros every bit her equal, and with that glorious auburn hair thrown in as an extra. Bert had done well, she thought.

Of course, it was looks they compared on first meeting. They already each knew the other was smart, accomplished and very, very dangerous.

"We'll get the drinks and snacks ready," Dent said. "Come help me, Elina."

The women went over to the bar, and the men headed for the seating. Sam and Jules jumped down from the sofa as they approached.

"Sam had a puppy, Bert?"

"Yeah. It's Sam for Samantha."

"Wow. Cute."

Portnoy looked around behind them to see if they would be overheard.

"Bert, you know what they say about redheads, right? God put a warning, right there on the top, so you couldn't miss it."

Mangum laughed. It was an easy laugh now, with everything decided.

"Yes, yes, I know."

"So what are you going to do? About assignments and such?"

"I don't know. I guess I'll have to talk to Frank and Henry about it. See what we come up with."

Portnoy nodded. Frank Latham, the Agency's head of operations, and Henry Grant, the Agency's director.

"Well, I wish you two the very best."

"Thanks, Claude."

At the bar, as they made drinks, Dent noted a stiffness about Stavros. Toward her, specifically.

"Don't worry, Elina. There are plenty of men about. I don't have any designs on yours. In fact, I wish you all the best."

That brought Stavros up short, but reminded her of what Mangum had said about Dent. It was all about her. Apparently men were interchangeable service items.

But wishing them all the best was sweet of her.

"Thank you, Gloria. I appreciate it."

"Not at all, Elina. I like Bert Mangum. He's a nice guy in a tough business. I hope you both are very happy together."

With that out of the way, Stavros relaxed, and both women were surprised to find themselves warming to the other. For all their differences, they both valued competence in others, and each was accomplished in her specialty.

"We have drinks and appetizers," Dent announced as the two women came over, each with a tray.

They set the trays on the coffee table, and the women took the armchairs opposite Mangum and Portnoy on the sofa. Sam and Jules lay on the floor.

"Well, isn't this the warm holiday scene," Dent said. "Drinks and appetizers on the table, dogs sprawled on the floor. All very heartwarming."

"But what's the holiday?" Portnoy asked.

THE FAVOR

"Old friends and new beginnings," Dent said.

"That's a good one," Stavros said. "I like that one."

They all toasted.

"And congratulations to the happy couple," Portnoy said.

Over dinner, they told their war stories. Times they wiggled out of a tight spot, or something funny happened. Stavros held her own in that conversation. The stupidest things happened on a space station full of transient crew on station leave.

After supper, Mangum turned the conversation to business.

"You made good time from Wilbourne."

"Yes, *Silverheel* is a bit quicker than a liner," Portnoy said. "Cut a day or so off the normal transit."

"What's your schedule now?"

"Captain Langdon wants to give each shift of the crew a night on station to blow off steam before going home. So we'll be two days here getting refueled and restocked, then *Silverheel* heads to Mardouk on Saturday."

Mangum nodded.

"What's your status, Gloria?"

"I'm on the *Gaston Galactic*, outbound on Tuesday. Then two weeks to get home. All by myself."

"Oh, I'm sure there will be plenty of men on the *Gaston Galactic*, Gloria," Stavros said. "You don't have to be alone unless you want to be."

Mangum was aghast Stavros had rubbed Dent's nose in her proclivities that way, but Dent laughed. The women had clearly reached an accommodation.

"Yes, there will be, won't there? That makes me feel better. Much better, actually."

Dent and Portnoy took their leave after the after-dinner drinks.

"That was very pleasant," Stavros said.

"Yes, Elina. I was afraid you and Gloria wouldn't get along."

"Oh, I think we understand each other, Bert. And we're both happy with that."

For Mangum's part, it had been interesting seeing Stavros and Dent together. Both incredible beauties. Both very competent, even dangerous.

But there was something– sharp about Dent. Something angular. Not in looks, but in personality. Mangum couldn't put his finger on it, but it was there. And it had been obvious to him when seeing them both together.

In contrast, Stavros had something else in that same spot. Something rounder. Something more comfortable.

Something more like home.

Back in their room, Portnoy and Dent also compared notes on the evening.

"Elina seems very nice," Portnoy said.

"Oh, yes," Dent said. "She's a sweetheart. I'm happy for them both."

"I heard you say that. You mean it?"

"Oh, yes. I'm very happy for them, Claude."

"I never thought Bert Mangum would settle down, though. I can't imagine it, myself."

"He's a couple years older than you, dear. You may get there, too, at some point."

"What about you, Gloria? When are you going to settle down?"

Dent laughed.

The foursome had several more meals together over the next

two days. Then Saturday evening came, and they were all in the private shuttle boarding lounge. Stavros' apartment had all been packed, and her and Mangum's baggage was all aboard already.

Dent was there to wish them off.

"All right, everybody. Have a great trip."

"You, too, Gloria," Stavros said. "You're leaving in three days."

"Yes, but you're leaving now."

Dent had hugs for them all, and played with Jules, and scratched Sam's head behind the ears.

"Goodbye, Sam. Take good care of them for me."

Then they were in the shuttle and on their way to the hub of the station.

"Ugh. I hate this part," Stavros said.

"What? Zero gravity?"

"Yeah."

"It's not so bad."

"Yes, but you do it all the time. I've only done it once before, on the way here."

That surprised Mangum, with all the time Stavros had spent in space, but then he realized all that time was here on Crossroads. She hadn't actually gone anywhere else.

"Well, it'll be nice to be home, anyway," Stavros said. "I'll just keep thinking about that."

Once the shuttle had reached the hub of the station, and there was zero gravity, the shuttle maneuvered clear of the station on thrusters. Only then could the pilot engage the shuttle's main thrusters, and apparent gravity returned.

At that point, the executive officer of *Silverheel*, also on his way back to the ship, pulled a small gift-wrapped box out of

319

his pocket and handed it to Stavros.

"I was asked to give you this once we were clear of the station, ma'am."

"Thank you."

Stavros turned to Mangum.

"I wonder what it is, Bert."

"It can't be much. It's a small box."

The box was only an inch and a half by three inches and two inches tall.

Stavros unwrapped it, then opened the box. There was a note inside, which she took out, and her breath caught when she saw what lay beneath it. She opened the note and read it.

"What a sweetheart."

She handed the note to Mangum:

Captain Stavros:

Congratulations! Post-dated to Glen Holbrook becoming Chief of Police. Please let us know when you resign the department.

Carl Ikenberry

"Captain?"

Stavros showed him the contents of the box. They were business cards for the Crossroads P.D., showing her as Captain Elina Stavros, Investigations Unit Head.

"But why hold it until I was off the station?" Stavros asked.

"Because he thinks you've made the right decision for your future, and he didn't want to tempt you to stay."

"Then why give me the promotion?"

"Because he thinks you deserve it. As do I, by the way."

"So when I get a new job?"

THE FAVOR

"Then resign the Crossroads P.D. Ikenberry will probably continue your salary until then as well, for that matter. And give you the differential in pay for the last three weeks."

Stavros looked down at the cards and shook her head.

"What an absolute sweetie."

The courier ship was a standard design intended for VIP transport. There were two first-class suites and crew quarters, and that was it for the accommodations aboard. Each suite had one bedroom, a living room/dining room combination, and a master bath.

With the small shuttle latched to the ship – an operation blessedly performed while under acceleration – and the passengers all aboard, *Silverheel* opened a rift in space-time in front of itself, passed through that rift and disappeared from reality.

The three of them – Portnoy, Mangum, and Stavros – usually took the big meal of the evening together in Mangum and Stavros' cabin. Portnoy had let them have the nominally larger cabin, which had four chairs for the dining table and not just two.

At those meals, Mangum would feed Sam and Jules, in their golden doodle personas, with plates on the floor. For breakfast and lunch, Sam and Jules, in their utility personas, would sit at the table with Mangum and Stavros.

The food on board the ship was very good, almost first-class quality, albeit with much less choice. The Agency had found good food on board ship reduced crew turnover on the erratic transit schedules mandated by operations.

The first day out they had a safety briefing on the use of the passenger emergency cradles. After that it was the boring routine of any interstellar crossing.

But it was with Elina Stavros, and Bert Mangum was happy.

Mangum at one point early in the transit mentioned to Portnoy that it was too bad Dent wasn't along. They would be two couples. Like double-dating.

"No, Bert. Thank you, but no. After the crossing from Wilbourne to Crossroads, I needed a break. That woman is insatiable."

"Tried to break the record again, did she?"

"Yes."

"And did she?"

"Yes."

"Oh. Oh, my. I understand. I *completely* understand."

"You do?"

"Oh, yes. That was our record."

After two weeks in hyperspace, *Silverheel* re-entered normal space. There was still a day's spacing to get to Mardouk.

Stavros was looking at the planet in the display.

"The last time I saw home in the display, it was getting smaller. I never knew whether I would see it again."

"Well, you're back."

She squeezed his hand, on the arm of the chair next to hers.

"It feels good."

As *Silverheel* decelerated past the planet, the small passenger shuttle peeled away and began to drop toward the surface, thrusters leading and decelerating hard.

THE FAVOR

On Mardouk

As *Silverheel*'s shuttle descended to the planet, they had already been in the system for a day, spacing from the hyperspace limit to the planet. Which means they had been in contact with the mail system.

Elina Stavros had a surprise for Bert Mangum as they descended to the planet.

"My parents are going to be waiting at the shuttleport."

Mangum hadn't given any thought to her family. An only child, his parents had died in an accident when he was in college.

"Meeting the new in-laws at the spaceport? We aren't even moved in yet."

"Oh, I know. But they haven't seen me in four years, so they want to greet us there. It won't be long. They know we have to get to your place and settle in first thing. We can have them for dinner or something later."

"I don't even know anything about your parents, Elina."

"OK. Quick briefing. They're both mid-fifties right now, and both are on their second career. Mom was a corporate accountant, and now has a small accountancy on the side. Small businesses and the like."

"And your father?"

"Was a cop in Ashur. Now retired from the force. He writes novels now. 'Cheap, trashy fiction' he calls it. Mostly spy novels and police procedurals."

"Your father writes spy novels?"

"Yeah. You know. Secret agent stuff. Sex and guns and all that. Lots of fun."

"Sounds like my life."

Stavros laughed.

"A little bit, anyway. His stuff is a little more out there. Aliens and stuff. You know."

"Like I said."

Stavros laughed.

Stavros' parents, George and Stacia Stavros, waited in the small private-spacing terminal, watching the shuttle come down.

"Now don't say anything about grandchildren, George. Every grandmother knows that adds at least a year."

"I won't if you won't, Stace."

Stacia pursed her lips. George sounded grumpy. He was sure no man deserved his beautiful little girl, and no man ever would. She hoped there wouldn't be any issue there.

"I hope she's selected a nice young man," Stacia said.

"Hmph."

Oh, dear.

Mangum and Stavros came up the escalator into the waiting area. Mangum had Sam on a leash, and Stavros had Jules on a leash.

Mangum gave them the once-over. She was a mid-fifties woman bordering on grandmother. Mangum could see where Stavros got her looks. He was a burly type, hair going to gray. It didn't look like his eyes missed much. Mangum could see where Stavros got her auburn hair.

"My, he's handsome," Stacia said softly to George.

George agreed. Handsome, but with an edge to him. Some indefinable thing. George couldn't say what it was, but he'd met many dangerous people in his life, and he knew one when he saw one.

Then Mangum and Stavros reached her parents. Mangum held back while Stavros hugged her mother and father. Sam and Jules both sat and watched.

"Hi, Mom."

"Welcome home, dear," Stacia said.

"Hi, Daddy."

"Hi, baby," George said, a bit huskily.

"Mom, Dad, I want you to meet my fiancé, Bert Mangum."

Mangum stepped forward and shook Stacia's hand first.

"Ma'am."

Then he shook George's hand.

"Sir."

"Everybody calls me George."

"It's good to meet you, George."

"Elina hasn't told us much about you, Bert," George said. "What do you do for a living?"

"I'm a trade representative for the Agency for Interstellar Trade."

George's eyes narrowed.

"You work for the Agency?"

"The Agency for Interstellar Trade. Yes."

Stavros stepped in.

"I have a present for you, Daddy."

George turned to her, and she handed him one of the cards Ikenberry had given her as a going-away present. He read it and looked up at her.

"Well, you outrank me now, Elina," he said huskily, his pride evident in his voice.

"Well, we know you two have to get moved in and settled and all," Stacia said. "So we'll let you go. But we had to see Elina for just a bit. It has been four years."

"Yes, Mom. But I'm back on Mardouk now. For good, I think."

"How wonderful."

"We'll have you over for dinner. Sometime soon."

The foursome walked across the waiting area to the autocab stand. George and Stacia saw Mangum, Stavros, and the dogs into an autocab and then got in the next one.

"Those dogs were amazingly well-behaved, I thought," Stacia said once they were on their way. "They heeled and sat and didn't jump around or anything."

George answered the unasked question.

"He'll do."

Stacia's eyebrows rose.

"Really? I didn't expect you to approve of *anyone* for your little girl."

George Stavros, in his twenty-five years as a cop in the Ashur P.D., had learned a lot about the central government of the Association of Planets. A lot of things he didn't talk about. And he knew that the 'Agency for Interstellar Trade' hired the best and the brightest people they could find.

Those who made 'trade representative' were the best and the brightest of them all. Whether man or woman, they were both competent and dangerous.

"I didn't either."

"Your father made me," Mangum said as they rode in the autocab to his condo.

"You think?"

"Oh, yes. George Stavros is a man who doesn't miss much."

"Well, after twenty-five years on the Ashur P.D., he knows a lot about the Association's central government."

"I shouldn't wonder. How discreet is he, though?"

"Daddy never told me anything out of line, and we're pretty close. A lot of times we knew something had happened, but he wouldn't say anything about it. At all. And he wouldn't put me at risk anyway."

"Good. Excellent."

The autocab pulled up at the portico of an exclusive condominium building in downtown Ashur. It was across the street from the capital's Central Park.

"You live *here*? At The 909?"

"*We* live here. Yes."

"Wow."

Mangum and Stavros walked up the front steps, Sam and Jules on leashes, and the doorman opened the double sliding-glass doors for them by pushing a button next to the doors.

"Good evening, ma'am. It's good to see you, sir."

"Good evening, Steven. It's good to be back."

They walked through the lobby to the elevator bank, and took it to the top floor.

"The top floor?" Stavros asked.

Mangum shrugged.

"It was an investment. I picked it up in a down market."

At the top floor, Mangum led Stavros to one of the condo doors. There weren't many at this level, and it was a corner unit. He opened the door – which had a bio-sensor lock – and waved her in.

Stavros walked into the condo as if she were in a dream. The immense living room had two glass walls looking out over the park on one side and the capital complex on the other, beyond which was a private balcony with a glass railing.

The condo was open plan, and the kitchen was beautiful, with all the latest high-end appliances and gadgets gleaming in quiet competence.

The condo was set up for entertaining, on a grand scale. All of it was expertly decorated, with subdued, expensive taste.

"Wow. Just wow. Somehow I didn't expect this, Bert. A penthouse in a first-class hotel would be slumming it compared to this."

"I had someone come in and do it all before I moved in."

"But this must all cost a fortune."

Mangum shrugged.

"It did. It's all paid for. We own it clear."

"On a government salary? How did you ever manage it?"

"Uh, yes. About that. We never did talk finances, Elina. You see, when someone tries to kill me, I usually take them captive. I take their banking information under Com-Ply."

"And then you transfer their assets to yourself?"

"Oh, yes. It's quite lucrative. Professional assassins make pretty good money."

"And the government lets you keep it?"

"I'm not sure the government per se knows anything about it. My superiors do, however. It's considered a perk."

"Some perk. So you spent all the money on a fancy condo."

"I spent *some* of the money on a fancy condo."

"Bert, what's your net worth?"

"I don't know, Elina. A lot. Much more than we need. I would have to ask my accountant. And my broker."

"Unbelievable."

"I'm also in a position to make market moves based on inside information."

"Like Crossroads."

"Yes. I shorted some things before the rumors started, cashed in on Evans Group and some shipping companies, then went long on them before we cleared it all up. I made a killing on that."

Stavros just shook her head. She walked over to the hallway to the bedrooms. The master bedroom – again, furnished with exquisite, expensive taste – had a glass wall looking out over the park.

The second bedroom was an interior room, but with a skylight, set up as a guest bedroom.

The third bedroom was a large office, with a glass wall looking out to the government center.

"We'll need an office for you, too, Elina. Maybe change out the guest bedroom for an office."

"I can probably just have a second desk in here, Bert. It's a big room, and it has windows."

"OK. We can try that. Depends on what you end up doing, I think."

The fourth bedroom, another interior room, had a bio-lock on the door.

"A bio-lock on an interior door, Bert?"

"Yes, Elina. And for a very good reason."

Mangum opened the door and Stavros stepped into a weapons room.

More an armory.

"I don't let the cleaning people in here. Some of these are not precisely legal for private ownership."

Stavros looked around in wonder. Yes, that rocket launcher was probably restricted.

"Gee, ya think? Bert, you could arm a revolution with all this."

"Nah. For that you would need a lot of the same thing, all in the same caliber. These are all specific use, one-off kinds of things."

Stavros continued to look around. Sniper rifles. Big-game

rifles. Combat rifles. Mortar launchers. Special things, like that fully automatic big-bore shotgun. That must be a handful.

The glass cases in the center of the room held pistols of all types and sizes. Heavy weapons. Tiny, concealable weapons. Weapons that looked like something else.

One whole wall was nothing but shelves of ammunition for all the weapons, carefully arranged and labeled by caliber, cartridge length, and bullet type. Lead bullets. Platinum bullets. Round-nose. Armor piercing. Super-expanders. Anti-personnel rounds. Smoke rounds. Sabot rounds. It went on and on.

"What do you do with all this?"

"Whatever the assignment is, Elina, I have what I need."

"And then some. Criminy."

Stavros looked at the walls. Something weird there. She touched one. It felt cold.

Stavros raised an eyebrow at Mangum.

"Quarter-inch steel plate, welded at the seams, then painted to look ho-hum."

"Yeah, a bio-lock doesn't do you any good if someone can punch through the wall."

"Exactly."

They went back out into the living room, where Sam and Jules sat on the sofa looking out over the city.

"What do you say to all this, Sam?" Stavros asked.

"It's good to be home, Elina."

The crew from *Silverheel* brought all their luggage to the loading dock of The 909, and the building staff brought it up.

Stavros meanwhile looked through the kitchen.

"Bert, there's no food here."

"Elina, I've been gone almost a year. When I left for

THE FAVOR

Crossroads, on what became the Evelyn Barnes affair, I had the cleaning service come in and clean everything out so I wouldn't come home to a science fair project."

"So what do we do for food?"

"I call the service and they restock the kitchen from my inventory list. In the meantime, we order in."

"Who do we order in from?"

"Anybody we want. Even Marceau's will deliver to The 909."

Stavros had heard of Marceau's, but had never eaten there.

"They deliver here?"

"Oh, sure. Sometimes Honoré will bring it by himself, just to say Hi. I'm a regular."

"A regular at Marceau's? Boy, I really married up, didn't I?"

"I'm just me, Elina."

"Yes, Bert. I know. You're just the man I love. The extras are nice, but they don't really matter. On a government salary, I thought you would live in some low-rent place in the sticks."

"And you'd have been happy with that, Elina?"

"Yes, Bert. I would have. Did I ask you anything about your finances before I agreed to marry you?"

"No."

"Right. Because it doesn't matter."

Stavros walked over and hugged him there, in the middle of the living room.

"All I need is clean sheets and my man. And I can compromise on the sheets."

Settling In

They did eat at Marceau's that night. Mangum had missed the five-star restaurant just down the block. What he considered the neighborhood eatery.

"Good evening, Mr. Mangum. It's been too long."

"Good evening, Francois. Yes, I've been off-planet for a year."

"I hope your business activities were profitable, Mr. Mangum. Your regular table?"

"Please."

"Of course. Right this way, ma'am. Sir."

The maître d' led them to a table in the far corner, and Mangum and Stavros sat in the far chairs, looking out over the room. Francois seated Stavros, left a menu, and departed.

"This is your regular table?"

"Yes. I can see the whole room, my back is to a corner, and it's next to the emergency exit. I can relax here."

Stavros nodded and picked up the menu.

"One menu?"

"Yes. Francois knows I don't need one."

Stavros couldn't read the menu, which was all in French, so Mangum had to translate. He made recommendations and they ordered.

"So what's on our schedule now?"

"I've been off-planet a year, with back-to-back assignments, so I have some serious planet time coming. Six months at least. Unless something big comes up and all the other top operatives are busy."

"Is Claude a top operative?"

"Oh, yes. He's very good, Elina."

"Better than you?"

"At that level, we don't make those comparisons."

"I see. Does he feel the same way about you?"

"Oh, yes. All the top people are very good, and we all know it."

"What about me?"

"You could probably continue in the Crossroads position while I'm on planet, and Ikenberry wouldn't care. I'm sure there's an assistant head of Investigations handling the job."

"That seems unfair, though, and I need something to do."

"I'll talk to my superiors. Best would be if we worked for the same outfit. They would understand strange schedules and disruptions and the like."

"Such as when you go off planet."

"Yes."

"And then do I stay here, or do I go with you?"

"I haven't thought that far ahead, Elina."

The food showed up and it was wonderful. First-class room service on Crossroads was very good, but you were still on a space station.

One couldn't compare that to a five-star restaurant in the capital city of a wealthy star nation.

Stavros got up to go to the bathroom in the middle of the night, and stood captivated by the view out the master bedroom windows.

On a lark, she walked out into the dark living room and stood, nude, staring out at the two-wall panorama of Ashur, capital city of a star nation, drinking it all in.

The 909 had room service much like a hotel, and the next

morning they had breakfast on the island bar of the kitchen. The kitchen had been laid out so they were looking out across the living room at the view.

"I don't think I'll ever get used to this view, Bert."

"Yes, it's entrancing. Sometimes I just stand there, staring out at it."

"I did that last night when I got up to pee. I thought I would just sneak a look and I was captured by it for half an hour."

Mangum nodded.

"It happens."

"So when do you go in to talk to your superiors?"

"Oh, I don't go in to the office, Elina. Too much risk of being made, either them from me or me from them. No, when I'm in residence on Ashur, I'm just that. In my residence."

"You work from here?"

"Oh, yes. I'll check in this morning after breakfast."

"Bert Mangum? Married?" asked Frank Latham, the Agency's head of operations. "I never thought I would see the day."

"Even the best operatives settle down some day," said Phil Marstock, the Agency's operations contact to its best operatives.

Marstock had been an operative himself back in the day – a legendary one – and had ultimately settled down to run the Agency's most critical operations.

"And if you read his recent reports carefully," Marstock continued, "it's been becoming clear for a while that he was headed that way."

Latham nodded.

"Yes, I can see that now, Phil. But I think he's not quite ready yet, as far as being out of ops. The question then is, what do we do about Stavros?"

"As far as a job, you mean?"

"Yeah. Mangum wants her to work here, and I agree with his reasons. She's an Association citizen, a local girl born here in Ashur. She already knows a lot, about us and Com-Ply and such, and we would be understanding of the sort of weird goings-on typical in operations, where some other employer wouldn't."

"What about a two-man team?"

"You think that would work, Phil?"

"Look at his reports of the Crossroads affair, Frank. Mangum has always been a bit cagey about some things in his reports. But she brought him the problem in the first place, did all the computer work – which is not Mangum's strong suit – and handled some of the wet work herself."

"She did?"

"Yes. Remember the meeting Mangum had with the station manager, Ikenberry? Stavros left the meeting for a couple minutes to deal with the RDT control unit that was closing in on them, and when she came back to the meeting there were nine guys dead in the corridor and she didn't have a scratch on her. I don't think they all shot each other. Mangum was clear it was her doing."

"I wonder how the hell she pulled that off."

"So do I. But, like I said, Mangum's always been a bit cagey about some things. You can see it if you look for it. This is an obvious case. The point, though, is she got the job done."

"OK, Phil. I agree with you. Let's do that then."

For dinner with Stavros' parents, they had dinner brought in from Marceau's. The 909 staff set up a table and chairs in the glass corner of the living room, with the view of downtown

Ashur all around.

"Oh, my. This is so beautiful," Stacia said when they were shown into the apartment by a bellhop summoned by Steven, the doorman of The 909.

"Nice place," George said. "But I really like the view."

"Come in, come in," Mangum said. "We'll have a drink before dinner."

Stacia looked over at the quiet kitchen, and gave her daughter a questioning look.

"Oh, we're having dinner brought in, Mom," Stavros said. "Then we can talk without all the fussing."

They sat in the living room and had a pleasant conversation about the condo, and being back on Mardouk.

At one point, Stacia had a question.

"What are you going to be doing for work, dear? Or are you going to take some time off?"

"No, I have a new job. I'll be working at the Agency for Interstellar Trade."

George glanced at Mangum and then back to his daughter.

"What's your job there?" he asked.

"Trade Representative."

George looked at Mangum, and Mangum gave him a slight single nod. He looked back to his daughter.

"It's clear there were things that went on on Crossroads you haven't told me about."

"Yes, Daddy, and I never will."

George nodded once.

"Good."

Stacia looked at George and raised an eyebrow.

"Elina is going to be working with Bert, Stace," he said.

"Oh. Well, that will be nice."

Mangum and George exchanged knowing glances. They

both knew they both knew, and they both knew neither was talking.

The food showed up. Marceau's captain of waiters, Honoré, showed up with another waiter and a service cart.

"Hello, Honoré. Long time no see."

"Yes, Mr. Mangum. It's good to have you back, sir."

They set everything up, then departed, leaving the service cart behind. Mangum would have The 909 staff return it and the table service when they were finished.

"Oh, this looks wonderful," Stacia said. "Where did you get the food?"

"There's a nice restaurant down the block," Mangum said.

George looked down at the table setting and noted the discreet embroidered script on the napkins. Marceau's.

"I'll say."

Dinner was nice. The food was excellent. The view was spectacular. After dessert and coffee, Stacia and George said their goodbyes. There were hugs and handshakes, then a bellhop for The 909 walked them down to the entrance and handed them into an autocab.

"What a wonderful meal," Stacia said on the way home. "And such a beautiful condo. Elina's very lucky."

"Bert's a good man. I like him. He'll be good for her."

Stacia stared at her husband like he had just grown horns.

"Well, I think that went well," Mangum said.

"Oh, yes. Mom was very impressed with everything."

"So was your father."

"Yes, I saw that. And he clearly knows what Trade Representative for the Agency means."

"Yes, he does, and he'll never say a word."

"Daddy gets it."

Mangum nodded.

"He's a good man. I like him."

Mangum and Stavros sat on a bench in the park across from The 909. They were watching Jules and Sam play in the park.

Jules, in the persona of a ten-year-old boy, was throwing a ball, and Sam was fetching it. There were several other dogs in the park as well, but none of them ever got to the ball before Sam did. After a while, they just gave up.

The sun was shining, Jules was laughing, they were holding hands there on the park bench.

It was a very pleasant afternoon.

Please review this book on Amazon.

Author's Afterword

Writing fiction is an interesting exercise. One reason for that is you're typically writing about extraordinary events in the world you've created. 'Day in the life' fiction, in which the main character goes about his normal ho-hum existence, never interested me.

No, by and large we read about, and write about, the exceptional case. The normal everyday lives of people in your manufactured world are at terrible risk. From bad guys, calamitous events, unusual happenings.

Of course, when you do that, the methods used by the main characters to extricate themselves and everyone else from the situation are also extraordinary.

It's something of a writer's dilemma.

One example is EMPIRE: Tyrant. One reviewer noted that Emperor Trajan is not a nice person. He implodes an occupied building, killing guilty and innocent alike. He nukes a city of twenty-two million to put down an insurgency. He destroys a space station with two million people aboard to make a point. How can he be the hero?

Um, the name of the book is 'Tyrant.' It's printed on the cover and, in the paperback version, at the top of every odd-numbered page. Trajan is a man sworn to protect hundreds of trillions of people, and he will do so, whatever it takes.

I have stated elsewhere that I am not generally interested in dystopian science fiction, when reading or writing. I prefer things to work out for the good guys, to be left with, or to leave my readers with, generally positive feelings about the outcome. To have it all 'come out right' in the end.

Then we have the Agency series.

I am, broadly speaking, a libertarian politically. A classical liberal, if you would. Yet our heroes in the Agency series routinely question people under drugs, the administration of which they have received no permission for. Our long-established constitutional rules about no self-incrimination and the like, it seems, do not apply either. Dystopian, surely.

Further, they have no problem with extra-judicial execution. Oh, they are agents of their governments, to be sure, and those governments have authorized their actions, but executing the bad guys out of hand is surely an extreme case. Of course, the stakes – interstellar war in Eve Of War and a terrible drug that enslaves millions in The Favor – are high as well.

Do I answer these questions? Do I deal with the inherent contradictions in their values? No. I tell stories. Sometimes those stories raise questions. Good. You, dear reader, and I both get to think about them. They are age-old questions for which I have no easy answers.

My characters, though, must operate in these environments, and they accommodate those inconsistencies each in their own way. Love, honor, duty, and loyalty, the four main pillars of civilization and my consistent themes, play a role in those accommodations.

But do not expect easy answers to age-old questions from me, dear reader. We can explore those questions together in my stories, but there are no easy answers.

And there never have been.

We are left, as before, to find our way as best we can.

Richard F. Weyand
Bloomington, IN
December 6, 2022

www.ingramcontent.com/pod-product-compliance
Lightning Source LLC
Chambersburg PA
CBHW061322170626
46817CB00001B/265